A Stitch in Crime

Other books in the Quilts of Love Series

A STITCH IN CRIME

Quilts of Love Series

Cathy Elliott

Abingdon fiction™
a novel approach to faith

Nashville

A Stitch in Crime

Copyright © 2015 by Cathy Elliott

ISBN-13: 978-1-4267-7365-5

Published by Abingdon Press, P.O. Box 801, Nashville, TN 37202

www.abingdonpress.com

Quilts of Love Macro Editor: Teri Wilhelms

Published in association with the Books & Such Literary Agency

The persons and events portrayed in this work of fiction are the creations of the author, and any resemblance to persons living or dead is purely coincidental.

Library of Congress Cataloging-in-Publication Data has been requested.

Printed in the United States of America

1 2 3 4 5 6 7 8 9 10 / 20 19 18 17 16 15

Dedication

For Dolores Guill, beloved bosom buddy.
Though not a quilt maker, you represent the Maker well.

Acknowledgments

Bigzilla thanks to my editor, Ramona Richards, for your thoughtful and laser-like insights. Working with you is a delight. Kudos to Teri Wilhelms for those cutting but kind edits and to Mary Johannes, for the stunning cover. Love the bit o' bling.

My appreciation to the folks at Abingdon Press is also huge. I am grateful to partner with you and be a part of the Quilts of Love series.

As always, I must thank my wonderful agent, Janet Kobobel Grant, who believed in me first. I wonder if other agents secretly mourn that they aren't you?

Up-front thanks to you, the reader. If you bought this book, have been a part of stocking or selling it, or supported it in any way through recommendations or promotion, I am in your debt. Please consider me your friend. I consider you mine.

To write *A Stitch in Crime*, I had an army of troops in my camp every step. My gratitude flows to the thankful-you-have-my-back brigades, including:

My Experts Brigade:
Sergeant Michael Peery of the Shasta County Sheriff's Department. Your tireless responses to my crime questions rescued me from who-knows-what kind of weird scenarios. You helped me beyond measure and any mistakes in police procedure are mine alone. Thanks.

Esther Strathdee, BSN, PHN, RN. Thank you for sharing some of your vast medical knowledge so the events surrounding a visit by my disheveled Dr. Wellman might seem as real to the reader as they were to me.

George Winship, Editor, *Anderson Valley Post*. You updated my outdated take on the role of a small town reporter, AKA – Multimedia Journalist. Thanks for being so generous with your time and expertise.

Pam Allred of Sun Country Quilters in Red Bluff, California, who gave me the skinny on chairing a quilt show. Thank you for being such a rich resource. And to Charlene Brians who allowed me to join her in a quilt show booth, answering my myriad questions between passersby.

A special crown of achievement goes to quilt expert extraordinaire, Linda Gholson of Prineville, Oregon, who made Thea's "Tail in the Rail" prototype quilt and organized instructions for the reader. You are amazing.

Honorable mention to Rebecca (Becky) Lamb, who suggested the perfect title. I'm using it at last. Thank you, Becky.

My Writer Brigade:
Special thanks to my mentor, Cindy Martinusen Coloma. Your wisdom and friendship enrich my journey. And to Maxine Cambra, my vital first reader who gets my voice.

Thanks to the Quills of Faith Writers group who inspire me to march onward. And to the Redding Writers Forum for your constant support.

My Family Brigade:
Heartfelt thanks to my sweet mother, Evelyn, who still teaches me about unconditional love. To Mike and Pam, Dan and Nancy, Eric and Heidi, and the grand-gems, Sidney and Nicholas. Love-love you all.

And to my Gospel Brigade:
Cottonwood Community Church and my sweet home groups. You keep me focusing on the Great Author, and I am so grateful for your loving support and prayers. Eternal thanks.

1

Perhaps if she simply avoided eye contact.

Thea James turned her back on the partygoers, paying attention to the dessert buffet instead. The Quilt-Without-Guilt Guild had surpassed their Christmas potluck standard. Among a bounty of petite cakes, cookies, puffs, and bars, Thea found her own offering, a plate of blueberry tartlets. They appeared untouched. Strange. She pulled them to the front of the culinary display.

"Thea! Why are you hiding out in the desserts when I need your help?" The familiar voice of fellow guild member, Heather Ann Brewster, hinted at desperation.

Turning with reluctance, Thea morphed into hospitality mode. "Blueberry tartlet?"

"What?" Heather Ann viewed the diminutive dessert, gave a small shudder, and then had the grace to look apologetic. "Ah ... no, thanks. I haven't browsed the appetizers yet. Anyway, I can't think about food now. I'm too upset."

Thea shoved her reluctance aside. "What seems to be the problem, Heather Ann?" This time.

"You know the publicity banner we had made? The one advertising the quilt show next weekend? The one supposed to be hanging over the entrance to Old Town?"

"Supposed to be hanging over the entrance? I thought they put it up yesterday." Thea calculated the days left until the show opened. Today was Sunday, and tonight's kickoff quilt show soirée started the festivities. The main event was scheduled for next Saturday. Folks needed to be aware of the date so they'd attend en masse.

"City utility workers were supposed to put it up. Oh, and it's beautiful, Thea. In bold letters it says, '1ˢᵗ Annual Blocks on the Walk Quilt Show, Pioneer Park' and the date."

"Good . . . very good. So why isn't it hanging up?"

"I had the letters made in red, too. Sort of reminds me of Janny Rice's redwork quilt, you know? Perhaps she'll place with hers. Beautiful embroidery." Heather Ann seemed lost in the vision, green eyes staring at nothing.

"Heather Ann. Focus, hon. You said there was a problem. As the quilt show chairperson, I want to help." Well, that was a lie. Helping was overrated. Thea wanted to eat some desserts. And she wasn't the chairperson. Another fib. Rather, the co-chair, along with Prudy Levasich.

Where was the elusive Prudy, anyway? Probably showing off her twin sister, Trudy, visiting from the East Coast. The co-chair's co-twin. If Prudy stuck around now and then, she could co-solve these problems with Thea.

"You have to do something! The Larkindale City Planning Commission won't let us put up the banner." The desperation returned to Heather Ann's tone, sending her voice to a higher key.

"Why not?"

"It's not up to code. They said the banner needs holes cut in it so the wind will flow through and not blow it down."

"Makes sense. Without the holes, it could act more like a sail," Thea said. "Can't you cut some?"

"I guess." Heather Ann looked uncomfortable. "But I don't know how big to make the holes. Or how many. The banner was expensive. I don't want to ruin it."

"Very responsible." Thea considered the options. "I have an idea. Call the Larkin Lake Resort. They're always putting banners up for some event. The Fly-Fishing Derby. And the Daisy Pedal Bike Race, right?"

"Oh, you're good." Heather Ann's expression turned eager, like a puppy about to score a treat.

"Whatever size they advise, be sure you use the white space and don't cut into those big red letters you chose. That way people will only see the letters and not notice the holes." Thea gave Heather Ann an encouraging pat on the shoulder. "Sound okay?"

"Sounds great. Thanks so much, Thea. I'm on it." Heather Ann dashed away, blonde ponytail bouncing, presumably to make the call.

Or grab a few appetizers.

Which seemed an even better idea to Thea.

"Well, aren't you just the CEO. Or is that dictator?" Renée Fowler pushed up against Thea in jest, as she used to do when they were teens.

"Oh, stop." Thea grinned at her best friend since fifth grade, recently returned home from a long honeymoon tour of Europe.

She had missed Renée terribly. But something seemed off between them. Had the travels changed Renée? She certainly looked different. More elegant. Her brown hair, cut in Paris, was styled in a fashionable pixie cut. But weren't her large gray eyes filled with disapproval now? Or was the still single Thea a little jealous of her friend's marriage and new life?

Thea studied the crowd. "A wonderful turnout, don't you think? I've been watching for him but have yet to see Dr. Cottle. Did he already check in?"

"How would I know, Thea?" Renée asked. "I may own the Inn, but I don't keep up on what time every guest walks through the door."

Not a hint of a thank-you for recommending Renée and Howie's Heritage House Inn as lodging for their illustrious judge and guest speaker, Dr. Niles Cottle. Typical treatment from Renée since her return to Larkindale.

Thea waved to a friend of Gram's. "Everyone seems to be enjoying themselves. And no better place to do it than in Mary-Alice Wentworth's garden. Exquisite, isn't it?"

Glorious roses edged a pavestone patio, which surrounded a sparkling pond, highlighted by the spectacular fountain in the pond's center. Water poured endlessly from an urn held by a graceful granite lady. The effect was more than tranquil. It was hypnotic. Tables with bistro chairs dotted the grounds, and this evening's attendees alternately chatted in groups or relaxed with a cool drink. A number of quilts were displayed near the walkway, staging a quilt show preview and adding a folksy feel. Thea's mother's string quartet played various classical selections with so much enthusiasm the occasional sour note went unnoticed.

Except maybe by Renée, who now winced as if she had stepped on a nail.

Uh-oh. Thea grabbed the dessert plate and shoved it at her friend. "How about a nice blueberry tartlet?"

"Tartlet?" Renée's distasteful look increased. "What's in the filling? And look how thick the crust is, Thea. You must use very cold dough to make a flaky crust."

Crestfallen, Thea placed the plate back on the table. "Tasted good to me."

"They probably *are* good, for Larkindale. I do like the antique serving plate though," Renée said. "My tastes have refined so much from my exposure to other cultures. Like what I'm wearing, for instance." She smoothed out her simple black dress. "In Europe, everyone wears something elegant like this. Understated, you know? Your dress is much too frilly. Too yesterday."

"Oh." Thea's cheeks burned. Was it no longer okay to like yesterday's fashions best? Her vintage cocktail dress had been a steal from the family's antique store, James & Co. Antique Emporium. Certain the cut was flattering to her figure, Thea also thought the cobalt color and purple tulle overlay brought out the periwinkle blue in her eyes. Both Mum and Gram had agreed.

"But the pouffy skirt is a great illusion. One's not sure if it's so full because of your curves or the dress's design." Renée put a hand on her hip and once-overed her friend. "I could never pull it off. It would just hang on my slender frame. But those strappy sandals are cute. A nice change from your clogs."

Thea was beginning to wonder why she was friends with Renée. And where was Dr. Cottle?

Thea studied the gathering again but didn't see him. Their hostess, Mary-Alice, was also missing. Perhaps she was inside greeting him this minute.

Leaning toward Thea, Renée said, "Here comes your Cole Mason. So handsome. Did you see him chatting with Mayor Suzanne Stiles for more than a half hour? You better watch out, Miss Thea. Step it up or you'll remain *Miss Thea* for a long, long time."

"He's not my Cole Mason, and he can talk to whoever he likes!" Thea almost hissed at her friend as Cole approached them. His roving reporter role tonight was to cover the quilt show kickoff soirée for the *Larkindale Lamplight's* society pages. Surely he wouldn't report any petty problems from putting on the show. It could result in a definite damper on attendance at the official opening.

Moving past a sullen Renée and closer to Thea, Cole flashed his disarming dimples. Then appearing stunned, he stopped and said. "You look so . . . nice! Am I writing about the wrong subject for the *Lamplight*? How about a full-page spread of you in your dress?"

Renée rolled her eyes.

"No comment," Thea said, laughter in her voice. "What *are* you planning to cover?" Making her a feature story was not an option. He had to be kidding. Especially if she looked as chunky in her dress as Renée seemed to say. And the camera added what? Thea sucked in her stomach.

Cole's attention had diverted to the treat table. "What do you call this delicious-looking sweet?" He plunked a pink petit four on a faux-china plate. "I don't want to get the name wrong in my article."

Relieved, Thea named each dessert. Cole listed it in his notebook and took still shots with his smartphone. Without embarrassment, he snuck a few more tempting treats.

"And this . . . ," she swept her hand in front of the tartlets with a flourish, "is what I made. Blueberry tartlets. Care to sample one?"

So far, Renée stood silent. But apparently she'd reached her etiquette limit. "You don't want to eat those, Cole. They're made by our peanut-butter-and-pickle sandwich queen here. Need I say more?"

"Good recommendation. I'll take two." Cole stacked the tarts on the last empty spot on his plate.

The tiny triumph tasted like sugar. But Thea wondered if Renée, with her newly acquired European sensibilities, was right.

"Perhaps I should have used raspberries instead of blueberries," Thea said. "Might have looked more appetizing."

"I doubt it," Renée said. "Probably would have looked like coddled blood."

Coddled blood? Coddle? What was familiar about that word? Then Thea shivered, remembering Dr. Cottle was still a no-show. What if something horrible had happened to him?

She surveyed the party once more. Mary-Alice's favorite nephew appeared to have captivated a small audience, his hands in motion, probably spouting his expertise on the family quilt, "Larkin's Treasure." The string quartet sawed with vigor. Thea spotted Prudy hard at work, gabbing with the guests. Or was it Trudy? Thea's Aunt Elena, along with a few others, admired a magnificent Grandmother's Garden quilt displayed on the walkway.

But no Dr. Cottle.

Cole's voice cut through her concerns. "You know, these look so good, I think I'll take another one in case we run out before I've had my fill." He balanced another tartlet atop the others and winked at Thea.

Renée blew out a sigh. "You are quite the risk-taker, Mr. Mason." She waved a dismissal and strolled toward the mayor, probably for a little update on her conversation with Cole.

That's it. That's all I can take. I'm leaving before one more person says boo to me.

Cole's hand briefly touched the middle of Thea's back, stopping her flight, his dark eyes inquisitive. "Are you quite sure she's your best friend?"

No. She wasn't sure anymore. But what could she say? Thea groped for a reason for her friend's bad behavior. In the search, she found an emptiness she couldn't name.

"Renée's . . . not been herself since she got back from Europe."

"A lingering case of jet lag. That's probably it," Cole said.

Thea looked up, grateful for his kindness.

"So where's the famous Dr. Cottle?" Cole asked, changing the subject. "I've heard he can read the stitches on a fastball from the nosebleed section at Yankee Stadium."

"So they say. He's a major leaguer on quilts and quilting in our state," Thea said. "In fact, I should go see if there's been any word of him. Folks came tonight to hear his talk about the Wentworth legacy quilt."

"You go then. I'll pacify myself with a blueberry tartlet." Cole stuffed a whole one in his mouth and started chewing, pleasure written all over his face.

Did he like it or was he trying to cheer her up?

Maybe she didn't want to know.

Thea excused herself and strode purposefully toward the house. *No eye contact. No eye contact. No eye contact.* She managed to slip through the French doors, muting her mother's Mozart, and putting a wall between herself and the problems outside.

She closed her eyes. *See no evil.*

Beyond the glass door, a distant voice called out, "Has anyone seen Thea?"

She clicked the door closed.

Hear no evil.

2

Wandering through the great room and past the kitchen, Thea didn't see Dr. Cottle or Mary-Alice. In fact, she didn't see anyone.

Stepping into Mary-Alice's sitting room, she found herself blessedly alone. Thea stared out the window, willing Dr. Cottle to come, wondering if something sinister had befallen the famed quilt expert. *Get a grip, Thea.*

Thea pressed her nose against the leaded windowpane, searching for any sign of him among the passersby. Various vehicles drove past the Wentworth Mansion, but she didn't see a man wearing those trademark sphere-shaped spectacles.

Thea sensed someone behind her and whirled around. As she did so, she stumbled against an elderly woman, who fell backward into a potted ficus tree.

"Mary-Alice!" Thea lunged and grabbed a bony elbow, rescuing the woman from a close encounter with some potting soil. Thea slipped her arm around Mary-Alice Wentworth in a supportive gesture. "Sorry, I didn't hear you come in."

"I'm the one who should apologize, interrupting your quiet time." Mary-Alice shook out her skirt. She appeared unflustered, in spite of the episode.

Thea brushed a brown leaf from Mary-Alice's soft, gray curls and straightened the elder's necklace with its attached silver key. Thea was soothing herself as much as her friend.

"I was hoping for a glimpse of Dr. Cottle," Thea said. "We can't start the festivities without him."

"Too late, my dear." Mary-Alice's eyes hinted at mischief. "I think we already have!"

"I guess it's true. In fact, our celebration seems like a success." But Thea didn't believe her own words. How could it be anything but a disappointment if the guest of honor didn't appear?

"You've done a wonderful job arranging it," Mary-Alice said.

"Thanks. But I'm only a co-chair." Thea hoped she sounded suitably humble. "Prudy, my quilt show co-partner, deserves some of the credit, no doubt."

"Oh, no doubt." Mary-Alice gave an impish wink. She sat on an elegant Queen Anne chair and opened a drawer in the matching desk. "Now, where did I put that letter?"

"What letter?"

"The one from Dr. Cottle." Mary-Alice riffled through the drawer's contents, then opened and explored another.

Ah, yes. The late Dr. Cottle. Thea caught herself as if the thought might become true in more ways than one. How silly.

To divert herself, she watched Mary-Alice's feverish search, then turned back to the window, flooded by an uneasy feeling. Thea squinted to scrutinize the passing population again. Not a single Cottle. No one even Cottle-like. She gave a dejected sigh.

"It's not here. I must have left it upstairs in the bedroom." Mary-Alice's voice disrupted Thea's thoughts, bringing her back to the lost letter.

"Do you want me to help you look?" Thea noted the open drawers and mussed desktop.

"Bless you, my dear. But you have better things to do than help a forgetful old woman find her missing mail."

"Pish-posh, as Mum would say. I'd be happy to help." Thea leaned over and squeezed the elder's hand, which wrinkled like crepe paper.

Mary-Alice surveyed the room. "I was so sure it was here." She lifted the blotter on the desktop and checked underneath.

"What's in the letter?"

"Something about the quilt, 'Larkin's Treasure.' New information about the old mystery of great riches attached to it. And so interesting, too. But . . . oh, my." Mary-Alice looked up, disheartened. "I'm afraid I've forgotten what it said."

Made by a granddaughter of Larkin McLeod, the beloved wife of town founder Hastings McLeod, "Larkin's Treasure" was considered one of the finest examples of late nineteenth-century textiles. Plus, legend allowed the old crazy quilt contained a secret about great riches.

Mary-Alice, a direct descendant of the McLeod line, had tired of guarding the old family heirloom from thievery and donated it to the State Quilt & Textile Museum. However, for the weekend's festivities, arrangements had been made to loan "Larkin's Treasure" back. It was now safely locked inside a display case in Larkindale's own Hastings McLeod Museum—the only key clipped to the chain around Mary-Alice's neck.

"I'm sure we'll find the letter soon." Thea started toward the sofa and tripped on the corner of a thick throw rug, stubbing her sandaled toe. A sharp pain shot through her foot, and she bit her lip to keep the tears at bay. She waited a moment for Mary-Alice to stop ransacking the room and offer a word of comfort. But the woman foraged on.

"You know so much about the history of the quilt," Thea said, while rubbing the damaged digit against the back of her leg, "you'll be able to enchant everyone with the story."

"It's kind of you to say, my dear. But you should hear Kenneth. Why, he's out back right now, enthralling the guests with talk of secret maps and family feuds and all sorts of nonsense about 'Larkin's Treasure.' He can certainly spin an intriguing tale. In truth, my great-nephew's almost as knowledgeable about the old quilt as our visiting expert."

What visiting expert?

"If you'll excuse me, I'm going to check in my bedroom to see if it's where I left that pesky letter." Mary-Alice turned toward the staircase in the foyer. "Stay as long as you like, my dear. I always find this room restful."

Thea sat on the edge of a chenille-covered chaise where she could still see out the window and arranged her voluminous skirt about her legs, crossed at the ankle in a most ladylike fashion. She appreciated the effect of sparkly sandal straps around each foot, and she noted no evidence of trauma to her offended toe.

The sound of Mary-Alice's footsteps faded as Thea studied the sitting room.

A grandmother clock emitted a clear tick, audible above the sounds of the soirée. Thea's glance took in the charming fireplace with marble tiling and dark oak surround. She could imagine Mary-Alice stitching away on her latest quilt project on cool winter evenings, fire crackling, hot tea on a tray, and her little dog, Moxie, at her feet.

Where was Moxie, anyway? Maybe the wiggly, white puffball was secured in the big bedroom Mary-Alice once shared with her husband of nearly fifty years. How lonesome she must feel without Professor Wentworth. She lived alone in this cavernous old house, once filled with the sounds of many feet on the stairs. Of course, Mary-Alice would say she wasn't alone.

"I do get lonely for my husband, Seth, but I am never alone. The Lord is always with me," she often said. "And He's a marvelous companion. Life with Him is worth living."

The clock chimed half-past the hour. Seven-thirty. Thea dragged her thoughts back to the present problem. What was keeping Cottle? She should get back to her guests. And whatever mayhem might wait in ambush. Thea again squinted through the windowpanes. Completely Cottleless.

Enough. She needed to take her mind off the Cottle crisis, even an imaginary one. Though it didn't help when Moxie's little erratic yaps started from somewhere upstairs. In response, Thea's brain birthed the vision of a few baying Baskerville hounds. And mists and danger and. . . .

17

Perhaps she could discover if Mary-Alice's missing letter was still in the sitting room. Thea wandered onto the wool rug, this time careful to clear her silver sandals over the thick edge. She patted along the top of a bookshelf, then chided herself. Much too high for her petite friend to reach. Thea noticed a short stack of periodicals on a lower shelf. Maybe it got stuck in a magazine? She flipped the pages of the *Saturday Evening Post, Quilting World, Christianity Today*, and a couple of local publications. No letter.

What about the antique linen press? An unlikely prospect, but Thea opened the door to reveal the stack of colorful quilts. On top was a scrappy, log-cabin quilt, reminiscent of Thea's own first creation and quilt show entry. She pulled it out of the cabinet and stroked the soft fabric, admiring the design. Something fell from the folds and scored a direct hit to her exposed pinkies.

Thea leaned down and found an envelope lying at an angle atop her foot. "Hello, what have we here?" Addressed to her hostess, the envelope's return address was the official logo of the California State Quilt & Textile Museum.

This must be the lost letter! Would Mary-Alice mind if Thea examined the contents? She hesitated and turned over the envelope, wondering what to do.

Then, from deep inside the house, she heard a high-pitched sound, chilling as a chalkboard screech.

A blood-curdling scream.

3

Something's happened to Mary-Alice!" Thea shoved the quilt and letter back into the linen press and charged upstairs. On the landing, she stopped to listen. Moxie's muffled bark a steady staccato. A sound of someone's cry, "Oh, no. Oh, no. Oh, no . . ." drifted from Mary-Alice's room. Thea's stomach spun into an agitation cycle as she willed herself forward. Moxie's yapping increased.

Thea knocked lightly, then pushed open the heavy double doors. Nothing seemed amiss, except for some open drawers—perhaps Mary-Alice's continued search for the letter. On second scan, Thea saw a woman flattened against the far wall, sniveling as she stared across the room. Had she been ransacking it? Thea noted the woman's fawn, forties-style suit and the tiny pillbox hat angled atop auburn curls. At any other time, it was a look to enchant an antiquer's heart. But Thea was far from enchanted right now.

"Excuse me, but did you just scream?" she asked.

The woman nodded once, adding no more information, other than continuing her horrified gaze at something beyond the bed. The barking seemed to be coming from Mary-Alice's walk-in closet. Thea turned the knob, and the door swung open. Moxie's nails clicked against the hardwood as she sped beneath the bed.

Thea edged around the bed, peering past the ornate footboard. Mary-Alice's inert form lay sprawled across the oak floor. Next to her mistress, the faithful Moxie made soft sounds of distress.

"Oh, no!" Thea said, echoing the strange woman's words. Had her elderly friend suffered a heart attack?

"She's dead, isn't she? There's . . . blo . . . blood on her blouse." The woman pointed a shaky finger.

The scarlet smear on the collar alarmed Thea. Had Mary-Alice hurt her head in a fall? Or had the unthinkable happened and someone else caused the fall? Someone like the woman weeping against the wall?

"Move, Moxie. You're in the way. Off you go." Thea knelt down and, giving the dog a small shove, picked up Mary-Alice's delicate wrist. A feeble throb told her to hope. "I think she's alive. Call 911!"

The woman ignored Thea's directive and mumbled, "I didn't do anything. It wasn't me. I don't know what happened to her. I just popped in to freshen up and found—"

"Toss me the phone, then!" Thea held out her hand.

No response from the woman except her continued denials. It was maddening.

A noise at the double doors caused Thea to look up.

Kenneth Ransome, Mary-Alice's great-nephew, burst into the bedroom like a human cannonball. "Is somebody hurt? Where's my great-aunt? Who made that unholy yowl?" His overbite almost a snarl, he glared at the woman now cowering beside the bathroom wall.

"Over here, Kenneth." Thea strained her neck and waved him over. "It's your great-aunt. There's . . . an accident."

It had to be true. Who would want to harm Mary-Alice Wentworth?

"An accident?" Kenneth rushed around the bed to Mary-Alice's side. His bulk nearly knocked Thea flat. Squatting, he began to stroke his great-aunt's arm with a meaty hand, tender against her silky sleeve.

"Oh, no!" he said, repeating the words of the day. "Wake up, Auntie. Don't leave me!" He stopped stroking her arm and waved his big hand back and forth in a fan-like gesture.

Nice try. Their hostess was still out cold.

"She's not in a coma, is she? Could she just be overcome with the heat?" He gave Thea an expectant look from beneath bushy brows. "Don't old ladies have the vapors or something?"

Thea stared at Kenneth. Funny, he didn't look like he'd been reading Victorian novels. She must remind herself never to depend on him in a disaster.

Where was the telephone? The empty charger sat on the bedside table.

"Do either of you have a phone?" Thea asked, first facing the woman, then Kenneth. Apparently not. Nor did Thea. She remembered seeing a cell phone in the sitting room.

Frantic, she said, "Kenneth, stay with Mary-Alice. I'll go downstairs and call 911." Then she wavered. Would an emergency response take too long? In a house full of people, surely someone knew life-saving techniques. Maybe it was the best way to begin. She darted for the doors and froze.

A number of guests had silently squished inside the bedroom, building a blockade. Thea held out her hands, imploring. "Is there a doctor in the house?" The familiar cliché left her lips before she could check herself. And just her luck, too. Cole Mason stood among the crowd.

"Dr. Wellman is downstairs," Cole said. "I'll bring him right up." He worked his way out of the room, directing others out as well. "Mary-Alice needs some air. Let's wait downstairs."

Thea called out her thanks and returned to Mary-Alice, wanting to do *something*. Perhaps a pillow under her hostess's head?

No. What if there was a neck injury? Thea grabbed a thick, mohair throw and covered Mary-Alice's limbs. What else could Thea do for her friend? Say a prayer?

The crowd withdrew, one by one, though some still sought a glimpse of Mary-Alice. The woman-stranger hiccupped and clamped a hand over her mouth. Then, with one economizing move, she wiped a few tears with her suit sleeve.

"Who are you, anyway?" Kenneth stopped patting his aunt's arm and stared at the woman. It seemed he might say more, but something turned his attention back to Mary-Alice. "Wait! She's coming around."

Mary-Alice groaned and turned toward her nephew. "Kenneth?" Her voice was just above a whisper. "What happened?"

"You don't remember?" He tucked the soft throw around her shoulders. "Never mind. Just rest. I'll take care of you, Auntie. I promise."

"I'll take care of my mother, thank you." A new voice inserted itself into the scene, causing Thea to look up. A fiftyish woman wearing an emerald green pantsuit marched across the room, speaking with authority, "Kenneth, go back to the party and do what you do best. Blow out a bunch of blarney about the old quilt."

Louisa Wentworth Carver, the current relative residing in the mansion, snapped back the white, whole-cloth quilt adorning Mary-Alice's bed, a take-charge maneuver. She stared hard at her cousin through eyes accentuated by dark brows, lips red as a stop sign. Her chin-length blackened hair contrasted a dried-plaster complexion, giving her a Goth look.

Thea glanced at Kenneth, puzzled. How odd Louisa hadn't even bothered to come to her mother's side. Did her dislike of her cousin keep her from offering assistance?

"We were doing fine without you," Kenneth said. He smiled back down at his aunt, showing twenty-something front teeth. "Weren't we, Auntie?"

"Oh, sure. I can see that." Louisa plumped the pillows up until they stood at attention. "What I don't see is why I have to hear about my mother's misfortune from strangers."

"They're not strangers." Thea bristled. She rose and marched around to where Louisa was straightening the sheets. "They are friends. And family. Like you."

Louisa sent Thea a glare of disapproval. "Of course. Pardon me for not noting all the good will in this house when my poor mother is lying in a bloody heap on the floor." She gave the mattress a slap and spoke directly to Kenneth, ignoring further interaction with Thea. "Now, lift her up here and carefully! I'd help you, but I have a bad back. Mother will be much more comfortable in her own bed than lying on the hardwood."

"You're not seriously suggesting we move her, are you?" Kenneth asked.

Louisa straightened, as if set to debate. "As her daughter, I have the authority to—"

"Stop arguing, you two!" Mary-Alice's weak whisper silenced them both. "My head. . . ." She closed her eyes again.

Thea longed to cradle her friend's head and deck her daughter at the same time. Before she could do any decking, Dr. Wellman entered the bedroom, followed by Cole.

"Where's our patient?" Wellman, wearing the look of an unmade bed, had once been Mary-Alice's personal physician. Now retired, he only made house calls when dinner was involved. But he always carried his medical bag, just in case someone needed his expertise. The old doctor hurried over to where Mary-Alice lay and stooped, setting down his bag. He rummaged inside and pulled out his stethoscope.

"Now this might be a little cold." Dr. Wellman pressed the tool to his patient's chest. The tubing snaked across her blouse. "Are you awake, my dear?"

"Barely." Mary-Alice spoke with an effort, eyes still shut. "Listening to my family fight makes me want to sleep until next week." She attempted a weak smile.

"Too bad." Wellman glanced up at those gathered nearby. "Maybe you can give us some privacy while I conduct my examination. I'll let you know when I'm through."

He bent down, and as they left the room, Thea heard him ask, "Do you know my name, my dear? Or, better yet, can you remember yours?" followed by a chuckle.

Thea closed the door and joined the others in the spacious hall. Kenneth, face colored with concern, kept watch on the bedroom. Louisa tapped her foot. The strange woman stood away from the rest, an outsider. Cole took out a small, spiral-bound book and jotted notes.

Wait a minute.

"You're not going to write a news article about this terrible experience, are you?" Thea knew he was good at his job, but was this necessary?

"Don't worry, I'll keep it off-the-record." Cole winked at Thea. "Just a few notes, in case the police get involved."

"Police?" Kenneth looked stricken. "Are you saying my great-aunt's fall was not an accident?"

"Not exactly," Cole said. He paused, apparently thinking it over. "But when Mary-Alice remembers what happened, there may be no choice but to involve the police."

"Oh, no, oh, no, oh, no!" The strange woman clasped and unclasped her hands. "I need to go . . . to . . . er . . . visit the powder room. Excuse me." Surprising them all, she turned and shot down the hallway with hurried steps.

"Wait! Wait!" Arms flailing, Kenneth lunged after the escapee. He grabbed her sleeve before she disappeared down the back stairs and dragged her back to their little circle.

"Do you mind?" She jerked her arm away, her first sign of spunk. Kneading the offended limb, she gazed at the stairwell with longing.

Thea and Cole exchanged astonished looks as if agreeing the situation was going badly off-script.

"Sorry, ma'am," Kenneth exaggerated the second word. He moved to bar her way in case she got stair-happy again. "Who invited *you* to our family crisis?"

The woman winced at his words, returning to her mouse-like self. "Of course. How . . . how rude of me." She backed up a bit from Kenneth's looming figure. "My name is Odette Milsap. How do you do?" Odette put out a timid hand.

"What are you doing here? Upstairs?" Kenneth asked, snubbing the shake. "Specifically, what were you doing in my great-aunt's boudoir?"

"Good question." Louisa, in lady-of-the-manor mode, crossed her arms and shifted her weight to one hip.

"Oh, no." Odette's eyes filled. "I'm just a visitor. I didn't hurt anyone. Especially not Mrs. Wentworth!" She sniffed and dug in her pockets. "I'm harmless as a kitten. At least, my Charles used to say so. God rest his soul. He's been gone for five long years."

"Lucky dude," Kenneth said in a low voice.

In spite of her annoyance with Odette, Thea could see they were all ganging up on the woman. Putting aside her wish to join the gang, Thea switched subjects. "Would someone please go downstairs and inform the other guests what we know so far? I'm worried the small crowd who saw Mary-Alice passed out on the floor may have already gotten some gossip going."

"Good thinking. I'm in." Cole closed his notebook and deposited it back into his pocket. He gave a guy-slap to Kenneth's broad back. "Why don't you and I do the honors, Ken? I could use your help."

"Well . . ." Kenneth didn't seem so keen on the idea. Or maybe he just didn't like being called Ken.

"What if someone saw something important?" Cole asked.

Kenneth considered. "Okay. I'm in, too."

"Great." Cole steered Kenneth across to the staircase, asking him questions as they went. He glanced back at Thea once, gesturing toward Odette with his chin, an encouragement to get the scoop.

The stranger's expression seemed wary, and she turned toward the stairs again as if to exit but was unable, corralled. Not only by Thea's presence, but also by Louisa's, who edged closer, staring at Odette, indictment in her eyes.

A bad situation had just worsened.

The bedroom door opened, and Dr. Wellman poked his head out. "Louisa, I wonder if you might come in and talk to your mother. She is refusing my recommendation to go to the hospital for an evaluation."

"But she's okay?" Louisa dropped her Cruella De Ville countenance. "Does she need to go?"

"I expect she's fine. Resting comfortably in bed, petting her puppy. And except for a bad headache, seems almost herself now." Wellman stole the rest of the way into the hall, securing the bedroom door behind him. "She's rubbing the back of her head. A little bleeding, not much. But head wounds can be risky."

As much as she didn't want to ask the question, Thea wanted the doctor's expert opinion. "Do you think someone might have, you know, hit her?"

What if it was true? Okay, maybe not the anxious Odette. But someone else? What if there was a psycho at the soirée?

"Couldn't say. I expect she fell. She doesn't remember."

Thea cut her eyes to Odette, who apparently was attempting to fade away by inching backward. Did she know something about Mary-Alice's fall? Something she wasn't telling?

"What about a stroke?" Louisa asked. "Maybe she lost her balance and hit her head."

"I see no sign of a stroke. But they will rule it out at the hospital." Dr. Wellman tiptoed back to the door, beckoning Louisa to follow. "She's got an ugly knot on the back of her head. And head traumas are deceiving. Even if she feels fine, she may not be. I want her checked out by a medical team just to be safe. I'll make the call." He patted his pocket, indicating he was armed with a cell phone. Then the doctor disappeared into the room, leaving the door open just enough for Louisa to enter.

"How will I get her to go?" Louisa looked at Thea and shrugged. "You know Mother never does anything unless she wants to do it."

"You're right." Thea thought a moment. "Tell her you're packing a bag for her trip to the hospital in case she has to stay. Then pick out things she wouldn't want to take. On purpose."

"I get it." Louisa smiled, looking quite unlike her uncivil self. "She won't like me choosing for her. She'll soon be busy controlling the situation, I expect. Thanks." She disappeared into the bedroom.

Pleased she could be of assistance, Thea turned to tackle the Odette dilemma. Down the hall, the woman inched along the polished oak floors toward the back stairs.

"Halt!" Thea said.

Halt? Who says halt these days?

Odette halted. She spun slowly around until she faced Thea, who flaunted her sternest, don't-mess-with-me manner.

"Odette Milsap. We need to talk."

4

L et's sit, Odette, if you don't mind." Thea plopped into one of two upholstered chairs situated in a seating area nearby, glad to give her aching toe a time-out. A table topped with a Tiffany-style lamp separated the chairs. She could imagine Mary-Alice reading her Bible right in this cozy nook.

Or praying. Which was a given.

Thea wished Uncle Nick were here. As a retired police officer, he'd know just how to handle things. What would he do in this situation? She brooded over the question, then settled on a solution: interview everyone close to the crime, if it *was* a crime, while the details were fresh. Every minute mattered when gathering clues.

Without anyone else to ask these questions, Thea felt compelled to do so before Odette slipped out of the house. Did she live in Larkindale? Thea didn't think so. The woman might leave for good and take the truth right along with her.

A mantle of responsibility wrapped itself around Thea's shoulders like a heavy cloak. She had to do this for Mary-Alice.

How much time did she have to grill Odette before someone else barged in?

Thea heard voices raised downstairs and expected more guests were upset by now. Mary-Alice was a great favorite among the townsfolk.

If the town matriarch *had* been attacked, Thea wasn't the only person who wanted to know the details and call the person into account. Was it Odette Milsap? Still standing alone nearby, she looked guilty.

Waving Odette over, Thea said, "I need to ask you some questions." Amazed Odette obeyed, Thea watched the woman's half-hearted trek to the seating area. She guessed her to be about mid-forties since there was no gray in her hair. Thea tried to decide if Odette's auburn tresses beneath the pillbox hat were just a little too red.

If the color was phony, did it have any bearing on the case? Thea couldn't see how. Her own blonde locks were scheduled for highlights next week. She dismissed that line of questioning.

"What do you want to know?" Odette asked, sitting in the proffered chair, resigned, as if ready for her reprimand. Odette must realize some explanation was required after being caught in Mary-Alice's bedroom with her hostess unconscious on the floor.

Better to talk to Thea than either Louisa or Kenneth.

She was doing a kindness, actually.

"Did you have anything to do with Mary-Alice's injury?"

There it was—the big-money question. Thea congratulated herself for leading with a verbal right hook. But, was it a knockdown?

"No! Absolutely not!" Odette said. "I told you so."

"Yes, you did. Several times. I'll take you at your word." Thea hoped her inquiry might elicit a few lucky details. Since she didn't know what she was doing. "How did you come to be here this evening? I arranged this little party and don't recall an Odette Milsap on our guest list."

"A last-minute thing. My niece invited me. You probably know her. Sissy Sloane."

Sissy Sloane, owner of the Quintessential Quilter shop in historic Old Town, had helped Thea select fabric for her first completed quilt, Kitty in the Cabin. The same wall hanging would soon be displayed in the Blocks on the Walk Quilt Show. Sissy's wise counsel and her store were at the heart of quilting in Larkindale.

Thea warmed to Odette, considering her connection to Sissy. "I don't understand why you left the party. All the quilters were in the garden. Including your niece."

Odette shifted in her seat. "I'd hoped to talk to Mary-Alice alone. Put in a good word for Sissy's Drunkard's Path quilt entry. It would mean a lot for her business to win Best of Show."

"You didn't get the chance?"

"People always surrounded Mary-Alice, three deep. She's like a celebrity."

Thea had to agree. Their hostess *was* popular, especially at quilt-judging time. Being Mary-Alice's best friend was always the height of fashion in Larkindale, but at quilt-judging time, it was positively haute couture.

"So you decided to waylay Mary-Alice in her room?"

"Oh, no!" Odette said, reverting back to her original exclamation. "Someone told me she'd gone inside. So I went to find her, hoping for a word alone. But I didn't see her anywhere."

"What did you do?" Thea leaned forward.

"I was curious and . . . uh . . . decided to explore. Just a little." Odette blushed. "I slipped up the back staircase through the old servant's wing. Nobody saw me, I'm pretty sure."

Had she bumped into Mary-Alice, instead? Thea shuddered at the idea. Who'd want to be caught slinking around the mansion? Especially by the owner?

But maybe it's what happened. And Odette responded with violence. Thea remembered the woman's anger when Kenneth stopped her escape.

Why would she stay in Mary-Alice's room, whimpering she hadn't done anything? A guilty person would run away, right? Or was Odette too smart to run?

Finding it hard to believe anyone so obviously associated with Sissy Sloane could harm anyone, Thea rejected the image of an aggressive Odette. Still . . .

"Did you see anyone while you were exploring?"

"Let me think. . . ." Odette squeezed her eyes closed for a moment before blinking them back open. "I believe I heard footsteps on the servant's stairs. The way I'd come up."

"Was it Mary-Alice?" Thea scooted to the edge of her seat.

"Possibly. I hid behind the closest door before he or she appeared."

"You didn't see the person?"

"No. Just heard footsteps moving down the hall toward the master suite."

Then maybe it *was* Mary-Alice. This conversation created more questions than answers. Rats.

"Did you think it was a male or female?" Thea asked, probing. "Was it the sound of a woman's high heels or a heavier footfall?"

"No idea. I wasn't trying to identify the person, just save myself from humiliation." Odette began to pick at her skirt, as if it were covered with Lilliputian bits of lint. Her voice husky, she said, "I nev . . . never expected to be cross-examined about it."

The comment stopped Thea. Was her attempt at interrogation too harsh?

Just then, Cole climbed halfway up the staircase, calling, "What's the latest? How's Mary-Alice? And how long until you come back down, soirée czar? People are asking after you, especially your friend, Renée."

Thea had hoped Renée might step in as co-hostess during her absence. They always used to cover for one another. Was it still true today?

Excusing herself, Thea got up, walked to the railing, and looked over at a grinning Cole. Her heart gave a little lurch. Those dimples should be illegal. She grinned back.

"Mary-Alice seems okay. Louisa is packing her overnight bag. Our patient will be taking a detour from her bedroom to the emergency room," Thea said. "Dr. Wellman wants a second opinion, just to be sure."

"Good news then," Cole said. "I'll ask your mum to strike up the band. Maybe Mary-Alice will be home before the party is over." He started down the steps, then stopped, looking back at Thea.

"What about the mysterious Ms. Milsap? Anything interesting up here?"

"We're having a nice chat," she said. "I'll fill you in later. How about you? Anything interesting down there?"

"Folks are worried about Mary-Alice, mostly. I called your Uncle Nick to come oversee things. Your mother suggested it."

Thea blew out a sigh she didn't know she was holding in. "Thanks. I'm sure he can sort everything out. Even if he has missed most of the event."

"Not to worry." Cole patted his pocket with the spiral notebook. "I've got it all down in black and white."

Thea was about to revive the not-writing-an-article-argument when he gave her a wink. "What can I say? It's a living." He turned, tapped down the stairs, and disappeared.

As Thea returned to her seat, Odette asked, "Is he your boyfriend?"

Not knowing how to answer, Thea thought about the uncertainty of the relationship between her and Cole. If it could even be considered a relationship. On occasion, they caught a matinee, lunched together, or joined Aunt Elena and Uncle Nick for a family dinner. He moved about in her world, sometimes mildly flirtatious. Sometimes keeping a little distance. He hadn't declared his feelings—for or against them as a couple.

So she wasn't sure if they were dating. Wouldn't it be presumptuous for Thea to call Cole her boyfriend? To call him hers at all?

"Sorry for the interruption," Thea said, passing over the boyfriend question as if it hadn't been asked. "I think you were telling me about hiding from Mary-Alice in one of the bedrooms."

Odette didn't answer right away, examining her French manicure, nail by nail.

Thea looked at her own nails, proud they had grown a bit beyond her fingertips. Maybe she wasn't ready for a manicure, but as a recovering nail-biter, this was progress. She blessed her own heart for a job well done.

Thea quit admiring her nails. "So, Odette. You were hiding in a bedroom?"

A loud sigh from Odette seemed to say she was reaching the end of her endurance. She glanced again at the stairs before giving her answer. "I don't know how long I was in there. The truth is, I took my time looking around. It's like a museum around here. Have you noticed the gorgeous quilt in the small room? It looks like an Irish Chain."

"It's actually a hand-quilted Double-Irish Chain."

"I've never seen a finer example," Odette said. "The stitching is so precise."

"When did you leave the room?" Thea asked, not wanting to get trapped into a quilt discussion when everything around them was coming apart at the seams.

"Oh, dear . . ." Odette searched the ceiling as if answers were hidden somewhere in the beams. "I heard footsteps again, fading down the back stairs. I figured the person had left, so I peeked out into the hall."

"What did you see?"

"Nothing. No one. All clear."

"Then what?" Impatient, Thea tapped her foot, causing instant toe torture. She stopped tapping.

"I checked out all the rooms since I was already there," Odette said, appearing pleased. "They were so tastefully furnished!"

"Uh-huh." Thea's annoyance at Odette's invasion of Mary-Alice's private rooms again simmered near the surface. "And?"

"I thought I heard barking down the hall. So I went to the suite."

"Did you have the courtesy to knock?"

Eyes wide, Odette said, "Oh, I'm sure I must have."

Right. Maybe in your daydreams.

"When I walked in, the dog went crazy. I tried to shush her, but she kept barking. I was about to leave, but it was such a gracious room. Did you notice the gorgeous whole-cloth quilt?" Odette waited for an answer. Then as if realizing her error, gave a nervous giggle. "Silly me. Of course you did. We were both just in there."

Honestly. The woman was a master of misdirection.

"Yes, it's a lovely quilt." Thea tried again. "What happened next?"

"I wanted to visit the bathroom, just for a minute. Maybe check my makeup. But the dog..."

"So you didn't check your makeup?"

"Oh, yes. I coaxed the yappy dog into the closet, then took a quick look in the bathroom mirror. And it was lucky I did because I had a piece of kale on my upper right tooth." Odette pointed to the insulting incisor.

"Good heavens. Just tell me what happened!"

"I came out and saw Mary-Alice on the floor."

"And?"

"And I screamed."

Thea was about ready to scream, too. Instead, she flopped backward in the chair and clamped her mouth shut. Getting information out of Odette was like removing a molar with eyebrow tweezers.

The door to Mary-Alice's room opened. Louisa rushed across the threshold toward them, anxiety in every movement, worry written in her eyes.

"Is Mary-Alice worse?" Thea jumped up, a catch in her throat, not ready to hear bad news about her friend.

"Call the police!" Louisa's voice was tinged with hysteria. "Mother's diamond brooch has been stolen!"

5

"Well, what a relief!" Thea said.

"A relief? Part of my inheritance has been stolen right out of my mother's room and you call it a relief? I have a good mind to sue the whole quilt guild," Louisa said. "*After* the police finish with you."

"Oh, no!" Odette defaulted back to her script and shrank deeper into her chair, her head drooping. "I can't talk to the police," she said. Her voice was barely audible.

Louisa wagged her finger at the woman, saying only, "You!" as if she couldn't find words to describe her outrage.

Thea stepped in front of Odette. "Louisa, you're jumping to conclusions. I'm sure Odette had nothing to do with it." *Well, pretty sure.* "How do you know the brooch is stolen, anyway?"

"Because I looked in Mother's jewel box and it was gone. Since it will be mine someday, I feel it's my duty to oversee its whereabouts."

Thea remembered seeing Mary-Alice wear the antique brooch at the occasional town function. But not at this one. Could Mary-Alice have interrupted someone's search for the jewel?

Louisa touched a filigreed gold bracelet inset with jade circling her wrist. "Mother gave this bracelet to me last year on my fiftieth birthday. Once a gift to her from Dad. Beautiful and old, too. But with little value in comparison to the diamond brooch." She glared at Odette. "And I want it back!"

Thea turned and saw Odette picking unseen somethings from her skirt again. How could Sissy's aunt be involved in a jewel heist? Or in Mary-Alice's plight? Ridiculous. Still, she was found in Mary-Alice's bedroom. And had been reluctant to have the police called. Why?

Cole appeared atop the stairs with two blue-uniformed men and pointed out Mary-Alice's bedroom. Several more males and one female followed behind, carrying emergency gear.

"Good. Here are the police," Louisa said. She watched them disappear into her mother's room. "I guess they want to get her statement."

"Actually, those are the paramedics," Cole said. "Dr. Wellman wanted to take extra precautions rather than drive Mary-Alice to the hospital himself. Or have one of you take her."

"All uniforms look the same, these days," Louisa said, shrugging. "Police, paramedics, military, firefighters . . ."

"Heroes all. Though I beg to differ on the firefighter gear. No mistaking *them* for the boys in blue," Cole said. Then his expression turned wary. "You expected the police? Why would they be taking Mary-Alice's statement?"

Before Thea could explain, a stretcher guided by paramedics on both sides rolled onto the landing and a hush overcame the group. Mary-Alice wore an embarrassed look and a neck brace. Her tiny form was covered with a blanket and secured with safety straps for a journey down the stairs. Moxie was nestled in her arms.

Thea's eyes misted. She approached the stretcher and touched the elder's arm. "Mary-Alice, I'm so sorry this happened. But I'll do my best to show your guests the same hospitality you would. Though I'm sure everyone will want to leave early, since you . . . aren't feeling well. It won't be the same, old friend."

"Old is right," Mary-Alice said. A whisper of a smile passed over her face. "You'll do fine, my dear. I'll be back before the party's over."

"Oh, I do hope—"

"Auntie, are you alright?" Kenneth interrupted, breathlessly, back in their midst. He panted from his climb up the stairs before continuing. "Must she go to the hospital?" he asked, looking at his great-aunt strapped down and surrounded by emergency staff.

"Absolutely. Your aunt still can't remember what happened or how she came to be on the floor." Dr. Wellman leaned over the stretcher and spoke to Mary-Alice. "And you are a little unsteady on your feet. We want you safely transported to Faith Memorial. What if you fell ill in the car? I'd have a time of it tending to you and driving, too."

"Good thinking." Kenneth patted her hand with obvious concern. "I'll ride with you in the ambulance."

Mary-Alice gave him a weak, but grateful look. Thea wondered if she had already been given a sedative. Was her head injury worse than they first thought? How could something like this happen to the gentlest woman in town?

Of course, no one knew what had happened to Mary-Alice. Perhaps she became light-headed and fell. Or tripped over a rug. Thea knew a bit about such a scenario and flexed her toe, regretting it immediately.

"What a good idea, Kenneth. You ride along in the ambulance, and I'll follow in my car," Dr. Wellman said. "Unless of course, Louisa prefers to accompany her mother?" He waited for a response.

Smoothing her pantsuit, Louisa seemed to struggle with the suggestion. She cast an apologetic glance at Mary-Alice. "Normally, I would go, Mother. But since we must wait for the police, Kenneth can go in my stead. You should have some family with you during this ordeal." But she pronounced the word *family* with something like disdain. As if Kenneth were faux family at best.

"Walk us to the ambulance and then bring the dog back inside," the doctor said to Louisa. "You can come visit your mother after the police are finished. Naturally, you'll be worried. We all are. . . ."

"Naturally," Louisa said, without a hint of sincerity.

Mary-Alice moved her head as if she meant to say something, but moaned instead. Kenneth shushed her, kindly. Then the paramedics carried the stretcher downstairs with Kenneth, Louisa, and Dr. Wellman trailing as the rest watched their descent.

Nick Marinello, Thea's uncle, appeared at the bottom of the stairs. Casually dressed in a checked shirt and sneakers, hands clasped in front of his khakis, he waited for the stretcher and paramedics to clear the stairwell and aim toward the mansion's exit.

When she saw him, Thea's shoulders straightened as if a big burden had fallen away. She mused that with his dark Italian looks, he could be more closely related to the chocolate-haired Cole Mason than to Thea. She watched him take the steps with a slight limp, the result of an old gunshot wound. The injury ended his career on the police force. His demeanor was professional, and there was no hint of the teasing relationship Thea and her uncle shared. He stopped at the top.

"What just happened here?" Nick asked. "And how can I help?"

Thea barely had time to explain about Mary-Alice's fall before Louisa broke in.

"My antique diamond brooch has been stolen! You have to call the police before the thief gets away." She glowered at Odette, who covered her face.

Nick looked from Louisa to Odette as if making a judgment call.

"Downstairs, everyone," he said to the remaining four, ushering them toward the banister. "I'll call Detective Brewster. Don't anyone leave the premises. The police will want to interview each of you when they arrive."

Behind her, Thea heard an "Oh, no!" sounding like a shattered sob. She stopped and waited, reaching for Odette's elbow as she drew near. Thea had just put Odette through all those questions and now the woman would have to answer many more from the police.

Soon everyone would know of Odette's secret trek up the back stairs.

6

Thea found herself back in the sitting room facing Detective Brewster. He sat at Mary-Alice's desk, the too-small chair angled outward to better face his quarry. On the desktop, a portable recorder seemed poised to penalize, and Thea hoped she wouldn't say something stupid or use bad grammar. How long did they keep those tapes, anyway?

The detective fixed his piercing gaze on her as if he already knew every dishonest thought she'd ever had. No fooling him. No need to try. Thea blinked rapidly, her eyes crying "uncle." Powerless to look away.

Must be nice to have x-ray vision.

Brewster asked if she had seen anything out of the ordinary and jotted a few notes on a notepad. Thea related the discovery of Mary-Alice on the bedroom floor while Odette Milsap stood by, whimpering against the wall. And finally, Thea outlined her long chat with Odette. Imagining the detective would be impressed with her sleuthing skills, she allowed herself an inner gloat.

Brewster took a few more notes, his expression unreadable.

Thea tried not to shift in her chair. She should be comfortable in his presence. He was, after all, married to Heather Ann Brewster, long-time member of the Quilt-Without-Guilt Guild. One of Thea's team, a star player in staging the quilt show. Surely, the detective understood Thea's role as the show's co-chair and problem solver better than most, because of Heather's involvement.

"Did you notice anyone arguing, fighting, or acting upset with Mary-Alice tonight?" Detective Brewster asked, tapping his pen against the desk. Then, maybe realizing the noise would record on the tape, he drummed the pen against his leg instead.

"Fighting with Mary-Alice? You're kidding, right?" Thea said. She watched for his reaction. There was none. Okay, he wasn't kidding. "Uh . . . I can't imagine anyone upset with her. But let me think." She concentrated hard. "The only arguing I saw was between her daughter, Louisa, and Kenneth, her great-nephew."

He paused mid-tap. "Tell me about it."

After relating the uncomfortable scene between the cousins in Mary-Alice's bedroom, Thea said, "Kenneth's distress at his aunt's fall . . . or attack . . . was evident. But the theft of her mother's brooch seemed more important to Louisa than Mary-Alice's health."

Brewster scribbled some more. "Any significance to this brooch? An heirloom? Valuable?"

"Oh, absolutely! In fact, Louisa told me the brooch was part of her inheritance. It's rumored to be worth over twenty-five thousand dollars. She was upset at its loss."

More like furious.

"I see. Then we are talking about grand theft/larceny. Along with the possible assault to Mrs. Wentworth—yet to be determined. Anything else to add?"

"Just one more thing. I forgot to mention it before. Odette seemed . . ." Thea stopped, suddenly uneasy at her eagerness to trash another person. She looked away. Was she becoming the hated snitch? Did this disclosure have anything to do with the crime? Did it even need to be said? Like mum always told her, "No one likes a tattletale."

"Odette seemed?" The detective's urging was like a command.

She looked back at Brewster, and he reconnected their mutual gaze.

Transfixed, Thea gave in, but tried to tenderize her tale. "It's not anything important enough for your notebook there. Just when Louisa insisted the police be called about the brooch, Odette seemed stressed."

"Explain."

Sighing, Thea gave a halfhearted account of Odette's fearful reaction to each mention of police involvement. "In fact, she said, 'Oh, no! I can't talk to the police.' But I don't know why. It probably has nothing to do with the brooch. In fact, I wish I hadn't brought it up."

"I see." Brewster stood, releasing Thea from his gaze. He excused himself and exited the room. The door didn't quite latch and swung open a crack.

Thankful to be out of his spell, Thea rose, stretched, and ambled toward the door. She should close it, right?

Right after she surveyed the scene playing out beyond the gap.

In the foyer, Brewster spoke in low tones with another officer and pointed toward the stairs, motioning to the upper floor. The officer nodded once, an affirmation.

Beyond, Odette sat on a Victorian settee, biting her cuticles and casting glances between the police officer and the front door. Perhaps Odette's interview was next. Thanks to Thea, it would be more intrusive than ever.

Thea shut the door and dashed back to her chair, dropping into it just before the door opened. As if she'd been there all the time.

The detective entered and sat, as well. He gave her a quizzical look. "Everything okay in here?"

What did he mean?

"Yes, fine. Just stretched my legs a little." Thea had the feeling he knew she'd been spying and her face flamed. "Besides, you didn't get the door closed. So I shut it for you."

"I see." Brewster hesitated a moment, his eyes holding hers in an I-don't-believe-you stare.

So now she was a tattletale *and* a liar.

He continued, asking a few more questions, jotting down the occasional note. Then thanking Thea for her cooperation, he concluded the interview by excusing her. She was free to go.

"And Ms. James," Detective Brewster said, rising first. "Leave the questioning to the police. Please." He opened the door. "If someone did assault Mary-Alice, you could be in danger, if you get in his way."

His way? Thea wandered across the room, distracted. Was that just a quirk of speech? Or did the detective think someone—a male someone—struck Mary-Alice Wentworth?

Maybe there *was* a Wentworth whacker on the loose.

"Again, Ms. James." Brewster held her gaze in the doorway, as if analyzing her thoughts. "Don't get involved. Let us handle it from here."

Thea dragged her eyes away, croaking out a timid "Okay, sure," and made her escape. Chastised and unable to look at Odette, Thea hurried through the hallway toward the safety of garden and guests, shaking off the shock of Brewster's warning, and biting her nails to the quick.

7

Outside in the deepening twilight, she assessed the soirée situation. Good heavens. What had happened to her bustling party atmosphere?

No happy chatter. No folks piling their plates with goodies. No Mozarty strains from violins. In fact, she didn't see a single music stand on the patio. Or Mum. Or the other members of the quartet. Were they being questioned somewhere inside?

Pity. Thea's inner cynic could have used the diversion.

She progressed past the illuminated pool, stopping for a moment to watch the granite lady continue her eternal task of pouring water. Thea still didn't see any guests, which added to the eerie atmosphere.

Path lights lit her steps past the pool until she spotted a small group of partygoers grouped together. They sat silent in lawn chairs, swirling punch in stemmed goblets, crossing and uncrossing legs. A few hanging quilts stirred as the evening breeze sighed.

Lighted by lanterns, a couple of bistro tables had been commandeered for private interviews, one guest to one officer at each. Thea noted a small tape recorder atop each table and gave a slight sympathy shudder. The sight of Uncle Nick as he helped a younger officer with an interview allowed Thea to relax a degree.

She surveyed the rest of the garden. What a fiasco.

Yellow plastic tape reading CRIME SCENE DO NOT CROSS adorned the exits to the property. At the main gate, a security light shone on Officer Threet and Justice, his K-9 partner, as they stood guard. Thea edged backward, and the German shepherd focused on her as if seeing his prey the first time. Not liking what he saw. She willed him her best "good boy" vibe. If she attracted his doggie disapproval, Thea could only hope in her case, Justice was indeed blind.

She peered around, again looking for her mother. And Prudy. Thea had hardly spoken to her co-chair all afternoon. She could use some help entertaining the guests. She'd promised Mary-Alice.

Her uncle strode across the Pavestone toward Thea and gave her a hug. "How did your interview go? Brewster was excited to question you, after I told him how much information you got from the intruder. You scored big."

"How flattering," Thea said. "I don't want to talk about it."

"That bad? You underestimate yourself. My niece, the natural-born PI."

Thea ignored his remarks. "Are the police almost done? I want to go home." She felt a headache start, pressing against her forehead like a too-tight bandana.

"When did you last eat something?" Nick took her hand, pulling her toward the tables of remaining food. He handed her a paper plate. "What's your pleasure, Princess? How about a nice, healthy spinach ball? Or one of those stuffed peppers?"

A voice from behind cut into their conversation. "A mini-empanada? There's some sort of crab mixture inside." Cole pointed to a plate holding two shriveled empanadas. "I had one earlier. Delicious." He grinned.

"I'm sure they *were* delicious. Earlier." But Cole's dimples had done their duty, mollifying Thea's mood. "Thanks, but I'll pass." Still, she should eat something. But what? Several hours in the elements did not make meatballs more appetizing.

"These are harmless." Nick sprinkled a few potato chips on her plate, along with several chocolate chip cookies. "You need to keep your blood sugar up."

How wise of her uncle. One didn't mess around with blood sugar. Thea took a chocolaty bite, trying not to moan at its deliciousness.

When she had downed the entire cookie and started a second, she said, "I don't see my peeps. Where's Mum?"

"She's been interviewed and excused, along with the other musicians. I expect she went home. Or maybe to the hospital to see Mary-Alice, if I know my sister," Nick said. "Afraid everyone has to be interviewed, Princess. Even your mum."

Cole drew bistro chairs around an empty table and they sat. Thea crunched chips and cookies. It was almost pleasant. The headache ebbed.

"Why can't they just go?" she asked, scanning the last of the guests.

"We have to take a statement from everyone before we can let them leave," Nick said. "At least get horsepower."

"Horsepower? Not sure I've heard the term before," Cole said, taking out his notebook and writing it down.

Nick reached across the table and broke off a chunk of Thea's last cookie. "Just cop slang for personal information. Cell number, birth date, Social Security number, driver's license info, and so on." He popped the cookie piece in his mouth and chewed.

"It wasn't how my lovely experience went," Thea said. She knew she was laying undue blame on Brewster. Her self-censure stemmed from her own bad behavior. She hoped Odette was okay. Maybe Sissy had taken her home by now.

"The officer will ask some basic questions, too. If he hits on anything important during questioning, he'll pass off the witness to Detective Brewster. For the old closed-door session." Nick winked at Thea, who groaned.

A couple walked over to the big gate where Officers Threet and Justice saw them out. Then Threet snapped the gate shut, a metallic clang ringing out, and returned to his previous stance.

"Do you think Prudy is inside being grilled? Er . . . interviewed?" Thea asked. "I've got to talk to her." When the ordeal was over, the food needed to be carried inside, tables cleaned off, and someone had to carefully take down the display quilts. She didn't want to leave a mess for Mary-Alice. Or endanger the quilts by leaving them out all night.

"I saw the twins leave about a half hour ago," Nick said. "I assumed one of them was Prudy."

Rats.

"What about Renée? She's my ride home." If her friend had already left, Uncle Nick could take her home. Yet another hash mark on his rescue tally. Or perhaps Thea could grab a police-ride-along with Detective Brewster. But would Heather Ann approve?

Cole reached over and touched Thea's arm. "May I escort you home? Right after we clean up this mess." More dimples.

Maybe this evening could be salvaged after all.

Just then, an officer ushered a person past them into the house, probably to meet with Detective Brewster. Even in the dimming light, Thea recognized Louisa.

Recalling her own interview, Thea felt her attitude slide back into the glum zone. "Why do all these people have to wait here and be interrogated? I doubt they even went inside the house. These are my guests, for heaven's sake!" She dropped her head in her hands. "My party is ruined."

Worse, Mary-Alice was hurt, her antique brooch was missing, and Thea had trashed Odette, *and* stubbed her poor toe . . . and . . . what? There was something else.

Oh, no. Thea sucked in her breath and stared bleakly toward the house.

She had forgotten all about Dr. Cottle.

8

As he backed out of her driveway Thea waved her thanks to Cole and watched his Durango's headlights recede. She closed the cottage door and latched the deadbolt. Drawing back the door's window shade a bit, she peeked out to catch a last glimpse of Cole's car as it disappeared around the curve.

He had been quiet on the drive home. Maybe sensing her bee-in-the-brain fixation on Dr. Cottle's absence from the soirée. What if the absent expert had arrived smack in the middle of the muddle, just in time for his own police interview? Would Cottle's concept of Larkindale be one of a backwoods, Podunk town? One where hostesses get bonked on the back of the head at random?

With the Wentworth Mansion as the setting for the soirée, he would have expected a grand gala event. Which didn't happen. In fact, if she hadn't completely forgotten about him in her anxiety over the evening, Thea might have had the presence of mind to pray for a Cottle cancellation.

Targeting some one-on-one time with her sofa, she turned and stumbled, tangling with her cat, who was busy executing feline figure-eights around her mistress's bare ankles. Thea righted herself and scooped Betty up, pressing a cheek against the calico's coat. "There you are, pretty kitty."

She held Betty like a newborn, tucked into her arms with paws and claws folded in, not wanting to risk a tear to her vintage dress. "You need a pet-a-cure, girl," she said. Fingering the heart-shaped ID tag on Betty's black collar, she read the name engraved on the metal out loud. "Pretty Kitty. That's you." She gave Betty a little squeeze.

Awkwardly, Thea turned on a red-shaded table lamp, bathing the room in a rosy hue, as if the sun was setting inside. She dropped her purse on the floor next to her quilt bag and kicked off her sandals. Still cradling the cat and using her elbow, she pushed a pile of clean laundry across the cushions and sank into the sofa. Stroking Betty's softness, Thea felt the cat rev up a purr. Betty closed her golden eyes in apparent bliss.

Did she have time to work on her current quilt project before bed? She loved the original Aunt Elena design, based on a traditional Fence Rail pattern. With a twist. A cat-patterned square her aunt put in each design for her niece. Thea had chosen the fabric herself from the back room at The Quintessential Quilter. The last of the jewel-toned fabrics from Sissy's private Smithsonian collection, reproduction textiles mirroring patterns from the nineteenth century. Fitting, she thought, since the theme of the quilt show was A Legacy of Quilts.

Thea wished she could have entered it this year. But it was unfinished.

The quilt top, backing, and batting were securely basted with contrasting thread, about two-thirds of the hand quilting done. Thea was anxious to get a few new stitches in before bedtime. But a clock on the side table told her the time was ticking fast, with few ticks to spare for stitchery tonight. Already 11:45 P.M. Rats.

Next to the clock, the answering machine blinked. Twelve messages. Double rats.

"Don't want to hear those messages, Betty. I'm sure they're just problems for me to solve. And it *will* be me. It's not like I have a contributing co-chair, do I?" Thea scratched behind the animal's ear. Betty opened one eye and flicked her crooked whisker.

"What? Too catty?" Thea asked, unable to quench a tiny grin. "Though I suppose nothing is too catty for you." She exhaled deeply and pressed the play button.

The first message was short. "Thea, this is Nina. I quit."

Thea groaned. Nina was on the Set Up/Tear Down Committee for the quilt show. What had happened to cause Nina to walk out when she was needed most?

According to the subsequent calls, a number of quilt show glitches had come up: more items were needed for the boutique, some theme props had been dropped off early and were stored in Wanda's garage, angering her neatnik husband, and a message from Lyndi Meeks, recapping a row with Nina, which caused her to quit the committee.

Thea's head throbbed. She pressed the answering machine's pause button, laid the cat on a cushion and, exhausted, padded into the tiny kitchen. Maybe some tea would soothe her psyche.

After running some water into the kettle, she placed it atop the stove and turned on the flame. She waited stoveside, rubbing her still-sore toe against the back of her leg, thinking about the day's even more painful events. Mary-Alice's fall and . . .

What *had* happened to Dr. Cottle? His presence had been so important. In deference to Mary-Alice, he'd even agreed to judge the Best of Show entry. Cottle's connection would lend an air of importance to the event. Maybe next year quilters would come from neighboring states instead of just nearby cities.

Why didn't he show? The image of an auto, plunging over a cliff, crashing into flames at the bottom, played across her mental big-screen, rousing Thea's inner 'fraidy cat. She must stop these wild imaginings.

"A load of codswallop," her British grandmother Elspeth would say. "Stuff and nonsense!" And she would be right.

The kettle whistled and forced Thea back to the present. Turning off the flame, she floated two orange spice teabags directly inside the metal pot. She wasn't preparing a proper cuppa and glad her mum wasn't there to see. In Thea's quest for hot, fragrant immediacy, she had omitted a few steps in the ritual.

And instead of choosing her favorite Dainty Blue patterned Shelley teacup, Thea dug deeper into the cupboard and drew out a lemon-curd–colored mug, picturing a threaded needle over a music staff. She read the familiar quote on the side, "Sew . . . a needle pulling thread." It always made her smile, bringing back thoughts of Renée and herself playing sisters in their junior high production of *The Sound of Music*.

Humming, Thea poured half-and-half into the mug's bottom and added the tea. The spicy scent wafted through the cottage like simmering potpourri. A couple lumps of sugar and the steaming brew was ready.

Once seated and a sip or two taken, she noticed her luxury-seeking cat had moved onto the pile of laundry and now rested between black sweatpants and some colored t-shirts. Though she brushed Betty every day, Thea was in danger of having a hair shirt to wear. Or more than one.

She relocated Betty to the floor. The cat stretched, kneaded the carpet, and cozied down.

Thea pulled the sweatpants and an oversized t-shirt out from the pile, stood, and changed, tossing her filmy frock across the back of a neighboring chair. She noticed her Winnie-the-Pooh slippers sticking out from beneath the chair, dragged them out, and slipped her bare feet inside. Getting comfortable on the sofa, she propped her Winnies on an ottoman.

Through squinty eyes, her gaze darted to the answering machine, its message light flashing frantically. Her hand refused to press the button. Didn't she have enough problems to solve?

Sipping tea, Thea thought again of carefree days when she and Renée were still close. She fixed her eyes on an antique print positioned above the TV. A gold filigree frame surrounded swirly glass from the 1800s. The old glass was one of her favorite things, almost like looking into a pool of ripples during a gentle rain.

The print portrayed two little girls playing dress-up in big hats, wearing long strands of pearls, their pudgy feet hidden in high heels. Lacy shawls and long skirts draped over the side of a large open trunk. When Thea had first noticed the picture at the Antique

Emporium, she was reminded of her best friend and times they had once shared. With Renée away on an extended honeymoon and Thea pining the loss, she brought the picture home. As a comfort.

It didn't comfort her tonight. Rather, it made her cross. The girls seemed to be arguing over the contents of the trunk. Was one of them acting snooty? The one who reminded her of Renée? Thea had never noticed the child's arrogant expression as both girls preened in front of an ornate mirror. Did this print also reflect what was happening between Thea and her best friend in present day?

Deciding her eyes were unreliable during a headache, she blinked several times, then pressed the play button on the answering machine. More messages, each outlining a problem . . . no, a crisis . . . only Thea or Prudy could unravel.

Correction: Only Thea could resolve.

Blah . . . blah . . . blah. She should be writing all this down. Closing her eyes, she leaned her head back against the cushions. There was always tomorrow to take notes.

The next message brought her to full alert. "Ms. James, this is Dr. Cottle's private secretary. As in, Dr. Niles Cottle of the California State Quilt & Textile Museum? I apologize for not calling earlier. Dr. Cottle has been delayed and is unable to attend Mrs. Wentworth's affair this evening. He sends his regrets."

Stunned, Thea replayed the message. If only she had known this earlier, she wouldn't have worried about their expert's absence. Okay, maybe she forgot about him for a while, but still. There had been plenty to concern her and Prudy, had her co-chair cared to be concerned, without the Cottle calamity.

Odd the secretary didn't leave a number. Thea would have to follow up. Later.

Two messages left. She pressed play and waited.

"Thea, luv. I'm worried about you," Mum said, her elegant English accent soothing. "You must be quite ravaged by the evening's kerfuffle, dear. Bad luck, indeed."

Though not born across the Pond, Mum's accent seemed real, if often clichéd. A result of her exposure to Beatlemania, reading

Austen and Wodehouse, listening faithfully to Marianne Faithfull albums, and watching the BBC. But the appeal and personality of her British war-bride mother-in-law, Elspeth James, influenced Mum the most. Prizing all things from the Motherland, she had perfected her faux English style over many years. Now, no one even remembered she wasn't of the Empire born.

Continuing, Mum mentioned she'd called to check on Mary-Alice "in hospital." The senior was resting, having a layabout. And Thea was to get some rest, as well. Right after ringing up her mum. No need to mind the time. "Hearing your voice is the nighttime tonic I need to sleep, luv."

Thea smiled. Mum always made her feel better.

The last message blared. "What happened to you, Thea? I left as soon as I was liberated from your little police party. Thanks so much." A few sentences and Renée had ruined Thea's mellowing mood with well-honed sarcasm. "Howie needed my help with all those extra guests at the Inn. Besides, I'm a newlywed, you know."

As if Thea needed the reminder.

She eyed the antique print again. The little girls seemed to be pulling each other's hair. Thea stared hard, refocusing, making a decision. If those children couldn't get along, soon they would be hanging in the antique store instead of her living room.

Maybe she needed to put the picture in the corner for a time-out.

But first, Thea had an important call to make.

9

Monday morning dawned much too cheerful, as if it had forgotten the drama of the previous night. Thea had not. The daylight's joyful disposition differed from her mood. Which darkened after an unanswered call to Prudy. It didn't help to listen again to all her messages and make "honey-do" notes. Especially, since it was apparent *she* was the honey who must do it all.

Some quick oatmeal sprinkled with brown sugar, pelted with raisins, and then gobbled without grace, did not satisfy her palate. Thea craved pancakes. She checked her watch—8:20 A.M. Probably Prudy and Trudy were at Curly's Miner Diner this minute, consuming a short stack, still early enough to get the Diner-deal. Thea determined not to look in Curly's window on her way to open the Antique Emporium.

Or take notice if she spotted Prudy's car parked outside.

She said good-bye to Betty and backed her carrot-colored Jeep Wrangler out of the driveway, peeking over as she passed the Durtles' freaky house next door. Run-down and overrun with cats—eleven at last count. But Thea tried to keep Betty inside. To keep her from hanging out with a bad crowd.

Thea had mixed feelings about her ancient neighbors. Despite her devotion to antiques, some weren't as collectable or lovely to display. Mr. Durtle seemed nice enough, his bent figure rising to wave at her as he puttered in the gnarly yard. The outside activity puzzled Thea since his yard never appeared to improve. Mrs. Durtle was another mystery. Wraith-like, with white hair unkempt as her garden, she often stared out through a large windowpane on the side of the house. The side facing Thea's driveway.

Today the glass was Durtle-free, giving Thea a little break from the bizarre. She sped down the road, passing the entrance to historic Old Town and turning toward Faith Memorial Hospital located on the outskirts of Larkindale.

She found a parking spot near the entrance and jumped out of the Jeep, instantly remembering the sore toe inside her clogs. Limping a few steps, Thea worked out the twinge, annoyed with an odd feeling of déjà vu. Not long ago she had tripped over a rubber ducky and injured her ankle. Before that, she was showing her sister a cool karate kick and struck the side of the dining room table, breaking her baby toe.

Maybe she should have taken karate classes first.

Still . . . what was up with all the foot failures?

With less than an hour 'til the Emporium opened, Thea dashed toward the double-doors, which swung wide in automated appreciation of her arrival. At the front desk, she learned Mary-Alice's room number. A plump lady in pink pointed the way. "Down the long hall clear to the end. Last door on your right."

Starting her trek down the never-ending hallway, Thea concentrated on some small quilts hung up between rooms, a nod to the upcoming Blocks on the Walk Quilt Show. Possibly Mary-Alice's influence, since she served on the hospital board. More quilts were displayed in the Larkindale Library and, of course, in the museum, where the Wentworth family's legacy quilt would be displayed.

Thea caught her breath. Rats! Tonight was the unveiling of "Larkin's Treasure" at the Hastings McLeod Museum in Pioneer Park. How could she forget? She slowed her walk to an old lady shuffle and ticked items off her mental list. The mayor would be there, which meant Thea needed to look her best. And Dr. Cottle, as overseer of the Wentworth quilt while on loan from the State

Quilt & Textile Museum, was *supposed* to come, too. Maybe so, maybe no. She'd need to ask Mary-Alice for his phone number.

The press would be there, meaning local and even state newspapers. Making Cole's attendance guaranteed. Again, Thea needed to look her best.

Good heavens. What would she wear on such an occasion? To compete with the fashionable Mayor Stiles? Her diamond stud earrings, of course. Or . . . ? Thea was suddenly stabbed with a sense of disloyalty. The earrings had been a gift from her fiancé, Jeff, who had died almost two years ago. Was it okay to wear them when spiffing up for another man? She decided to figure it out later and shuffled on.

Thea and her team planned for television crews, local and beyond, to cover the quilt show. The publicity would ensure a huge crowd on Saturday. And provide needed foot traffic for Larkindale's businesses, including her own.

What if the media became aware of last night's disaster at the quilt show kick-off? Even if Cole didn't share his on-the-scene experience, there would be a police log. And so many innocent people had been dragged through the entire ordeal. They would want to talk it out, right? This kind of publicity could ruin everything. Thea gulped.

Squaring her shoulders in a big-girl stance, she entered the room. Mary-Alice was alone, eyes closed, a childlike bundle under the white blanket. Instead of a typical hospital gown, she was wrapped in a lacy bed jacket of Tiffany-box blue.

Thea felt quite underdressed in her jeans and t-shirt. Slipping the purse strap off her shoulder, she noted the now exposed Blocks on the Walk Quilt Show logo on her lavender shirt. She'd purchased a different colored one to wear each day of the week, leading up to the show. What would Renée think of her style now?

Thea approached the patient, who awoke. "How nice of you to come and see me, my dear." She lifted a hand in greeting, the satin sleeve falling back from her slim arm.

Thea leaned over and kissed Mary-Alice's wrinkled cheek. "Did I wake you? How do you feel?" She pulled a chair closer, and it screeched across the tiled floor.

"Actually, I've already had breakfast, a visit from the doctor, and a chat with the nice Detective Brewster." Mary-Alice looked pleased. "Doesn't he have the most arresting eyes?"

Very punny. But at the mention of the detective and his hypnotic stare, Thea felt herself slide back into the discomfort of last night's interview. Wanting to skip the replay, she evaded the arresting eye question, instead asking, "What did Brewster have to say?"

A flicker of worry altered Mary-Alice's expression. "He told me my diamond brooch was missing. Strange. Earlier, I'd considered wearing it for the soirée. But it would have clashed with my so-called necklace." She smiled sadly. "The silver chain with the museum key, remember?"

Thea nodded. "By chance, did you take the brooch out and try it on?" If so, maybe Mary-Alice set it somewhere else other than returning it to its case. Somewhere Louisa didn't even notice when she inventoried her future inheritance.

"I don't think so, but the memory's still a little foggy, my dear." Mary-Alice tapped her temple with a bony finger. "The doctor said it should clear up in time."

"Of course it will. Did Detective Brewster say anything else?"

"Just asked how I came to be on the floor in my bedroom," Mary-Alice said and shrugged her narrow shoulders. "If only I could remember!"

"I know, my friend. But how you ended up there is a mystery to everyone." Thea took Mary-Alice's hand in her own. "I wonder if the police have learned anything to help you put the pieces together."

"If they have, Detective Brewster didn't tell me." The senior sighed deeply. "Though he did say they found my cell phone outside. On the other side of my neighbor's fence. Can you imagine? Someone must have thrown it out my bedroom window."

So the perp had flung Mary-Alice's phone over the fence. Why? To make sure Mary-Alice couldn't call for help?

"Most likely, I simply slipped and fell. And mislaid my beautiful brooch. It was a gift from my husband, Seth, you know," she said. Her lips quivered a little. "And now, here I am in the hospital, making a huge hubbub for everyone." She looked at Thea, her gaze seeking comfort.

"Not true, Mary-Alice. We're all just thankful you are going to be okay," Thea said. She could see the woman was upset, on the edge of tears. Thea tried a new tact. "By the way, I didn't see Kenneth or Louisa in the waiting room."

"Louisa will be here for lunch," Mary-Alice said. Her expression brightened. "She's busy this morning, overseeing the soirée clean-up for me. Isn't it nice of her?"

"Oh, yes," Thea said. But she meant, "Oh, no." Where was Louisa in the wee hours when Thea and Cole carried in the remaining food, washed off tables, took down quilts, and swept the stone pathways? Sitting on her bum, watching the telly? To put it Mum-style. Uncle Nick helped, too, and the housekeeper, Annette. No Louisa in sight.

"Kenneth needed to stop at the police station to make a statement. Then he had to go into town for something. He said he might end up in Sacramento if he couldn't find just what he wanted," Mary-Alice said.

"What was it?"

"No idea. He didn't want me to worry about anything, dear boy." Mary-Alice gazed out the window as if anticipating his arrival. Then she turned back to Thea, thoughtful. "Did you know he once had the lead in a Little Theatre production? He's a talented actor. But spends too much time alone." Mary-Alice sounded wistful and her kind eyes watched Thea. "I do wish he'd find a nice woman to marry."

Oh, no! Does she mean me? With Kenneth? An inner "eww" oozed over her, and Thea's stomach turned a bit queasy, as if her insides were gherkins splashing about in a half-full jar.

I knew I should have had pancakes.

Thea glanced around for a place to sit down, then realized she was already seated.

Mary-Alice looked alarmed. "Oh, my dear! I didn't mean to suggest *you* for Kenneth," she said, pressing Thea's hand. "You have quite a nice young man, already, don't you?"

"Ye-es . . . ," Thea said. "I guess." Maybe not entirely true, but who was she to dispute her dear friend's opinion?

This time, Mary-Alice changed the subject. "Now, tell me what happened last night, my dear," she said. Her pale eyes took on a new sparkle, greedy with curiosity. "Don't leave anything out."

Thea proceeded to summarize the evening's events. Her questioning of Odette and the apparent regrilling by Brewster. Thea sugar-glazed her own interview, mentioning more about the officers taking statements in the garden, aided by Uncle Nick.

"I almost forgot," Thea said. "Officer Threet stood guard with his K-9 partner, Justice, and there was yellow crime tape strung everywhere."

"How festive. I do so love yellow ribbon."

"Pardon?" Thea wondered if her friend's head bump had harmed her hearing, too.

Mary-Alice laughed. "I'm teasing you, my dear. We need some levity. What a terrible evening. How did Dr. Cottle take it?"

"Well . . ." Thea had skipped over the Cottle quandary during her narrative. She explained now, winding up with the ill-timed message from the doctor's private secretary, cancelling his appearance at the soirée. "If I'd known he wasn't coming, I wouldn't have worried he was in an accident or something."

For a couple minutes.

"You poor dear," Mary-Alice said.

"I know," Thea said. And allowed herself a momentary pity party. She'd put enormous effort into her Cottle-concerns. "By the way, do you have a contact number for Dr. Cottle's private secretary? She didn't leave one."

"Of course. Would you mind reaching into the cabinet, my dear?" Mary-Alice gestured toward her bedside table. "My handbag . . ."

Thea unlatched the faux wood door and located the bag. She held it open for her friend, who pulled a small address book from a side pocket. Mary-Alice turned a few pages, searching for the secretary's number.

Thea was just thinking the purse's contents were a little too orderly when Mary-Alice said, "Here it is! But didn't you say the message was from a woman?"

Nodding, Thea leaned over the bed rail, trying to see the name.

"I never spoke to a woman. Or a secretary. I don't believe he has one," Mary-Alice said. "My liaison was Dr. Cottle's Administrative Assistant, a Mr. Ralph Galliano."

But *someone* had left the message on Thea's phone. Who?

10

Thea turned her vehicle beneath the arched sign declaring, "Welcome to Old Town Larkindale." She scanned the high spots but didn't see any quilt show banner yet. Whatever was Heather Ann doing with herself? Breakfasting with the twins?

She sped past Curly's Miner Diner with only a brief look through his windows. No Prudy in sight. No Trudy either. Though Thea probably couldn't tell the difference since the twins were now dressing alike. Ridiculous behavior for women of a thirty-something age. A tiny heart twinge pricked Thea's memory of late-night phone chats with Renée, plotting their matching outfits for school the next day.

Parking her Jeep in the alley, Thea mounted the steps to the raised cement walk and hurried past other historic storefronts facing the town square. She passed The Babbling Book. The twenty percent off sale signs posted in the window didn't tempt her to stop. Just beyond the bookstore, she ignored the tug of Adeline's Apothecary & Post Office Annex. No time to her habitual "howdy" with Adeline.

Instead, she continued her trek and looked to the left at her favorite sight, her eyes on the grand old flag. Towering over the square, its base encircled with vivid purple and yellow pansies and pink verbena, the sight made her heart stand at attention. The

Colors stood at rest, reminding Thea today would likely be hot. In more ways than one, if she ever got hold of Prudy.

Sprinting along the walk, her socked feet slipped, unsteady inside the brown leather clogs. Thea had to slow her pace or risk a fall in front of a few customers who waited for the stores to open. At 9:52 A.M., she unlocked the Antique Emporium door, entered, and shut herself inside with an apologetic smile to a tracksuited lady reaching for the knob.

"Eight minutes and we'll be open," Thea mouthed to the woman through the oak-framed glass, holding up the appropriate number of fingers and relocking the door.

The woman dropped her hand, disappointed.

As Thea tossed her purse on the front display counter, she glanced up at the old Seth Thomas mantel clock. Its ancient hand clicked off another minute, adding unwelcome pressure she didn't need. Not after last night's fête fiasco and unfortunate interview with Detective Brewster.

A knot formed in her throat, but she swallowed it. No time to dwell on it now.

Thea flipped some switches, turning on the overhead deco chandeliers, then headed for the coffee cupboard behind the soda fountain. She and her sister, Rosie, spun round and round on these same rotating barstools as children, hearing them rumble, while waiting for their favorite drinks. The thought made her thirsty for a cherry cola. And for the old days when their Andy-of-Mayberry type Gramps was the soda jerk.

A lot had changed in only a smattering of years: the deaths of her grandfather, father, and then, only two years ago, her fiancé, Jeff. Dear memories came alive every time she opened the Emporium door, its glass lettered with gold calligraphy:

James & Co. Antique Emporium
Fine Antiques & Collectibles
Since 1948

Thriving for many years under Gramps's steady hand, now Thea struggled to keep the store afloat amid online antique auctions and a bad economy. High gas prices kept people home, as well. If only the Blocks on the Walk Quilt Show went off well, attracting a new population of tourists to Larkindale. Then Thea could relax. And so could the other Old Town business owners.

Echoing in the cave-like Emporium expanse, Thea heard the clock click off another minute. She jerked open a cupboard and pulled out the first coffee can she touched—toasted almond. Not her favorite, but it must be somebody's passion. Grabbing an empty coffeemaker carafe from the nearby table, she rinsed it out and filled it with tap water. Thea liked to provide a cup of flavored coffee to her customers at no expense.

If folks wanted the real coffeehouse experience, just a few steps into the Espresso Café and they could order designer drinks. The Café consisted of the Emporium's soda fountain and some space filled with round tables and mismatched chairs. About 11:00 A.M., Emby Minsky, Larkindale's favorite flower child and baker, took up residence behind the fountain and set out her pastry wares. The spicy-sweet scents pulled passersby into the Café like a Pooh-Bear to a honey pot. And often, customers ambled right on into the antique store for a little shopping therapy.

Thea toggled the "on" button, and the coffeemaker gave a few groans. Perhaps she should invest in one of those single-cup-at-a-time machines. But then, this one worked so hard. And produced the best aroma. She patted the top of the coffeemaker.

After positioning the "Please Help Yourself" sign on the table, Thea put out a few more paper cups and napkins, some creamer and sugar. Then clogged over to the gilded mirror hanging behind the fountain for a customary hair and makeup inspection.

Remove raisin bits between teeth. Check. Brush mascara flakes off cheeks. Check. Wait a minute. Was that a blemish starting on her chin? She peered closer. Then jumped back, startled by a sharp rap-rap-rap on the front door.

The woman in the tracksuit frowned from behind the glass along with a couple others who pointed at their watches. Thea stared at the old clock face as it clanged the first of ten chimes. A few other clocks joined in the chorus.

Uh-oh. She wasn't quite ready to open. Thea felt her chin, positive she had the beginning of a blemish. It must be thwarted before tonight's unveiling at the museum. Cole would be there. And so would Suzanne Stiles.

And Renée.

Blowing out an incensed breath, she marched to the door, held up one finger, and turned away as a man rattled the knob. She snatched up her purse from the counter and dashed into her office. Unlocking the safe, she pulled out the cash box and shoved her purse in the blank spot. Thea rushed back out front and had just slid the container under the counter when the phone began to ring.

What if it was Prudy?

More doorknob rattles told her to let the machine take a message while she admitted the customers. She prayed it wasn't another grump-o-gram like those she'd gotten last night. Except for Mum's, of course.

Before the door was fully open, two of the customers pushed against it to get inside. The glass hit Thea in the face with a thwack. She stood for a moment, stunned, like mountain sheep after ramming horns on a wild animal TV show. Then massaged her nose.

Would her accessories for tonight include both a bruised schnozzle and a blemish? Set off by diamond stud earrings? What if her nose had broken?

With its slight sprinkling of freckles, her short, straight nose was one of the few features she didn't dislike. She'd inherited it from her beautiful mum.

What if she had to wear a nasal cast?

The first woman who had waited the longest asked, "Are you okay?" She stepped onto the mat, causing a cheery jingle to compete with the ringing phone. "That wasn't me beating down your door, by the way. It was those rude people." She indicated the couple, now exploring a corner full of vintage furniture.

Thea stooped to anchor the door with a 1920s-era Boston terrier doorstop. She stood up, breathed deeply through her wounded nose to be sure she could, and inhaled the fresh coffee fragrance. Lovely. Her nose was working.

"I'm fine. Never better," she said. "Sorry I was late opening. I'd been to see a friend in the hospital and . . ." She stopped herself.

Should she be sharing this? What if the lady asked who it was and happened to know Mary-Alice? Would she want the whole gruesome story of the assault? Maybe the woman was in Larkindale for the quilt show.

If Thea wasn't careful, she could start a rumor.

Even worse, she could tell the absolute truth.

11

The woman brushed aside Thea's apology and said, "It's okay. I know how it goes. And you were only a minute or so late." She looped her handbag strap over her head and across her chest, messenger-bag style. She wiggled her fingers and grinned. "I like to shop hands-free. Now I'm ready."

"Can I direct you toward anything in particular?" Thea asked, wary, wondering if the woman would ask for vintage quilts. If so, then Thea had been right to stop herself.

"Hand-tinted prints. Primarily ones with people. Or animals. Got any?"

"Way in the back." Thea pointed toward a gallery wall and her blood pressure slowed to a drone. "All our hand-tinted prints are grouped together. Nutting, Sawyer, Davidson, and so on."

The phone had stopped ringing. Beeps and chirps signaled a message recording. Thea was grateful she couldn't hear a voice; it might be bad news. She would listen to it later, with no customers nearby. Right now duty called.

Rather, duty hollered.

She turned the sign in the window from Closed to Welcome, then took her place behind the counter. After pulling out the cash box, Thea deposited the money into the filigreed cash register. She paused to appreciate its regal beauty. Like a sentinel, it stood guard on the counter, ready to remind the customers to pay for their items before they left the Emporium, rewarding them with a melodic ding when they did so.

Perusing her mental list, Thea remembered last night's request for more boutique items. Apparently, it wasn't enough she had donated an ornate Singer hand-cranked sewing machine with original parts, including the sought-after instruction manual. Noooo. Now she must cruise the antique store and search for other temptations for the attendees.

She cruised up and down the wide aisles with dealer booths on both sides, alternately picking up a Shirley Temple doll, a Harker mixing bowl, and a French graniteware lunch box. She swung the box by its handle, admiring the chicken-wire pattern on the enamel. Would anyone pack a lunch in it now? Even something as cute as this? With Tupperware in the cabinet? She moved on to other booths.

Since A Legacy of Quilts was the quilt show's theme, Thea needed to look for items to complement the Quilt-Without-Guilt Guild's handmade potholders, aprons, table runners, and pillows. Vintage stitchery stuff. And things light and easy to transfer to her Jeep. She chose a pink, sixties sewing basket as a carryall.

Her first selection for the basket—a set of embroidered tea towels featuring cuddly puppies doing chores every day of the week. If they'd been kitties, the towels would already be hanging in Thea's kitchen. She added numerous cards of sparkly vintage buttons, a glass sock darner, and a 1919 John Deere tape measure she'd been scouting for some time.

Rats. She wanted it for herself. But she tossed it into the sewing basket anyway.

A small object inside a display case caught her eye. An old Amish thimble with the identifying mark stamped inside the brass edge. Thea sort of wanted that, too. But the plastic thimble she'd bought at The Quintessential Quilter worked fine. She unlocked the case, reached in, and soon the thimble joined other notions in the pink basket. About to lock up the case again, she noticed a lovely set of

J.A. Henckels decorative scissors from Germany. Thea looked at them with longing.

So beautiful. So sharp. She put them in the basket. So gone.

Back at the counter, she noted the booth number and price on each article, and tallied the total. Whoa, hefty. Would the dealers donate these items? If they didn't, then she must foot the bill. It was a tidy sum to spend, counting the sewing machine. But in Thea's world, it didn't come close to the value of the many hand-pieced and hand-stitched beauties donated by the quilters. She had only made one quilt so far, but it took hours and hours.

And hours.

The woman shopper appeared in front of Thea holding a small, framed something. "Your nose looks pretty good."

"Pardon?" Thea had forgotten and ran her finger along the bridge. Was her nose out of joint? Nope. She tried to keep from grinning at her own inside joke.

"The redness is becoming. Like you've been out in the snow," the woman said.

"Thanks, I think. What did you find?"

"I love this. Love-love-love." She placed the picture on the counter. "I'll buy it."

"Nice," Thea said. It was a hand-tinted print featuring a domestic scene. A long-skirted lady examining a lace scarf pulled from a tall bureau. "Congratulations on a great find. A signed David Davidson print, 'Treasured Scarf.'"

Hmm . . . treasure. Pondering the word as she wrapped the print in bubble wrap, she was reminded tonight was the unveiling of "Larkin's Treasure" at the museum. Thea needed to check on the refreshments, figure out where to store the theme props to keep Wanda's marriage together, and confirm Dr. Cottle's appearance later with his assistant, Mr. Galliano. Plus, make a run out to the museum to check on everything before she rushed home to make herself presentable.

She wrapped faster.

Where was Lyndi Meeks? Emby didn't open the Espresso Café until 11:00 A.M., but Thea wished for the older woman's calming effect now. And a little TLC. And pancakes.

The happy customer paid for the artwork and clutched it close, stepping aside at the door, allowing others to enter. Two more customers arrived, followed by Emby. Lyndi and another part-timer, Mariana Ortiz, trailed a few yards behind, deep in a discussion. Hallelujah.

Thea waved Lyndi over and smiled at Mariana who went to store her things. Emby, clad in her usual batik skirt and peasant blouse, pulled her cart laden with premade desserts for the Café inside. A blast of sweet-smelling aromas engulfed the entryway.

"Whazzup, boss-lady?" Lyndi asked, placing a hand on her hip, her red and gold Bakelite bracelets clicking together. She laid her free hand on the glass countertop and tapped long fingernails. Thea watched the nails, also painted red and gold. They tapped a familiar rhythm, which reminded her of the Lone Ranger's horse galloping in time with the *William Tell* Overture.

Staring at Lyndi's beautiful manicure, Thea withdrew her own chewed fingernails from sight. Lyndi's bright nails matched her cardinal-colored shirtdress and gold belt. And today, her purple hair exploded into a short, spiked frenzy on top, teased without mercy. It crowned her otherwise long locks, giving the illusion of a matching chrysanthemum-shaped hat.

Unable to drag her eyes from the spectacle of hair and color, Thea decided Lyndi must have an identity crisis. Her clothes said fifties June Cleaver. But her hair said eighties rock group.

"Uh . . . you changed your hair," Thea said. "It's so . . . free."

Lyndi stopped tapping. "I know, right? I look just like Albert Einstein. Makes me feel smarter, too." She grinned and adjusted her rhinestone-edged glasses. "Did you get my message about Nina quitting the show?"

"Yes, but I'm not sure I understood what happened," Thea said. Even listening to the message again this morning had not cleared up the mystery. "Last night was pretty crazy."

"A calamity, most definitely," Lyndi said. "Nefandous, even."

"Nefandous?" Thea tilted her head. "Vocabulary word for the day? What's it mean?"

"Unspeakable." A satisfied smile rolled across Lyndi's face, but stopped when she seemed to recall something. "And it *was* unspeakable for poor Mary-Alice. Those police interviews were nothing to speak about either."

"True." Thea shuddered. Wanting to leave the whole nefandous calamity behind, she moved on. "Would you explain to me again why Nina quit?"

Hard to believe anyone would tussle with Lyndi since her good humor was legend in Larkindale. When she had volunteered to head up the quilt show's Set Up/Tear Down committee and oversee the heritage quilt displays at the Hastings McLeod Museum, Thea was thrilled. A big burden off her shoulders. And a generous gesture since Lyndi was still a rookie in their material world.

"Nina didn't like the way I placed the newsprint under the display areas. But I thought it would work better," Lyndi said. "So did Sissy."

"Just a difference of opinion. Happens." Though if Sissy agreed, it said a lot.

Briefly distracted by Mariana's petite form at the coffee table, Thea pulled her eyes back to the reality of Lyndi's Technicolor drama. "Sorry. You were saying?"

Lyndi pushed the red rhinestone glasses back up her nose. "Nina got so mad, she shoved me. I knocked over some quilt tripods and accidentally ripped up a lot of the newsprint."

"Goodness, don't worry about it. Are you okay?" No one had told Thea the quilters might turn on one another. Being co-chair was supposed to be no work at all. She'd been misinformed.

"Then Nina grabbed me," Lyndi said, rubbing her forearm. "Sissy had to separate us. My first catfight. I'm so ashamed of how I acted." She hung her purpled head and her red shoulders drooped. "The worst part is, Nina quit. Both the committee and the quilt guild."

"Don't be so hard on yourself, Lyndi. You weren't at fault."

"Like, you're not saying that because I work for you?"

"Of course not." Okay, maybe a little. Thea considered. "We need to find someone to help you. Too much work for one person."

Who could she tap at this late date?

"No prob. Sissy is assisting. We've got it covered." Lyndi beamed. Even the rhinestones in her glasses appeared to be flashing support.

"Hey. You need me to watch the counter? Lemme put my stuff away."

"Sure, thanks." Thea watched her bounce back to the office, then scanned the store. The man and woman seemed in cozy conversation, parked on a Victorian sofa. The two new customers browsed through some booths. Mariana cruised nearby, ready to help. In the Café, Emby busied herself arranging bakery items. And Lyndi—aka Thea's rescue—would soon return. Alone now, she seized the moment to punch the answering machine's play button. Lowering the volume, she hovered near the tiny speaker.

A perky voice said, "Hey, Thea. It's after 10:00. Isn't the Emporium supposed to be open? Where have you been? Don't you think it's time for us to meet about the quilt show?"

It was Prudy. At last.

12

With Lyndi counter-sitting and Mariana cruising the Emporium aisles, Thea hunkered down at her desk with the office door closed. She picked up the phone and called Prudy, catching her on the second ring.

"Thea, long time no see. Where ya been? We have a quilt show to put on, you know," Prudy said.

Surely the twin teased. Far too cheery. Though if Thea had been simply squiring her own sister, Rosie, around Larkindale and the forested hinterlands, eating at Curly's, without a quilt show millstone dragging behind, she might be every bit as bubbly.

It was unspeakably nefandous. Or was that a double negative?

"Prudy, can we please meet today? We need to coordinate our tasks so everything gets done." Thea struggled to be civil. "How about lunch at Curly's?"

A great idea. Thea could confirm the twins had ducked in for an early-bird special. And she could scarf down some pancakes.

They agreed to an 11:30 A.M. meeting time at the Miner Diner. Which left Thea wondering if she'd been wrong. It wasn't likely someone would return to the same café for lunch when she had breakfasted there only a few hours before.

Next, Thea called Wanda Wooten, who had also left a troubling message last night. Wanda, a favorite Quilt-Without-Guilt

Guild member, chaired the Theme Props committee. When they spoke, Wanda seemed close to hysteria. Her husband wanted the props out of their garage. Now.

"But Wanda, it's only for a week," Thea said. "Some are valuable antiques. In families for generations. We need a safe place to store those items where they will be protected."

"Well, they aren't going to be safe from my husband for much longer," Wanda said. "He wants to park his new pickup inside the garage, and there's no room. He's threatening to relocate everything to a dumpster down the street."

Uh-oh. "It's okay, Wanda. Tell him the props will be out of the garage today. Or this afternoon. Well . . . evening, for sure," Thea said, scribbling on a note pad. "I have a plan."

She had no plan. How was she going to pull this one off? Maybe an idea would materialize if she worked on her quilt. But no time for that now. She could think more clearly once she had a second breakfast.

Thea looked at her notepad to see what she had written. Pancakes.

Abandoning the telephone, she pulled her purse out of the storage cabinet and traipsed out front, stopping at the counter where Lyndi polished the old register. For a gal who looked like she was always dressed for Mardi Gras, she had a good work ethic.

Lyndi might look like a character, but she possessed character, as well. And that's why Thea gave her charge over tonight's vintage quilt display inside the Hastings McLeod Museum. And on Saturday, Lyndi would oversee the hanging of many more competition quilts, displayed outside in Pioneer Park and businesses in Old Town Larkindale.

"When are you heading over to the museum?" Thea asked.

"In a couple hours, after some backups come in to work," Lyndi said. "Mariana is staying all day, so we're covered there." She placed the pink sewing basket on the counter, full of quilting related items. "Donations, I presume?"

"Maybe." Thea grinned. She held up a finger, indicating she'd be right back, and ambled over to the soda fountain where Emby hummed a happy tune. Thea felt a surge of affection for the dear woman, forever lost in the sixties, overflowing with goodwill.

"What's happenin', Thea?" Emby stopped fussing with the baked goods, a sweet smile ready for her friend. "Cinnamon bun, honey-bun?"

She threw her long, thick braid over her shoulder before pushing a glass-domed plate full of glazed buns toward Thea. "My treat."

"Rain check?" Thea asked. Tempting, but a short stack called her name. "And you've got the cookies for tonight's quilt unveiling at the museum, right?"

"Right on. I'll be there. Cookies, too. It's going to be far out." Without warning, Emby floated around the fountain and engulfed Thea in a hug. "You're doing a great job, you know."

"What's the hug for?" Thea dabbed at her eyes, embarrassed.

"You looked like you needed a hug. Frankly, so did I." Emby gave her one more squeeze, a little shove, and then said, "Now off with you. Peace."

"Peace," Thea said and held up two fingers in the obligatory sign. Turning back to the counter, she picked up the pink sewing basket. Waving at Lyndi on the way out, she headed for her Jeep Wrangler.

―※※―

Opening the Jeep's back, Thea searched around for space to put the donation items. Not much room, since she hadn't unloaded all her groceries from the last trip to the market. She hadn't had time to sort out the canned goods—some went to the Christian Cupboard, some to her own. Plus, she'd tossed in two oversized rugs for a cleaning at Laundryland. Thea's reputation for never emptying her car had gotten around, so she preferred the passenger seat clear in case someone looked inside and got the wrong, or right, idea. No need to reinforce the rumor.

Wait a minute. The back seat might be full, but the floor was open for business. She secured the back, opened the rear door, and placed the sewing kit securely on the carpet. Then hopping into the driver's seat, Thea pulled out onto Main Street and circled around the town square. A hay-colored Jeep approached from the other direction. Though Thea didn't know the driver, he raised his hand in greeting. She waved back.

According to Uncle Nick, a Wrangler aficionado, all Jeepers were expected to uphold the tradition of the Jeep Wave. Always. Thea figured it was important to keep a good rapport with other owners, should her Jeep break down along the road. So she adhered to the rules and didn't waver.

Thea found a parking spot directly in front of Curly's and pulled in. Her stomach grumbled as she entered the diner. The scent of bacon frying, pies fresh from the oven, and pot roast all combined to torture her taste buds. She hurried past the fountain, its bronze miner panning for gold, the water spilling over the pan into a tiny pool. Thea found an unoccupied table and sat, shaky, too hungry to open a menu.

Curly arrived tableside, a red bandana tied around his head, his long ponytail captured in a hairnet. He wore a white apron around his waist and a short-sleeved flannel shirt. Pushing a plastic glass of ice water across the table, he stared pointedly at her nose and said, "You look a little worse."

"Do you mean . . . worse for wear?"

"I mean worse. Worse than the last time I saw you." Curly pulled out his pad. "What'll you have? Hearty or healthy? You look like you could use both."

"I've been thinking about your blueberry pancakes all morning, Curly. I'm almost drooling." Which was not a good look on anyone. "I better wait to order. Meeting someone." Thea gave him a weak smile. "How's it going with you?"

"Terrible," he said, his expression not changing.

"Oh, I'm sorry."

"Don't worry. I'm good at it. Who are you meeting? Your fella?"

"I wish. No, Prudy Levasich. And probably her twin sister, Trudy, too." Thea sighed.

Curly pulled a long, white something out of his apron and tossed in it on the table in front of her. "Well, that's the last straw."

No kidding.

Thea unwrapped the straw and watched him go, chuckling to herself until Prudy's outline in the doorway wrecked the mood. She appeared slimmer than Thea remembered and she'd seen her only last week. Maybe Prudy had worked herself into a smaller dress size, laboring on the quilt show.

But doing what?

Prudy entered the Miner Diner and scanned the thickening crowd. Her usually loose dark hair was pulled back into an elegant ballerina bun. A flowing tunic top over black leggings completed her dancer look. Had she already dressed for tonight's "Larkin's Treasure" unveiling?

Thea pinched her cheeks and fluffed her hair. Then stood, beckoning. Prudy finally noticed and walked across the café. She slid into a seat opposite Thea.

"I love your hair pulled back," Thea took her seat again, eyes on Prudy. "You look . . . like a model."

"The hair's a please-your-twin-sister thing." A trace of a smile crossed her face. "She is so into doing everything the same. It's just easier to play along. But I have to say, these outfits Prudy picked out are pretty cute."

"Pardon? You're not Prudy?"

"Are you kidding? God forbid." Trudy's words were as cool as her tone. "We look alike, but we're not alike. At. All." She dug into her designer bag, pulling out her cell phone, and checked for messages. Apparently, there were none because she tossed it back into the purse's depths. "So where is our waitress?"

She scanned the diner, searching, then signaled to someone. "There's Prudy. She wanted to freshen up before seeing you," Trudy said, inspecting Thea, as if wondering why her sister would take the trouble.

As her twin made her way to their table, Thea could now see some slight differences between the gals. Though dressed exactly the same, Prudy was the loser in presentation. Her hair and makeup compared favorably enough, but her figure appeared a bit thicker. Where Trudy wore an air of cool aloofness, Prudy seemed anxious, excusing herself to other customers as she weaved her way over. She pulled out the chair between her sister and Thea and plunked down in a most unballerina-like manner.

"Thea, finally we are together! So much to discuss," she said, as if she had been chasing her co-chair around town. "Let's order first. I'm—"

"Starved, right?" Trudy completed her sister's sentence with a reproving glance.

"Right." Prudy sent a fond smile back.

Trudy didn't return it, opening a menu instead, and ran her finger down the page.

Prudy dropped her eyes and fiddled with her purse, slumping a little.

For the first time since she'd known Prudy, Thea felt a prick of sympathy from the sister's snub. Embarrassing. Weren't twins supposed to be the closest of siblings? It seemed like only Prudy was close.

First impressions. Thea knew they didn't always tell the story.

"Brutal business last night. When did you get away?" Prudy asked. "We left as soon as we could. I figured one less person there to worry about was a good thing. Or in our case, two less. No need to thank me."

What was she talking about? Thea could have used *more* help last night. She was just about to say so, too, when Renée happened by their table.

"Hello, ladies. Mind if I join you?" Renée asked, seating herself in the final empty chair. She placed her tote on the floor. "Hope I'm not interrupting."

Before anyone could respond, Morlene Pickett, Curly's anorexic waitress appeared tableside with her pad and pen at the ready. Okay, maybe not truly anorexic, but she seemed all pointy angles and bony elbows. Her straight, scrawny legs reminded Thea of fence slats. Perhaps Morlene had taken her new name a bit too personally when she married Mr. Pickett.

"What'll you have?" A few black hairs peeking out of Morlene's bleached mustache showed the need for a little tweezer time. As she rattled off an enticing list of lunch specials, Thea stared at Morlene's upper lip, unable to look away.

"I know just what you'll order, Thea," Renée said. "Pancakes. Though it might not be the smartest choice, if you get my meaning." She arched perfect brows to punctuate her point, her half-smile filled with something like pity.

Morlene turned to Thea. "Pancakes, then?" She wrote on her pad.

"Well—" Thea hesitated.

"Think about Mayor Suzanne Stiles chatting for ages with that hunky Cole Mason last night, Thea. He sure seemed to enjoy it." Renée crossed her lovely hands in an angelic pose. "Naturally . . . it's your call."

Thea's cheeks grew warm. "Actually, I've decided on the Lite Plate. Medium well on the meat, please." Snapping her menu closed, she handed it to their waitress. Then straightened her cutlery, avoiding Renée's stare.

"You sure?" Morlene asked, her pen poised.

"Positive. I need the protein," Thea said. It felt like a lie but was probably true. She still had a meeting with Prudy to get through.

Morlene lined through what she had written and made a new note. She took orders from the twins, who both decided on the bacon cheeseburger with sweet potato fries.

Rats. Their orders sounded delicious. Now Thea was stuck with prisoner food while everyone else awaited a feast. She had failed to defend her pancake position. What happened to her courage? In the face of Renée's rude remarks, Thea's bravado had melted away like whipped butter on a short stack.

In a surprise move, Renée ordered the French Dip to go. "It's for my husband, Howie. And a side order of Curly's curly fries, too." She stood and glanced around the table. "Enjoy your meal, ladies. I've gotta run over to Designs by Deb and choose new pillows for the Inn."

She informed the waitress she'd be back to pick up Howie's sandwich order in fifteen minutes. Morlene gazed at her wrist-watch, a look of panic flooding her face, then rushed toward the kitchen, her slat legs a blur of motion.

Renée followed a few steps behind, moving to the exit with grace. Had she learned to walk in Paris? Thea sighed and watched her go, left to tend her inner injuries with only Prudy and Trudy for comfort.

If they were the consolation prize, Thea was not consoled.

To loosely quote Curly, this day looked worse.

13

Hoping to get some work done while they waited for lunch, Thea pulled a sheet of paper from her purse. A list of quilting concerns for the upcoming show. She smoothed it out on the table. "Prudy, you're a hard gal to track down. I was beginning to think I'd have to put your picture on a milk carton."

Prudy laughed. "I felt the same way about you."

Thea held her tongue in check, grinding her teeth until she could be cordial. "Thanks for meeting with me. If we can tidy up a few details before tonight's unveiling, the rest of the week should be less frantic."

"I thought so, too. Though, honestly, I'm so excited to show you my entry, Thea. This watercolor quilt is the best work I've ever done. Maybe an award winner because it has a twist," Prudy said, sitting up straighter. "Even Trudy thinks so, and she's won lots of awards."

Trudy admitted to both her many quilting awards from back east and admiration of her twin's show entry. "Hard to believe my own sister, Prudy Levasich, made such a beautiful quilt. By herself. Folks used to call her Prudy Leave-a-stitch because of her sloppy handwork." She shrugged her shoulders. "I don't know where all this amazing skill came from."

Once again, Thea wondered at the apparent competition between twins. Like a tennis match, volleying the ball back and forth. First, Prudy lobbed a supportive comment across the table and then Trudy slammed a negative one back. Hard.

The score? Prudy shut out with a big zero.

"I'm just a rookie quilter," Thea said. "But my Aunt Elena says the consistency of my stitches keeps getting better and better the more I practice. I'm sure it's the secret for Prudy, too."

Good heavens. Had she just sided with Prudy-the-annoying?

"Anyway," Thea said, "I'd love to see your quilt. Why don't you bring it over to the museum later for a little preview?"

"Oh, no you don't! I'm waiting 'til the last minute. To make a big impression on the judges," Prudy said. "Who's judging, by the way? Since Mary-Alice is out of commission? Do we want someone to step in right away?"

At last, Prudy had mentioned Mary-Alice. Though with zip compassion.

"Why do you ask? It's only Monday. Maybe she'll be recovered enough to act as judge by Saturday. Isn't it what we want? A fully restored Mary-Alice?" Thea took a sip of water, watching Prudy. She had certainly dismissed Mary-Alice's role as judge for the Blocks on the Walk Quilt Show. Fast. What was the hurry?

"Yes, yes. We do," Prudy said. "Of course, we do. It's just . . ."

"Just what?"

Trudy broke in. "Prudy planned to volunteer me as a judge in Mary-Alice's place since I've had quilt-judging experience." She schooled stern eyes on her sister. "I told you it would be a conflict of interest. But do you ever listen?"

Prudy studied her placemat, silent as a shameful thought.

Attempting to come to the rescue once more, Thea dug around in her handbag and found what she sought. "Here, Prudy," Thea said, handing over a slip of paper. "This is the number of Dr. Cottle's administrative assistant, Ralph Galliano."

Taking the slip of paper, Prudy opened it. "Why are you giving me this?"

"Just divvying out the duties. Can you call him and see if Dr. Cottle will be at the unveiling of 'Larkin's Treasure' tonight? He never showed last night for the soirée at Mary-Alice's."

"I didn't realize, I guess. We left pretty early," Prudy said.

"Yes. I know," Thea said. "When I wasn't worrying about Mary-Alice, I worried Dr. Cottle met with an accident. Then I got home and found a message on my phone. His secretary said he couldn't make it." Thea inclined her head, remembering. "But this morning, Mary-Alice said this Galliano person was supposed to be the liaison. Not a secretary. Who didn't mention her name. So . . . it's a mystery."

"Can't he have a secretary *and* an administrative assistant?" Trudy asked.

When she put it like that, it sounded so reasonable Thea felt silly. Of course he could have both. Dr. Niles Cottle was an important man.

"Good point," Thea said. "But if we don't connect with him soon, it will be Cottle's picture on the milk carton. 'Missing: quilt expert.'" And missing judge. What would they do if both Mary-Alice and Dr. Cottle weren't available for the quilt show?

Thea would think about *that* tomorrow.

Prudy folded the paper and tucked it in her purse. "I'll give him a call and leave you a message about what he says. You'll be home later, right?"

"Aren't you coming over to the museum to check on things this afternoon?"

"Don't see why I should. You're going to be there. Too many cooks you know."

Thea was dumbfounded. "But you are the co-chair."

"So are you." Prudy looked all innocence, as if they were truly sharing the load. "But I'll be happy to call this person for you. After all, I'm here to help."

"But . . . but . . . ," Thea was saved from further sputtering by Curly's appearance at their table. His hand supported a giant round tray, held high, as if flipping pizza dough.

"Welcome back, ladies," he said, grinning at each of them.

So Thea had been right. The twins probably put away piles of pancakes while Thea visited Mary-Alice and attended to the antique store. And solved quilt show hiccups.

"It's been a couple days, hasn't it, Prudy?" Trudy said. "Since we ate here?"

Double rats. If she was honest, Thea's attitude needed a troubleshooting session. Perhaps she should apologize to the twins. But then they would know she'd been holding a mythical breakfast against them. And who knows what else?

She considered other options, remembering a Bible verse Aunt Elena mentioned recently, "Anxiety weighs down the heart, but a kind word cheers it up."

That was the answer. Thea needed someone to give her a kind word. Or was she supposed to utter a kind word to Prudy? That couldn't be right. Either way, she should definitely ditch the anxiety part. Decision made, Thea felt a bit more cheerful.

Curly deposited a plate of plump burger and sweet potato fries in front of Trudy. He pulled a plastic ketchup bottle from his apron pocket and plopped it near. Then he placed the same order in front of Prudy, who grabbed the ketchup and streamed the stuff all over her fries.

"Is that your orange Jeep parked outside?" Curly asked Thea, and she nodded.

"New rig?" he asked.

"New for me. And the color is called Crush. You know, like the soda," Thea said.

"Nice ride," Curly said. "But I wondered, if we all drove white cars, would we be a white car nation?"

Chuckling again, Thea waited as Curly set down her plate with a flourish. "Here's your order."

Blueberry pancakes. With a side of whipped butter.

Even though Thea's mouth watered, she said, "I ordered the Lite Plate, Curly."

"Are you positive? The slip said 'pancakes.'"

Each holding a fry, the twins stopped midmunch to watch the diner drama. Thea glanced at them and thought how alike they were except when they opened their mouths to talk.

But her observations were better left unspoken. Or as Lyndi said, "Nefandous."

"My mistake," Curly started to pick up the plate of pancakes. "I can have the Lite Plate to you in a jiff."

Thea grabbed the plate's edges and held on. "No, it's okay. I don't want to put you to any more trouble. These will be fine." She looked up at Curly and tugged at the plate.

Was this going to come to blows?

Curly released the dish. "Thanks, Thea. Considerate of you. It's hopping around here."

Placing a wire holder containing three flavors of syrup down next to her short stack, he said, "If there's nothing else, everyone enjoy your lunch."

The twins, both edibly occupied, paid no attention.

Thea, unable to believe the happy mistake, looked up just in time to see him wink at her before heading back to the kitchen.

14

Back in the Jeep, with a tummy full of sweetness, Thea contemplated her next move. She had discussed a few quilt show issues with Prudy and wrenched her promise to stop by the museum this afternoon. Before the evening's unveiling at 7:00 P.M., Prudy might be able to tweak something in Thea's absence since it appeared their schedules didn't gel. At least one of the people in charge should be available most of the afternoon.

She tapped on the steering wheel thoughtfully. The boutique items needed to be delivered. But she could do it tomorrow. Her pledge to relocate the theme props from Wanda Wooten's garage hung over her like an unseen bogeyman.

And that couldn't wait until tomorrow.

Think... think. What would Mary-Alice do?

Thea closed her eyes and sent up a prayer. Then started her engine and backed out into Main Street. As she crept back into the light flow of traffic, a man in a pickup waved at her from the opposite lane. Why was he waving? He wasn't in a Jeep. But still, he looked familiar. Thea squinted for a better view.

Uncle Nick. Waving her over. What did he want? No matter. In Thea's world, any Uncle Nick encounter meant a happier heart. And he might be the one with a kind word. She parked in front of The Quintessential Quilter, and he pulled in two spots down.

Before she finished unbuckling her seat belt and checking the rearview mirror for blueberries between her teeth, Uncle Nick had her door open.

"Hi, Princess!" he said, extending a hand to help her out. "You look at the top of your game today. No easy feat after last night." Nick closed her door, tucked her arm in his, and gestured toward the town square. "Got a moment for your old uncle?"

Old, indeed. Nick Marinello looked quite the opposite with his handsome Italian features. Dark mane of curls, scarcely grayed at the temples. Teasing brown eyes with crinkles at the edge. And his fit form growing ever fitter in service to others. Thea sometimes wondered if Aunt Elena had any outside competition for his affections. She was the less attractive of the pair. But to Uncle Nick, his wife was his dream woman.

Years ago, Mary-Alice confided to Thea her uncle had a deep understanding of his God-given role as a husband. To love his wife as Christ loved the church. And watching the beauty of it play out in Nick and Elena Marinello's life together told Thea she could settle for no less.

Arm in arm, they walked across the street, Nick's slight limp not holding him back. They passed between vibrant flowerbeds, finding an unoccupied wooden bench. Fancy black wrought-iron legs and armrests gave it a vintage feel. Sitting down, Thea's bare arm touched the iron. She jerked it back.

"Ouch!"

As she rubbed the burned place, Thea wished her breeding allowed a more colorful reaction. Some might say a robust response took the sting right out of a sore spot. Was it true? She hadn't yet dared to confirm it. Her cheekiness would disappoint Mum, and Gram would be gobsmacked. Besides, Thea didn't want to nourish that part of her nature by letting it run free like a herd of mustangs. Uncontrolled language wouldn't be as majestic as wild horses. Or majestic at all.

Still, she needed a better word than "ouch." Maybe Lyndi could find a word of the day Thea could adopt for special occasions.

"Are you hurt? You're zoning out on me. Could be heat stroke. It's a scorcher." Concern written in his eyes, Nick scooted to the edge of the bench as if ready to jump up. "Want some cool water from the fountain?"

"No, thanks, I'm fine," Thea said. "Sorry, the heat makes me crabby."

The sun blazed, and she felt unwelcome rivulets of moisture trickling down her scalp. Perfect. Now she'd need to wash her hair before tonight's event. The heat made her drowsy, as if she had a fever and needed to lie down. The big lunch and soothing sound of water flowing in the fountain nearby combined to push her thoughts toward a nice nap.

"Crabby. And tired," Thea said. Her eyelids drooped.

"If you are tired right now and tired again tomorrow afternoon, you'll be . . . ," Nick paused, grinning, with a wait-for-it air, ". . . retired!"

Thea shook her head in disbelief. "You are so bad!" But her mood brightened some.

"There's my girl and her beautiful smile. Now, how is everything going with the quilt show? Did you track down Prudy? And her sisterly shadow?"

Once Thea started talking about the Prudy problems, she couldn't quit. She outlined a long list of tasks left to do, not only for the big day on Saturday, but to make ready for the unveiling tonight. Her frustrations poured forth faster than the famous Glitter Creek flood of 1955. Not as if she'd been there. But it was as if her words rushed out and rose up and deposited a stack of difficulties right there in Uncle Nick's lap.

He blinked a few times. "I didn't realize," he said. "Your Aunt Elena has a much smaller role. And you know her. She makes everything seem easy." Nick patted her hand. "How can I help?"

Thea couldn't seem to turn off the complaint faucet and spilled out the problem with Wanda Wooten. "All those antique props for the show delivered to Wanda's garage. A lot of trouble for folks, too."

She wished Wanda could have kept her end of the deal. Now, what was Thea to do with them? She didn't have a garage. Or room in her Jeep to haul them anywhere even if she unloaded her groceries. And she certainly wasn't going to ask the Durtles next door. Even if they never seemed to use their tumbled-down garage to house their Lincoln Town Car, its paint job overtaken by oxidation.

Looking down, she sighed and gave an inner shrug. "I thought they were safe and out of the way until we'd need them on Saturday."

"What? Al can't get his new pickup into the garage or something?"

Thea looked up, amazed. "Right. How did you know?"

"Saw him last week at Curly's. He'd packed up his shiny pickup and was headed out of town for the weekend. Scouting some new areas to hunt this fall."

"Hmm." Thea said. "Probably the same time Wanda told everyone to bring over their props. While Al was out of town."

"You don't take away a man's garage when he's got a new truck. Especially if he's out of town," Nick said. "Unwise. You need to get those props into some other storage right away."

Thea had to agree. "That's exactly my problem, Uncle Nick. I promised to take care of it today, though I don't know how. I felt so bad because her husband was mad. I don't want Wanda to be out of favor with her man or for him to spread his anger around town. It might hurt the quilt show attendance. Got any suggestions?"

Wondering if all this stress might give her a migraine or something worse, Thea found a biteable fingernail and chewed. She always thought more creatively when she was eating.

"Princess." Uncle Nick's pulled her finger away and guided her hand to her lap. "I thought you had let those babies grow out."

"That was yesterday, before the soirée. This is today."

"If I didn't realize it before, now I *know* you are under extreme pressure. It's like you are going it alone." Even though it was hot, Nick put his arm around Thea and pulled her close. She nestled into his familiar embrace, comforted.

"Tell you what, I'll take care of Wanda's problem with the theme props. That will be one less thing for you to agonize about," Nick said into her hair.

Her smelly hair, most likely. But oh well.

"Where are you going to put the stuff? Some of it's so old and some is valuable. In your garage?"

Nick gave Thea a squeeze before releasing her. "Maybe. Not your concern."

"But you have both your pickup and a Jeep. And there's Aunt Elena's lovely car, too. Shouldn't you leave room in your garage?"

"I'll figure it out, little controller," he said. "Now remind me of Wanda's address while I walk you back."

Nick rose and stretched out his hand, pulling Thea to her feet. They strode back to her Jeep and he opened the door.

"Thanks, Uncle Nick. I can't even tell you how much I appreciate this."

"Glad to be of service." He grinned and helped her into the driver's seat. "You know, Princess, I worried about you after last night's grilling. Rough for anyone. And no one wanted the soirée to end up like that. Or for Mary-Alice to be hurt."

Thea stiffened at the mention of Mary-Alice. "Do we know if she was assaulted yet? What does Detective Brewster say? Or did she just fall?"

Nick outstretched his hands, palms up. "The jury is still out." Then he touched Thea's arm. "Will you promise me to be careful, Princess? If somebody was bold enough to hurt Mary-Alice, he may use bolder methods to stop anyone who gets close to his identity. Or gets in the way."

His words brought back Detective Brewster's similar warning the previous night, to keep out of police business. When cautioning her away from the case, Brewster had said much the same thing. In the same way.

An involuntary chill ran up Thea's back in spite of the heat.

Things were definitely getting hot in Larkindale.

15

Thea's afternoon visit to the Hastings McLeod Museum had been fast and frenzied. The number of people in and out of the building was hard to count. A few folks delivered quilts for hanging, others set up the rented quilt racks in rows to complement the rest of the Museum's Gold Rush display. Emby and company busied themselves, covering the long refreshment table with scrappy quilts in soft pastels, using them as tablecloths. At one end, an old hand-crank sewing machine served as vintage décor. Thea knew Emby's cookies would be a last-minute addition. "Scrumptiously fresh" was Emby's motto.

No sign of Prudy, but Lyndi, Heather Ann, Sissy, Wanda, Aunt Elena, and others from the Quilt-Without-Guilt Guild pitched in to set up. Even Mary-Alice's nephew, Kenneth, appeared, carting in the quilts displayed at the Wentworth Mansion last night. Thea spoke to each volunteer, making sure needs were met. It seemed all the planning might achieve the success they sought.

Thea checked off all her list's vitals, then surveyed the bustling scene one last time. Her gaze rested on the display area. Would anyone notice if she peeked behind the heavy velvet drapes to preview "Larkin's Treasure" before the real unveiling? As she unhooked the rope cordoning a ten-foot protective space around the display,

Thea felt someone watching. She glanced up, linking eyes with the museum curator.

He gave her a red-faced glare.

Smiling sweetly, Thea replaced the rope and patted the post. Nice post.

She turned away. Rats. She'd have to wait like everyone else.

Disappointed, Thea slipped out the exit and jumped into the Jeep instead. Then lead-footed it home to slap herself into event-worthy shape. After all, someone might interview her on camera. What if she looked less attractive than Mayor Suzanne Stiles? God forbid her outfit might provide more fodder for another Renée snarkfest.

Arriving home, Thea went right to her closet. She pulled out outfit after outfit, critiqued and discarded them one by one. Wrong color, too warm for summer, forgot to fix the zipper, or wore it at another recent event. It was as if the boring cliché applied to her—a closet full of clothes and nothing to wear.

Besides, her attire leaned toward vintage. Would she fit in? Would her outfit photograph well? Or would she look like an Audrey Hepburn wannabe? She wondered what the other ladies would consider fashionable for a night at the museum. Thea told herself it didn't matter and settled on a smart look from the 1950s. A good decade.

After a shower session and some get-down-primp-time, including extra cover-up on her pink nose, Thea was dressed and ready. What had she forgotten? There *was* something. But since she couldn't name it, she picked up her phone to tuck inside her vintage straw clutch.

Holding the cell phone jolted her memory. Prudy had promised to give her a call or leave a message about Dr. Cottle. Had Thea missed it? She checked the answering machine. No messages.

Perhaps Prudy thought she was supposed to leave a message if Cottle could *not* come. An encouraging thought as unveiling time approached with no bad news call.

Or, if Prudy planned to be at the event tonight, she would share her information then. What was the answer?

It wouldn't help anyone if Prudy left a message after Thea left the house.

She turned on the porch light and switched on the side table lamp for Betty. At the door, she wished her feline a fond farewell. "Later, pretty kitty."

Betty gave her a dirty look.

Thea considered spinning the soundtrack to *Cats* on the CD player to fill the house during her absence. But Betty never seemed to appreciate music much. How about a good kitty-friendly flick from Thea's collection? *The Aristocats*? Or *Puss in Boots*? *The Three Lives of Thomasina*? She checked her watch. No time to find one now. Besides, she knew her pet would soon be in a cat-atonic state, nestled in the pile of soft, sleepable laundry.

"Better enjoy it tonight, Betty, because tomorrow, I'll be in folding mode."

Betty turned up her nose and, tail held high, ambled right past the sofa as if the laundry would be piled there for many days to come. Betty could sleep on it later. Maybe even tomorrow. So there.

She knows me too well. Thea closed and locked the door.

This time, when she pulled into the Hastings McLeod Museum parking lot, Thea's excitement bubbled up like fizz in a fresh glass of soda. Arriving an hour early with keen hopes for a lovely evening, she got out of the Jeep and took one last glimpse in the side mirror.

Looking good. No, looking fine.

Thea dabbed a rosy lipstick called "Love's Muse" on her mouth, puckering up at her reflection. Kissable. Not as if she was looking to be kissed or anything. Or be anybody's muse. But didn't the Girl Scout motto say, "Be prepared"? She'd just read it in the 1947 *Girl Scout Handbook* the other day, poking around in an Emporium booth. Always good to be prepared. Plus, she could use the lip color to detract from her pink nose.

She fluffed out her full black skirt—late fifties style, without the poodle. With her crisp white blouse and short-sleeved bolero jacket, Thea was looking more Sandra Dee than Audrey Hepburn. She had punctuated her outfit with a black velvet headband adorned with a fuss of black netting, soft feathers, and beaded accents. Grasping her red Rodo clutch, Thea crossed her fingers for luck. Raising her chin high, she strode toward the museum entrance.

Designed to unite architecture with the surrounding pines, the Hastings McLeod Museum gave the impression of a ski lodge. A spacious wing for exhibitions had been added over time, also featuring offices and a kitchen. A woodsy dining area overlooked Pioneer Park. Shade trees, picnic tables, and the occasional barbeque pit made the park popular with families. Beyond, Glitter Creek boasted fine fishing and the ever-elusive sparkles for modern-day gold panning.

Tonight, "Larkin's Treasure" would get top museum billing. Bit parts would be played by a number of quilts representing a legacy of Larkindale quilting. The show would continue on through the week, culminating in the big Blocks on the Walk Quilt Show. Guild members and other participants would submit their entries for judging at a one-day outdoor show in both Old Town Larkindale and Pioneer Park.

An amazing venue for any show. But Thea had to mentally pinch herself because everything had worked together. "For good," Mary-Alice would say, completing Thea's thought, "for those who love the Lord."

Thea sighed. If only Mary-Alice could have attended tonight. The unveiling of "Larkin's Treasure" should have been *her* triumph. She had long looked forward to it, planning for more than a year. Thea chided herself for not remembering to call her friend before heading here. Mary-Alice could have felt more a part. At least, she might have appreciated a diversion from the sad loss of her brooch.

Still, Thea knew her friend would be faithful to hold up tonight's event in prayer. And to pray for every person involved. Right there from her hospital bed. In the doing, the dear woman would be a part of everything.

The museum's A-framed entry sported lots of glass and dark wood trim. As she approached, Thea noticed a professionally printed sign showing through the front door:

Special Unveiling of the Historic Quilt
"Larkin's Treasure"
Tonight at 7:00 P.M.
By Invitation Only

A thrill of excitement tickled Thea's shoulders and she opened the door, catching her breath at the sight. Just inside, an exquisite panoramic quilt depicted historic Larkindale. A row of small rectangle quilts stitched by different guild members, each featured a building from Old Town. Hung against navy velvet, tiny twinkle lights winked through the background, turning the entrance into a fairytale.

Nice work, Lyndi.

Stepping into the foyer, Thea took in the museum's transformation from this afternoon's construction zone to homey elegance. She recognized a familiar forty-niner tune playing overhead. "Clementine." Uncle Nick, in charge of the PA system and tonight's emcee, had chosen music to celebrate Larkindale's Gold Rush beginnings. And emphasize the antiques showcased throughout the building.

"Oh, my darlin', oh my darlin'," Thea sang a little off-key. The place was as empty as the Emporium at closing time, but the combination of music, museum antiques, and quilts of the old west set a perfect mood for the coming crowd.

Leaning over a glass-topped display case, she viewed a diverse collection of mine lighting. Primitive iron miner candlesticks, made by blacksmiths, had evolved into aluminum carbide lamps, and Thea wondered at the stories these items might hold. Next to a High Grader lamp, a little card revealed the lamp's secret spot to hide bits of gold as miners exited the mine. Did the mine owners know and just look the other way? Maybe some did. Or didn't.

She felt at home with all the ancient items in the many cases, forgetting the quilts for a moment. Distracted by the variety of mining pans, some bent and near to crumbling, Thea imagined a mythical miner panning with one of these pans outside on Glitter Creek, adjacent to Pioneer Park. Such hard work. But the tourists still panned, hoping for a few flakes or the occasional gold nugget.

Lingering over a display of quartz in gold jewelry, an elegant brooch and earrings, prompted Thea to touch her own diamond studs. Could she pull off wearing something so ostentatious as these antique dangles? Would Renée approve?

Something tapped on her back, and Thea tensed. She spun around. "Uncle Nick! You startled me." She exhaled, shifting from shock to reassurance.

"Sorry, Princess. But you wear 'startled' well. In fact," he stepped back and cocked his head, "maybe you should be on display instead of a bunch of rusty old miner pans." He reached over and flicked the feathers on her headband. "Nice touch."

"Thanks," Thea said. Her uncle always made her feel like gold. "And thanks for putting together this music. So cool," she said as "Sweet Betsy From Pike" rang out. "I owe you for dealing with my props problem this afternoon."

"Want to see where most of it is now? Come with me." Nick pulled her past a wall of framed Gold Rush prints. They came to the first group of quilts, zigzagging down a row on racks. "Check it out."

Thea stared in wonder. In front of the quilts, a small ensemble consisted of a scarred wooden table with two worn chairs. A well-preserved Indian basket sat on top, filled with someone's small quilt project.

"Looks like it's right out of a miner's cottage," Thea said.

"Inside the basket is one of your aunt's unfinished baby quilts for the nursery at Faith Memorial," Uncle Nick said. "You gotta see this." He motioned her to follow him down the next row, where items grouped on both sides of the walkway added charm and historicity.

"Uncle Nick! It's perfect." Thea kneeled down to touch a rustic dollhouse, furniture carefully carved for a beloved child from a distant time. Behind the masterpiece hung an old Schoolhouse-patterned quilt. Across the walk sat a number of spittoons positioned at various heights. A lacy plant placed inside each container gave a lush, garden feel.

Looking briefly down each row, Thea identified most of the props that had pestered Al Wooten and deprived him of his truck space. An antique treadle Singer Sewing Machine, a steamer trunk with quilts folded inside, a petite church pew. Most had been decorated to appear a lady had just risen and laid aside her handwork.

"It's exactly right, Uncle Nick. I'd planned to set it all up at the end of the week when the rest of the historic quilts arrive. But why not now? You're a genius."

"It's nice to hear my name out loud," Nick said with a grin. "Seemed like a good solution since the stuff would be coming over in a few days. What isn't used here, I'll cart over to the library for their coordinating exhibition. You know I'm just a furniture-carting fool."

To Thea's amusement, Nick reached over and rearranged a doll quilt across the arm of a graceful old rocker with original green paint. An oak side table sat near. He surveyed his work, serious as an interior designer with a rich client. "Is something missing?"

"Just this." Aunt Elena seemed to come from nowhere to lay a handleless cup and deep saucer on the table. "Our lady is taking a well-deserved tea break from working on this Christmas gift for her little girl." She touched the doll quilt, smiling at them both in her gentle way. "Your uncle has a good eye. But shh . . . we generally keep it to ourselves."

"Learned from the best," Nick said, putting his arm around Elena. "My beautiful bride. She's responsible for adding final touches to all these little setups, by the way."

Stirrings at the museum's entry made Thea squint between two quilt edges so she could see the source of activity. A man carried in a TV camera, and another, some lights. An attractive young woman dressed in a blazer and wearing a name badge followed them, toting a hard case by the handle. Thea looked from the case to her uncle, puzzled.

"Microphones," Uncle Nick said, nodding toward the woman. "I'll go help. They'll want to set up before everyone gets here." He looked at his watch, "We have about forty-five minutes until the doors open. Better skedaddle."

Lifting Elena's chin with his finger, Nick leaned over for a fond kiss before disappearing beyond the quilts.

16

Alone with her aunt, Thea thanked her. "You made everything look perfect, Aunt Elena. Like a professional."

"It's fun. You've done a great job yourself." Elena's kind eyes focused on her niece. "Can you believe this all started with the announcement you wrote in the Quilt-Without-Guilt Guild Newsletter?"

"Wow, you're right. We've come a long way." Thea had been shocked at the initial amount of guild interest in organizing an annual Larkindale quilt show. But she never expected to become the project's chair. How had it come about, anyway? When asked to serve in the top spot, Thea felt flattered and important. Apparently, her vanity won over wisdom. Or maybe they'd caught her fatigued and frayed from running her antique business.

Without the strength to protest.

Or the brains.

At first, the task seemed titanic. She was a rookie quilter, for pity's sake. But when Prudy came on board, Thea saw it as a reprieve. Now she would have plenty of help conducting interviews with other quilters, choosing their best suggestions and putting them into action. Prudy could provide assistance as rules and guidelines were drafted, volunteers recruited, and a site for the show pinpointed.

But Thea's vision and the reality had disagreed.

"I know it hasn't been a picnic," Elena said while admiring a Flying Geese patterned quilt. "But the guild is behind you and everyone will do their jobs. In fact, I'm ready for my role tonight as the white glove lady." She stopped, reached into her pocket, and pulled out a pair of sheer, wrist-length gloves with ruffled cuffs.

"Just anyone try and touch a quilt or look at a label with their grubby paws," she said, slipping her hands inside. Elena took a super-heroine stance, gloved hands on hips, and shook out her salt and pepper curls. "Quilt-woman to the rescue!"

Thea gave an affectionate laugh. "No patchwork cape?"

Standing so, Aunt Elena looked more than a little out of character. And out of season. Easter had passed months ago. Her pale blue polka-dotted dress with peplum waist had been one of her own creations, using a classic Vogue pattern. Becoming to her middle-aged figure. The ankle-strapped, platform sandals were a favorite with Uncle Nick. They accentuated Elena's shapely legs, her best feature, according to her husband.

Thea disagreed. Legs. Good heavens. Who cared about legs? Elena's loving smile and beautiful brown eyes were legend in her niece's heart.

Still, with those frilly gloves and pastel dress, Aunt Elena looked almost ready for sunrise service. The only thing missing was an Easter bonnet. What about . . . ? Thea touched her headband embellished with froufrou feathers. No. Her black band wouldn't match Elena's soft bluesy look at all.

———

"Sorry, am I interrupting?" Lyndi had ventured down the row, a stealth approach, and now joined them. Her lavender sequined dress color complemented her purple coiffure nicely. "I have news, boss-lady. But it's not good."

Thea did an inner foot stomp. She didn't want to hear bad news. Thank heaven "Oh, Susannah" began to play overhead and she could listen to it instead, tapping instead of stomping her foot.

But Lyndi's urgent stare pressured Thea until she collected herself. The toe-tapping ended. "Okay, what's your news?" Maybe it wasn't so bad. Or would sound better with a banjo on someone's knee.

"This all looks totally awesome," Lyndi said, motioning toward the hanging quilts and the arrangements of antiques. "But . . ."

"But what?" Thea asked.

"Here's what I wanted to talk to you about. You will notice there are no barriers in front of these quilts." Lyndi chewed on her lower lip, a pained look on her face.

Thea inhaled sharply. She hadn't noticed. "Why not?"

"Dunno." Lyndi shrugged. "I ordered them. Sent a check. But they didn't come in."

Thea considered. These quilts were of historical significance locally and must be safeguarded from theft or damage. The Larkindale Town Council had guaranteed their safety during the exhibit at the museum. And the responsibility for the antiquities loaned for props lay right in the lap of the guild. Without adequate barriers, chances were greater something might happen to one or more of the precious items.

"Do we know when they might be delivered?" Thea asked, her mind racing from one weird solution to another, nixing them all. "Tomorrow?"

"Not sure," Lyndi said. "I was working here all afternoon, expecting them before we open the doors tonight. But I don't think it's going to happen."

Where could Thea find some barriers in a hurry? And so many? More importantly, why had she said yes to being quilt show co-chair? She eyed the old green rocker with its high, painted back and longed to sit and rock and close off everything but the sound of happy music over the PA.

"Okay, let me work on this. Meanwhile, let's agree to do extra guard duty during the program tonight," Thea said. "It shouldn't be a problem because the guests are invited and most are guild members, friends, and a few officials."

She couldn't imagine Mayor Stiles stuffing a doll quilt in her purse. More likely, she'd be guilty of a different kind of theft. Attempted robbery of Cole's affections.

The ladies broke apart their mini-meeting. Elena left to make a few finishing touches with Lyndi accompanying for a preview. Thea remained a minute more, enjoying the moments before the guests arrived. The media activity played out behind the curtain of quilts. The TV and newspaper people could wait. Besides, Uncle Nick was on the job.

She breathed in the smell of baked goods, the aroma drawing her away from the quilts and to the refreshment table. Emby must have just put out her famous chocolate chip cookies—chewy, nutty, and three chips to the inch. Plus, her tangy lemon bars, each topped with a whipped cream flower. Fancy. Thea also noted cake pops wearing little chocolate tuxedoes and a plate of sugar cookies decorated like tiny quilts. Even with plastic wrap loosely covering the goodies, a tantalizing fragrance hung about the table. Thea knew if everything else went wrong, Emby's desserts would be right on.

Just as Thea reached under the plastic wrap to sneak a cookie, Wanda Wooten, of props storage fame, arrived and interrupted the effort. Her gaze gleamed at the sweet spread. Thea pulled her hand back and tucked the wrap tighter around the platter, instead. "Can't have the air dry these out, can we?"

With a disappointed look, Wanda shook her head and her up-do loosened despite a number of overworked hairpins. "I can wait if you can," she said, not sounding convinced. She pulled her focus from the feast. "Thea, thanks for arranging to get my garage all cleared out this afternoon. You're a miracle worker. I left Al vacuuming out the truck in his man-cave, happy as a kid with a new toy."

Before Thea could give credit to Uncle Nick, Janny Rice, in charge of the award ribbons, joined them. Soon followed by Heather Ann Brewster. Emby rocketed out of the kitchen, placing bowls filled with foil-wrapped confections between platters.

With so many ladies surrounding the goodies, the table had morphed into madhouse-mode. They needed to relocate and give Emby some space.

Thea motioned for them to move back out into the museum proper where she could see the action. The camera crew had set up in front of the cordoned-off, draped display area. Like a debutante awaiting her presentation at a cotillion, "Larkin's Treasure" waited for its first public appearance in many years.

Uncle Nick tested a mic, blowing into it like an amateur, then saying, "One, two, three, four. Hope my speech is not a snore."

As more members of the Quilt-Without-Guilt Guild wandered in and out among the quilts, Thea explained about the absence of barriers along the rows to Wanda, Janny, and Heather Ann. And asked they spread the word—everyone had guard duty tonight.

"I'd like to see a couple quilters in each row, just to be sure nothing gets broken. Not expecting any pilfering. But no one wants to be sorry in the morning, so let's be safe this evening."

The ladies agreed and scattered for a sort of preview party before the festivities began. Several more quilters entered. Thea's Mum and Gram came in next, the elder in a floral dress and big hat. It might have worked for an Aunt Elena Easter bonnet, but Gram was particular about her hats and never loaned them out. Affectionately called the Mad-Hatter of Larkindale, she wore them often and proudly, in fierce deference to the Queen.

Today's chapeau sported a white plume curving around one side of Gram's face, ending at her chin. Queenly, indeed. Thea rushed over to greet them, exchanging hugs with her grandmother and air kisses with Mum.

"You look lovely," Thea said, releasing her elegant mother, dressed in orange silk slacks and shirt. Dark hair swept up in a ballerina bun, Mum's gold hoop earrings and wrist bangles gave her a continental air.

"Wait 'til you see Emby's refreshment table," Thea said. "Hungry, you two?" Maybe she'd have an excuse to nab a cookie.

"Oh, no, child," Gram said, between attempts to blow her hat-plume away from her mouth. "I just had a smashing thigh salad."

"Pardon?" Thea gave her mother a puzzled look. *Thigh* salad?

"We dined at the new Thai restaurant," Mum said. "Decidedly good, actually." As always, Nora James's affected British accent seemed more evident than her mother-in-law's real one. "Though, I must say, I'm positively panting for a cuppa."

"Oh, jolly idea. Perhaps I'll pant, too." Gram, relentlessly cheerful as usual, strained to see a tea caddy at-the-ready. "I wonder if there is any blackberry tea." She blew the plume away from her cheek again, where apparently it was involved in a ticklefest.

Thea tried to keep a straight face as her grandmother fought with the feather, now batting at it with her hand. "Here, Gram. Let me help you." She reached up and twisted the hat back a bit, so the offending feather no longer teased Gram's cheek. "There."

While Gram sputtered her thanks, Thea glanced past her relatives, toward the entry. The door opened, revealing Kenneth Ransome. Even dressed in a suit, he wasn't good-looking. Though to Thea, it seemed ironic since his last name, Ransome, rhymed with the word handsome.

In truth, Kenneth was as far from foxy as the East was from the West. Which reminded Thea of a Scripture Mary-Alice quoted. Good heavens, what was the verse? Something... something about God removing one's transgressions as far as the East was from the West. Thea smiled, remembering hope hugging her heart when Mary-Alice spoke the words aloud.

Thinking of her dear friend, Thea realized Kenneth might have an update on his great-aunt's condition. Steering Mum and Gram toward the tea table so they could quit panting, she headed in Kenneth's direction.

"Kenneth! How are you?" Thea probably didn't need to ask, his shiny forehead and limp hair told her enough about a husky man in a suit combined with a hot day. He must have been grateful to step into the cavern-like coolness of the Hastings McLeod Museum.

Kenneth eyed her as if she was lunch. Though he must have already had lunch by now. "Very well, thanks." He thrust a hand in her direction. "You?"

Thea remembered how only this morning, it seemed Mary-Alice hinted her nephew was a good marriage prospect. For her. Gulping, she stuck out her hand, too. Kenneth grasped it and pumped with vigor. If she'd been scoring his handshake, Thea would have awarded him ten points for firmness. But subtracted ten for clamminess.

"I'm so excited about tonight's unveiling of my great-aunt's old quilt," Kenneth said. "Hope everything goes better than last night."

No kidding. In Thea's world, the place could burn down and it would go better.

Kenneth scoped out the room, his gaze finally resting on the cordoned-off display area. The cameraman had swung his camera around, now appearing to shoot footage of the museum interior.

While Kenneth took in the exhibition, Thea pinched her cheeks and bit her lips to make herself ready in case of a close-up. Touching her ears, she felt Jeff's diamond studs. A little extra sparkle. Why not?

"This is great publicity," Kenneth said. "Though I wish Auntie could be here."

"Me, too," Thea said. "I've been thinking about her all afternoon. How is she doing?"

Kenneth's eyes turned warmer, going from gray to blue like a mood ring. "She's herself, full of grace and concern for everyone else. I took her little white dog in for a visit. Remember Moxie? They both loved it."

How thoughtful. Maybe Kenneth had more points on his score sheet than Thea had tallied earlier. He wasn't right for her, of course. But husband material for another? Who did she know who might be interested? Someone with low expectations?

Thea noticed him staring over her shoulder toward the entry. Faster than a clap of thunder, Kenneth's blue eyes became as gray as an overcast sky.

"What is *she* doing here?" Kenneth said, his voice a low rumble.

"Who?" Thea spun around, squinting at the entry, only seeing the security guard.

But then she saw. More bad news.

It was Odette Milsap.

17

Uh . . . follow me," Thea said. Desperate to keep Kenneth from attacking Odette, Thea hustled him toward Uncle Nick, who stood unsuspecting, going over his notes. "My uncle wants you to say a few words about 'Larkin's Treasure.' "

In a surprise move, Kenneth acted the gentleman and allowed Thea to reposition him in front of her uncle. Nick looked up briefly, then dismissed the interruption, returning to his note reading.

"So . . . ," Kenneth said, ". . . what's all this about me speaking?" A hint of pleasure in his tone, a humble smile, and apparently, he had forgotten all about Odette.

Thea checked his eye color. Blue.

"What are you talking about?" Nick said, still sorting through his index cards. He seemed agitated for some reason.

"You remember, Uncle Nick," Thea said. "I was telling Kenneth you hoped he might say a sentence or two about the quilt. Since Mary-Alice can't be here and all."

Standing behind Kenneth, Thea opened her eyes wide, catching Nick's attention by wiggling her brows, trying to send a message. If she'd known Morse code, she could have blinked out SOS.

"Yes . . . right . . . sorry." Uncle Nick jumped in, putting the cards in his jacket pocket. "Glad you could make it, Kenneth. Would it be possible for you to introduce the quilt to our TV audience before the unveiling? A couple of sentences are all we need, I'm sure." He looked at Thea who nodded. "Dr. Cottle can do the rest."

Rats. She'd forgotten about Cottle again.

"Did you say I'd be on television?" Kenneth asked. He pulled at his tie and licked his upper lip, his many teeth gleaming in the reflected camera lights pointed at the podium. "I don't know . . ."

"How nice you are all dressed up. It will be like the Academy Awards," Thea said. "Your great-aunt will be proud of you." It was true. Mary-Alice had some kind of unreasonable love for this hapless individual.

"There's a good man." Nick slapped him on the back. "Here's a piece of paper. We need a pen. Just write out what you'll say so we don't repeat the same thing."

"Well, I . . ." Kenneth froze, his face blank as the sheet Nick just handed him.

Thea pointed to her watch. "Fifteen minutes left. No time for writer's block." She opened her clutch, found a pen, and stuck it between Kenneth's fingers. "Cheerio, off you go," she said, mimicking Brit-slang à la Gram. Thea gave him a push toward a nearby bench, and he zombie-walked over and sat, staring across at the cameraman.

Perhaps he had stage fright.

"Okay, what was it, Princess?" Nick Marinello asked, having just watched her performance. And adding his own inspired improvisation.

"Oh, Uncle Nick, I can't explain now, but you were brilliant. Thanks for backing me. You are always bailing me out." Thea gave him a quick kiss on the cheek. "Now I've got to figure out where Dr. Cottle is and locate Prudy."

First, Thea scanned the room. More folks had arrived, but no Cottle.

And no Prudy.

Thea spotted Sissy Sloane, sashaying between guests, and edged up next to her. So short she could shop in the children's section, Sissy was built like a tree-trunk. Not chunky, but hefty. A little powerhouse. When visiting The Quintessential Quilter, Thea had often seen Sissy cart heavy bolts of fabric around as easily as carrying a roll of paper towels into the kitchen.

Leaning down to Sissy's level, Thea informed her of Kenneth's hostile reaction when he saw Odette. "Frankly I was surprised to see your aunt here tonight, Sissy."

"Frankly, I was surprised at what happened to her last night, Thea," Sissy said. "So, I wanted her to have some fun at this event."

Sissy seemed a bit aloof, standing with her little muscular arms crossed, her hair teased high, but not happy about it. Did she know Thea had grilled her aunt? Without the authority to do so? And that Thea's words to Detective Brewster may have ratcheted up Odette's interview?

Recalling how she had turned into a snitch made Thea ashamed all over again. When this week came to a close, Thea promised herself she would make it up to both Sissy and Odette.

"I know it was a hard night, Sissy. That's why I'm hoping you can keep your aunt occupied and away from Kenneth," Thea said. "So she can have a pleasant evening."

With a slight tilt of her head, Sissy agreed. A woman of few words. Or, no words.

Seven minutes left before the event officially began. Mayor Suzanne Stiles, her usual svelte and stylin' self, had already attached herself to Cole like a barnacle to a boat. She laughed at something he said, tossing back long blonde curls highlighted with self-confidence.

Suzanne's simple black dress clung just so, then flared into flattering folds, adding to an overall picture of appealing poise. She rose on tiptoes to whisper something in Cole's ear, covering the side of her mouth with a bejeweled hand. Too bad the jewel wasn't a wedding ring. Alas, Suzanne Stiles was all too available.

Wait. What about Kenneth? Wasn't he available, too? On second thought, as attractive as the match sounded, Thea knew the mayor had other prospects.

Other interests. Like Cole Mason.

With a lemme-at-her-stride, Thea crossed the room. But instead of confronting the mayor, she passed her by and sidled up to Cole, slipping a hand in the crook of his arm. He turned at her touch, giving her a genuine smile of pleasure.

"Hi, there, Ms. Co-Chair. You look sharp. Like a woman in charge."

Technically, it would be Mayor Suzanne Stiles, in charge of the whole town. Cole's comment wasn't overly flirtatious, but coupled with the flash of his dimples, Thea's heart broke into a little boogie-woogie rhythm.

To the right of Cole, the mayor chatted with other attendees. Thea, standing on his other side, imagined herself significant in his sphere. Was she? Or did she appear desperate? Hanging onto Cole like a lifeboat on a sinking ship?

She gently disengaged her arm-link with Cole. He didn't notice, pulling out his trusty notebook, pencil poised for literary action. Cole might be regarded as a local leading man about town, but since his day job required him to put together a piece for the *Larkindale Lamplight*, tonight he was cast as a mild-mannered multimedia journalist. A little videotaping, some still shots, accurate notes transferred to his laptop, and the article would be up on the web before morning.

Just fine with Ms. Co-Chair, as long as Cole kept his story positive.

Thea drew in her breath. Had he already written up last night's unhappy ending to the soirée? She prayed not. Seemed so unlikely after all his help tidying up Mary-Alice's garden, taking down quilts, some of which hung here tonight. Besides, he rescued her from Renée's rude behavior, driving Thea safely home.

When she considered his integrity and kindness, Thea relaxed. Cole would report the truth in a winsome way. He had no desire to damage her venture. Or bring disgrace to the town he'd adopted as his home.

Sure this was the case, Thea set those thoughts aside. "Clementine" had come around again in the song rotation, and she let it flood her brain and being, enjoying the ludicrous lyrics even more the second time. As she sang along to herself, Thea decided after all their no-show history, Dr. Cottle and Prudy must be "lost and gone forever. Dreadful sorry . . ."

Tsk-tsk. Their loss.

With only moments to go before the program started, Thea thought about all the work and planning bringing them to this pinnacle—the presentation of the beautiful "Larkin's Treasure" crazy quilt. Its intricate handwork, antiquity, and historicity would be displayed all week, clear through the Blocks on the Walk Quilt Show on Saturday. A brilliant beginning.

Though the soirée had been the true beginning. And didn't turn out so well. But how much good did it do to dwell on yesterday? Instead, she focused on the museum floor theatrics.

Mayor Stiles had turned her attention to the museum curator, a slight, mustached gentleman with a Frisbee-shaped face. Ted? No, Ned something. They seemed engaged in a fascinating discussion about who-knows-what until Uncle Nick interrupted. Wearing a look of regret, Suzanne ended her talk with the curator, then walked with Nick to the podium situated near the curtained display area.

Still seated on the bench, Kenneth mouthed some words toward a ceiling fan, checking his paper for prompts. His numerous teeth glinted, even at a distance. Behind the barrier, Louisa Wentworth Carver waited, regal as royalty in a sapphire suit. As Mary-Alice's daughter, she had the honor of drawing back one side of the drape. Kenneth would open the other when it came time for the quilt reveal.

Thea moved away from Cole, now in discussion with the curator and taking notes. She consulted her program. Uncle Nick would introduce Mayor Stiles for opening remarks. When she was done dazzling them all, the mayor would then hand the microphone back to Nick. And he would present Dr. Cottle from the State Quilt & Textile Museum. Thea scanned the room once more.

Scratch that. Totally Cottle-less.

It was already several minutes past the start time. Perhaps the delay was to give Cottle the opportunity to arrive. But his appearance was unlikely. She scurried over toward the podium, interrupting her uncle as he and the mayor hashed out the schedule.

Thea tugged on his sleeve. "Uncle Nick? A slight change in plan."

18

Thea explained that Dr. Cottle had not darkened the museum doorway so far. History told her he wouldn't make it. She and Uncle Nick agreed to move Kenneth's comments up in the revised schedule, revising it once more.

"No worries," Nick said. "This will all come together. I'll take it from here."

He turned toward Kenneth, motioning him up front. And then headed back Suzanne's way, apparently to inform her of the changes.

Thea noted her mum and Gram held paper cups of what must be tea. She scolded herself for not making sure china was used. Didn't the museum kitchen contain proper dishes? Still, it hadn't stopped Mum from sipping her tea with her little pinkie raised. Mum's idea of gracious living always won. Even if the battle was over a paper cup.

After a quick check of her quilters on guard, Thea was satisfied they all shared the protect-our-props mission. Though she wanted a chocolate chip cookie, she walked over to greet Louisa, standing alone, looking lots less ghost-like. Could it be a result of the television network's soft, "glamour" lighting? Or maybe from added applications of war paint to her Goth face.

"You look lovely, Louisa," Thea said, meaning it.

The red lips gave a little twitch, as if Louisa needed practice to smile. "Thanks."

"Big night for your family. So sorry your mom couldn't be with us," Thea said, a little reflective in spite of the bustle surrounding them. "How's she doing?"

"Better, I think." Louisa's expression turned resentful. "She still can't remember what happened to . . . to her."

Thea noticed the hesitation. Did Louisa mean Mary-Alice couldn't remember what happened to the brooch?

"The doctor was concerned she might have fractured her spine. She's too elderly to take such a fall."

"Did they find evidence of a fracture?"

"No," Louisa said. "But they mentioned the possibility of osteoporosis."

"I wouldn't worry about it. Your mom is much heartier than she looks," Thea said. "She fell earlier last night, and it didn't seem to bother her a bit."

"What? She fell earlier?" Louisa said in a higher key, turning to face Thea. "Why wasn't I notified? I want to know exactly how it happened. Now."

So the old, annoying Louisa of last night had reappeared. Whoopee.

Thea swallowed, wishing she hadn't said anything about the other fall. "Well, it was only a half-fall, actually."

"What do you mean?" Louisa's dark eyes grew darker still.

"You know the big ficus tree in the sitting room?"

Louisa nodded.

"She fell back into it. But only into the pot. Not to the floor or anything."

"Why did she fall into the pot? Did she stumble? Does she need a walker or something?" Louisa leaned forward, invading Thea's personal space.

Thea put her hands up, palms out. "No! She doesn't need a walker. It was all my fault." Stepping back, she took a deep breath. "I was startled and spun around and accidentally knocked her backward. She started to fall—"

"Nice goin', clumso." Renée's unwelcome voice cut in as she appeared next to Thea. "Haven't you grown out of that stage yet? Honestly." She rolled her eyes, giving a slight headshake of disgust.

"Are you kidding?" Louisa's look of loathing matched Renée's. "So you knocked my mother over? Pushed an old lady?"

Outnumbered, Thea tried to defend herself. "I . . . I . . . saved her, actually. Kept her from falling to the floor. You know I'd never intentionally hurt Mary-Alice. I love her! She's one of my best friends."

Unlike Renée. Whose carping comment caused Thea to think again of the little girls in her antique picture hanging on the wall at home. Now she visualized the child who looked most like Renée slapping the other child across the face.

Thea touched her cheek, and it seemed to sting.

Louisa turned her back, apparently unable to stomach Thea's presence any longer. Renée adopted an innocent look that said, "Who, me?" and concentrated on the TV cameraman, now in position to film.

An unbidden tear spilled from Thea's eye and she looked down, blinking, fussing with something in her clutch bag. Her emotions bounced around like marbles in a vintage pinball machine. But was she hurt? Or angry?

Uncle Nick took the podium. Abruptly, the music stopped, leaving only a few restless murmurs and floor creaks as the guests shifted positions. Since the remarks were supposed to be minimal, folks were scheduled to stand through the ceremony. It might have worked well, except they were running behind schedule. Thea thought about Gram and other seniors in attendance with only a few benches to share among them. What if Gram's bad hip gave her grief tonight? Insensitive on Thea's part.

"Ladies and gentlemen, welcome to this historic occasion," Nick said over the PA. "Thank you all for coming. Let's please give a warm reception to the Honorable Suzanne Stiles, Mayor of Larkindale."

Suzanne Stiles. Thea could almost hiss out the name. In fact, the mayor's name was quite hissable. Thea might hiss it daily. She watched Cole for an adoring reaction as the mayor laid out her notes on the podium. But saw only a journalist's typical curiosity as he raised his camera to film the speech.

Claps throughout the room dwindled and Mayor Stiles began. "Four score and seven years ago . . ." She stopped as the attendees laughed at the famous first words of the Gettysburg Address. "Oops. Wrong speech."

Was it fair that the hissable Suzanne Stiles possessed not only beauty and power, but a great sense of humor, too?

No, it was not. Thea found herself entertained. A little.

Shuffling her papers, the mayor started again. "Good evening, friends. I am pleased to be here to celebrate the grand unveiling of the Wentworth family's historic quilt, 'Larkin's Treasure.' For the past decade, it has been housed in . . ."

Blah, blah, blah. Thea longed for a temper-tweaker about now. In the shape of a thick, moist chocolate chip cookie. After enduring all those tongue lashes from Louisa and Renée, Thea needed comfort food.

"And," Mayor Stiles was saying, "I wish to congratulate our co-chairs for this wonderful exhibition and for organizing the first annual Blocks on the Walk Quilt Show—Thea James and Prudy Levasich. We appreciate your tireless efforts on behalf of Larkindale. And we all say, 'Thank you!'" She raised her hands high, clapping with enthusiasm, and everyone joined in the applause.

"Come on up here, Thea. And where's Prudy?" the mayor asked, waving Thea to the podium, where she accepted a handshake from Suzanne. They posed, hands clasped, and the cameraman came in close. Thea beamed because she wasn't sure what else to do. Plus, it would look good on camera, right? Another tear escaped; and she wiped it away.

Suzanne made no more mention of the absent Prudy, and the moment became Thea's alone. The crowd cheered, and Mum smiled like a lunatic, clapping the loudest. Gram waved her hat wildly. Even Cole—Mr. Tall, Dark, and Dimpled—grinned in an admiring sort of way and took a picture. With the citizens of

Larkindale on her side, Thea felt like an Olympic runner. She wasn't in the home stretch yet, but she could see the finish line.

Too bad Prudy missed this. Wonder how she'll feel if she sees it on TV tomorrow?

Thea suffered a small pang for Prudy as she sauntered over to stand by her mother, feeling like a star, thinking that Suzanne Stiles wasn't so bad after all. Even with her hissable name.

Uncle Nick introduced Kenneth next, who came to the podium, running fingers through damp hair and mopping moisture from his face with a napkin. His collar hung open, tie jerked to the side. As he grasped the outstretched mic, Thea thought he had the look of an aging rock and roller, spent after a concert. If Kenneth had belted out a few bars of "Jailhouse Rock" or better yet "Rock of Ages," she wouldn't have been surprised.

The camera moved in and Kenneth said, "It's my honor to be here and say a few words on behalf of my great-aunt, Mary-Alice Wentworth, who is unable to join us tonight." He peeked at his rehearsal paper, then looked back at the guests.

"As many of you know, 'Larkin's Treasure' was made by a distant relative of my great-aunt's more than a hundred years ago. It is said to provide the secret to vast riches," Kenneth said. "Tonight, maybe one of you can solve the mystery of the antique crazy quilt."

Nice comeback, Ken. The man continued to almost impress.

He took a few steps to the display area and said, "My cousin, Mary-Alice's daughter, Louisa Wentworth Carver, will assist me as we draw back the drapes. Louisa?"

The curator unhooked the ropes so both Kenneth and Louisa could enter. They stood side by side in front of the heavy, blue velvet drapes, united for the good of the family. Cameras flashed from the audience. The TV spokesperson moved into position.

Thea admired the deep blue color of the drapes. These were lush and generous, plenty of fabric across the top, extra long so they didn't look stingy. Where could she find affordable, velvet drapes in Larkindale?

"Are those curtains the ones called portals?" Gram asked in a low voice, as if she knew what Thea was thinking. "A bit dodgy, I say. Far too long for my taste. Why, they'd drag the dust bunnies about."

"Shh . . ." said someone nearby.

"Or was it poodles?" Gram said to Thea, not paying attention to the shusher. "Why would anyone name their curtains after a breed of dogs?"

"Puddled, Gram. Long drapes pooling on the floor are called puddled," Thea said in an exasperated whisper. She noticed Gram's queenly hat now sat awry on her gray curls, perhaps replaced too hastily after all the wild hat waving.

"Puddled, you say? Pish-posh. A beastly bother," Gram said. She turned to her daughter-in-law and said rather too loudly, "Nora, dear, we're not getting any poodles at the Lake House, are we?"

Mum reassured her mother-in-law no poodles of any kind were planned.

Uncle Nick took the microphone back from Kenneth and said, "Without further adieu, ladies and gentlemen, I give you 'Larkin's Treasure'!"

The guests applauded with enthusiasm. A rush of expectation washed over Thea. This would make up for last night.

Kenneth took hold of one drape and Louisa the other, and they pulled back the curtains. A tinkling noise said something was amiss even before the drapes were fully drawn. Once they had been, Thea heard a chorus of gasps. Including her own.

The front of the display case was shattered. Fragments of glass lined the floor at the case's bottom, some swept aside with the curtains.

The interior of the case was empty.

"Larkin's Treasure" was gone.

19

Thea wanted to wail, "Nooooo!" But she covered her mouth instead with her hand, trying not to hyperventilate. This could not be happening. Every event she had orchestrated so far had gone awry. First, the opening gala ended in disaster. And now Mary-Alice's family quilt—stolen.

Thea James. The gal with the tragical touch.

All around her, unrest reigned. The guests crowded in for a better look at nothing but broken shards of glass. Uncle Nick pulled out his cell phone and walked toward the offices, maybe to make a private call. Cole quit filming and, moving closer, took some still shots. The TV camera focused on the newswoman who held her microphone close to her lips. She spoke to the viewers with deft professionalism. "Reporting live from the Hastings McLeod Museum in Larkindale, this is Jessica Andrews on the scene. . . ."

Here was the bad publicity Thea had feared. She felt a sudden sick twinge, and her stomach's insides flitted like nervous moths. What would happen now? The town council had guaranteed the quilt's safety. Would they have to dip into Larkindale's shallow coffers? Hand over the piddling profits gained from various pancake breakfasts and spaghetti dinner fundraisers? Money targeted for new Junior Baseball League uniforms?

Questions fired against her brain faster than buckshot on the opening day of hunting season. And she couldn't answer any of them.

Good heavens. Now people might not come to the quilt show on Saturday. Why visit a town where elderly women were routinely whacked on the head? Or got their antique brooches pinched? Where historic treasures were pilfered right out of a museum display case? After months of the town folks' investment, their time and finances, this venture could come to nothing. Plus, Larkindale's reputation might take years to rebuild.

Thea rubbed her temples. Only moments ago, she had been floating on a cloud. Now she felt lightheaded. Maybe Thea was in a trance or a dream. Perhaps she would wake up soon.

She surveyed the scene before her. Nope. The drama was real.

Standing there stunned, Kenneth seemed unable to close his mouth. Louisa, in a rare show of tenderness for the loss of another valuable Wentworth heritage item, wept quietly. The museum curator, whose florid face now seemed even more so, ushered Kenneth and his cousin out of the cordoned area. Renée had disappeared as mysteriously as the quilt.

Appearing calm, Mayor Stiles conferred with Uncle Nick, who took the podium.

"Ladies and gentlemen. We are all dismayed at this turn of events. I must ask you to remain inside the building until the police arrive. Detective Brewster will issue further instructions then," Uncle Nick said, more than familiar with the drill.

"Oh, no!" a voice said. Thea turned to discover the exclamation's owner. Though she didn't need to, she already knew. Odette Milsap, her face pale, gripped her niece's arm, causing Sissy to squirm. Why was Odette so afraid of the cops?

With last night's police interview still green in her memory, Thea empathized with the woman. But she couldn't worry about Odette now. Instead, she worked her way over to check on Gram, whom she identified from afar by the festive hat feather. What if the shock of thievery was too much for her delicate British sensibilities?

Gram brazened her way through the crowd, bold as a bully, to get a better view. She came face to face with Thea in the middle.

"There you are, child," she said to her granddaughter, pulling her toward the ruined display. "We must keep an eye on the crime scene. So there's no damnation."

"Damnation?" Thea asked aloud, then shushed herself, hoping no one overheard.

"Exactly so. Like on the old show I like, *Robbery, She Wrote*. Damnation of the crime scene." Gram stretched on tiptoes, not easy in her sensible shoes.

"Do you mean contamination of the crime scene?"

"Spot on. Just what I said." Gram peered closer, her eyes focused in narrow slits. "Notice all the glass on the floor. Those curtain poodles hid it from us, didn't they?"

Thea did an inner eye-roll. Where was Mum? Somebody needed to rein in this senior Sherlock. Fast. Though Gram did have a point about the glass splinters. If not for the curtain poodles . . . er . . . puddles, they could have seen something was wrong and investigated. Without the press videotaping it.

The PA system kicked on again, this time with Mayor Stiles taking charge. "Friends, we apologize for how the evening is turning out. No one expected this. But we can rescue some of it. We can do what Larkindalians do best. Support one another and find the good in every situation."

Someone called out, "Hear, hear!" and the mayor smiled and gave him a thumbs-up.

Hear, hear. Thea felt a shred of a smile forming on her face, along with a new bit of admiration for the hissable miss.

"Our museum curator, Mr. Ned Hilderbrand, has assured me there are folding chairs in the storeroom that he will retrieve so our citizens may sit if they wish." The mayor asked for a few volunteers to help bring in the chairs.

"While we wait for the police to arrive, I propose we pass the time by enjoying ourselves as much as possible, under the circumstances. I understand the Espresso Café's own superb baker, Mrs. Emby Minsky, has provided refreshments: coffee, tea, and an assortment of sweets." Suzanne pointed in the direction of the refreshment table. "We have our wonderful Gold Rush display to examine, as well as all these antique quilts with local significance. I think we can have a little fun. What do you say?"

A few "hear-hears" and a couple "hip-hip-hoorays" later, and people were piling goodies on their paper plates and touring the quilt aisles with appreciation. The music came back on, enlivening the air with "Oh, Susannah." Which seemed to fit the occasion. By the time the police arrived, a bona fide bash was in progress.

"How are you doing with all this, Princess?" Uncle Nick asked Thea at the dessert table, picking up a small plate and covering it with assorted nuts. He hesitated. "Too healthy." He added a lemon bar.

"Me? Okay, I guess. Feeling a little better now." Thea had already scarfed down one chocolate chip cookie and was eyeing another.

"Dorothea, look at me."

When her uncle called her by name, or worse, by her *full* name, she knew he had something serious to say. Thea dragged her attention from the extra thick cookie and met his direct gaze.

"This is not your fault. Last night was not your fault. Understand?" The question flashed in his eyes, pressing her to take heed. "Someone else is to blame. You are not the guilty party here."

Was she feeling the guilty one? Of course she wasn't. But how could she, as quilt show co-chair, not take some responsibility? Especially for tonight's catastrophe? If she'd only hired added security, or stayed at the museum all afternoon to guard their precious antiquity. . . . Maybe things would have turned out differently.

"You haven't done *anything* wrong, Princess," Uncle Nick said. "I'm so proud of you. Both the soirée and this unveiling event have been beautifully put together. Didn't the mayor and tonight's guests just endorse you as a wonderful leader?"

True. Of course, their praise had come before they knew of the theft.

Enough. She needed to stop this balderdash, as Gram would say. Her uncle made sense. Thea gave him a fond hug and said, "Thanks, I needed to hear that right now."

"I'm sure the quilt will be found. Even before the show begins on Saturday," Uncle Nick said. "After all, the whole town will be looking for it."

"You're right!" Encouraged by the idea, Thea pondered the puzzle. "Why would anyone steal such a well-known piece of history? It couldn't be hung in a home or someone would report it."

Nick agreed. "If someone tried to sell it, I imagine such a transaction could be easily traced. Especially now, since it belongs to the state." He threw a few cashews into his mouth and chewed, thinking. "Perhaps our thief has a private collection."

"Could be. Lots of possibilities." Thea focused again on her uncle, tilting her head, amazed. He had totally distracted her away from diving into a sea of guilt. Nick's little lecture not only rescued but redirected her. Now, Thea found herself in the express lane to solving this mystery. Though, considering Detective Brewster's warning last night, she'd have to be a super-sneaky sleuth.

But wait. He'd been talking about the danger of outing a dangerous attacker or mugger or something. Thea's plan was to oust a simple thief. Last night Mary-Alice might have been assaulted. Her brooch had gone missing. And tonight, a valuable quilt had been stolen, almost right in front of them.

Surely those incidents couldn't be related.

Or could they?

20

Tuesday morning, Thea woke at 6:58 A.M., two minutes before her alarm was set to sound off. Thankful for the gentle inner rousting, she pushed the button to the radio setting and lay listening to music until time for the top-of-the-hour news. In truth, she had awakened many times through the night, as if her mind were impatient to crack the case of the missing quilt. Which was crazy because she had no case.

Thea flipped the down comforter over to expose a leg to the cool air. Resting it on the soft puffiness, she raised her head to look at the bed coverings. Good. Everything was as it should be. Blowing out a relieved breath, she dropped her head back on the pillow.

While she had slept, Thea dreamt her comforter was gone and in its place, "Larkin's Treasure" kept her warm. The quilt was heavy, weighing her down, and she couldn't move. So, she lay still and fiddled with the gold wedding band sewn into the intricate design, flipping it back and forth.

What did it mean? She wanted to get married? She should grab her grandfather's Martin guitar and start a band?

She struggled to an upright position, yawning and rubbing her eyes, just as the news came over the air. "Breaking local news. Police have no leads in the Hastings McLeod Museum break-in and robbery yesterday, where a valuable historic quilt was stolen from a display case. Once owned by the Wentworth family, the quilt was donated to the California State Quilt & Textile Museum more than a decade ago. It was recently loaned back for a special exhibition connected to the upcoming Blocks on the Walk Quilt Show."

Great. They just *had* to mention the show in the same report as the robbery.

Annoyed, Thea considered lying back down and pulling the covers over her head. But then she caught a glimpse of her matted hair-do in the wall mirror. Would more under the covers time improve her look? Not likely.

"Police say the theft occurred sometime between noon and 6 P.M. on Sunday," the announcer continued. "They were called to the scene at 7:50 P.M. and proceeded to interview those in attendance."

Another dreaded police interview. But not so hard on Thea this time. Or anyone else, she hoped, thinking of Odette. The detective and his officers had set up in the dining room with its lovely view of Pioneer Park through the ceiling-to-floor glass windows. Once the officer heard she had arrived around 6 P.M., and the curator confirmed, she was free to go.

Right place—right time? Or was she becoming skilled at handling the police?

"A possible entry point was discovered," the radio voice said, "but police will not say for sure whether it compromised the museum's security. The robbery is still under investigation. Anyone with any information is asked to call the Larkindale Police Department. Now, on to the weather report. . . ."

Resigned, Thea switched off the radio. That report might be enough to quench the spirit of the show. And deter visitors from attending on Saturday. Who would buy all those darling things in the Members Boutique?

It occurred to her maybe no one had told Mary-Alice about the quilt's unexpected journey to who-knows-where. Would she have heard it first from the radio broadcast Thea just heard? Surely, someone must have done the honors. Just in case, Thea wanted to see her friend this morning. Plus, there were some unanswered questions only Mary-Alice could counter.

And Thea needed to let her know Dr. Cottle hadn't come. Again. She learned of his projected absence the way Prudy had apparently planned—without enough notice for Thea to make other arrangements. Though Kenneth did pinch-hit with his well-said remarks.

Like before, Prudy left a late message on Thea's answering machine, unheard until the event was over. Cottle couldn't make the unveiling, but he would be at the judging on Saturday. Thea found it harder and harder to trust the elusive quilt expert. If he didn't make the show, it would be his third strike. Then . . . he'd be out.

And what was Prudy's problem? Was she afraid of Thea's reaction?

Am I so scary?

Thea looked in the mirror again, scaring herself with her morning mat-head, mascara under her eyes, and pillowcase wrinkles across her cheek. Fright night in the daylight. Maybe she *was* scary. Jumping up to shower, she readied herself for the day.

Dressed in another new t-shirt with the quilt show logo on the front, Thea put the finishing touches on her makeup. The shirt's blueberry color flattered her periwinkle eyes. The knowledge helped her face a challenging day as much as carrying a lucky charm on her keychain. Which wasn't much, she guessed.

She made her favorite breakfast, a peanut butter and sweet pickle sandwich, grilled. A few minutes over hot tea, some Betty time and treats, a look at her quilt show to-do list, longer than before, and Thea was almost out the door.

But first, she walked over to the antique picture of the little girls playing dress-up. She remembered last night's imagined slap from the Renée Fowler look-alike child. The picture had power, but Thea didn't want it to have power over her. She removed it from the wall and carried it out to the back porch. Leaning it against the freezer, she said, "You've earned another time-out, ladies." This time, it had better work.

Thea got to the hospital by 8:30 A.M., parked, and peeked into Mary-Alice's room soon after. The sun filtered through the trees outside the window, rays streaming down on the patient as if the angels favored her above all others. Her eyes were closed, and she looked peaceful.

Too peaceful.

"Mary-Alice?" Thea crept into the room. "Are you awake?" She was afraid to ask, "Are you alive?" What if there was no answer?

But the woman stirred, fluttered her eyelids, then looked toward Thea. Mary-Alice smiled. "Oh, my dear. I'm so glad you've come. Actually, I need your help."

"Of course! What can I do? Get your purse? Fluff your pillow?" Thea put her handbag on the side table and moved closer to the bed. Did Mary-Alice look better today?

Maybe a bit. Eyes bright, face not so pale. The sight buoyed Thea's spirits.

"No, no. I'm quite comfortable. Not that kind of help." Mary-Alice reached out a hand so veined it looked like a map of the mighty Mississippi. With all its tributaries.

"Come. Sit with me a spell," she said.

Pulling up the same chair and scraping it across the tiles as before, Thea sat. "How are you feeling, my friend? You look much improved. Maybe you'll be released soon and can go home."

"It would be a blessing," Mary-Alice said, her voice soft. "The doctor said maybe tomorrow if I keep doing this well." She smiled again.

"You said you needed help. What can I do for you, Mary-Alice?" Thea leaned in so she wouldn't miss a word.

"Well . . ." The elderly woman hesitated. "It's a lot to ask."

"Anything!" Thea said. "It would be my privilege." She wondered what this woman with servants to assist her, who had all the money she needed, and was beloved by all of Larkindale, could want from her. A good deal on a cool antique?

Wait. It might be. Thea had located special items for her friend before. Only earlier this year she found a wonderful antique linen press for Mary-Alice. What this time? How about an old safe? To hide away beautiful baubles like the diamond brooch?

A safe would have been handy to have a few days ago.

Or perhaps her friend wanted an appraisal of all the antiques at Wentworth Mansion. Thea did have the expertise needed to accomplish such a huge task. It would take time, which she didn't have right now, but what a lovely way to repay Mary-Alice for her many years of friendship. And wisdom.

"What with the loss of my brooch and now, the theft of 'Larkin's Treasure,'" Mary-Alice said, straining to sit. "Well, something's going on and I want to know what it is. But I need your help."

"My help?" Thea said, surprised. This was not the direction she had expected the conversation to take. "Don't you want me to appraise your estate?"

"How thoughtful, my dear," Mary-Alice said, sinking back onto her pillow. "But I'm not expecting to kick the can anytime soon." She chuckled, adding, "Or was it kick the pail?"

"Bucket," Thea said, trying not to laugh also.

"And there is the question of whether or not I was struck on the back of the head. Or did I just trip and fall?" Mary-Alice asked, continuing her original theme. "I'm still a bit foggy on it. Can't decide if I really want to know someone assaulted me. Or confirm I'm an awkward old lady. Neither one is pleasant." She looked up at Thea. "Know what I mean?"

Awkward, bumbling, clumsy . . . she remembered Renée's clumso-comment from last night. Thea knew exactly what Mary-Alice meant with the last part.

"So what can I do for you?" Thea said, repeating herself. Obviously, her friend had heard the news about the stolen quilt. On top of everything else. Worrying about a possible head-whacker on the loose was enough for anybody. Poor dear.

"I want to hire you to be my own secret PI. To make some inquiries about the brooch, especially. Like a young Miss Marple," Mary-Alice said, excitement in her voice.

What? Thea blinked back her shock.

"Why do you want *me*? I'm not a PI. Besides, the police are investigating," Thea said. Even though she had already promised herself to try and find the stolen quilt on the sly, she hadn't planned to delve into Mary-Alice's personal business. It might be creepy. Or dangerous.

Hadn't Detective Brewster been emphatic she keep out of his investigation? And yesterday, Uncle Nick had hinted the same thing in the town square. Thea figured her grilling of Odette had already gotten her involved. Maybe involved enough.

"You are the perfect person. No one would suspect you of collecting evidence for me. You'd just be talking to people about the quilt show. And you have wonderful diplomatic skills, my dear, when you choose to use them."

Mary-Alice looked out the window as if searching for something. A cherry-on-top reason to persuade Thea to agree?

"Besides," Mary-Alice said, turning back. "I trust you completely."

The woman was good.

"Can I ask you a few things before I answer?"

"Ask away."

"Not sure how to put this," Thea paused for a moment, taking a deep breath. "Do you think it is possible any of your family might have taken the brooch? Or knocked you out, for some reason?" She cringed a little at her own invasiveness. Maybe after her questions, Mary-Alice would unsuggest Thea make inquiries.

"You know, in spite of the lovely old brooch, I'm not personally attracted to diamonds." Mary-Alice gazed down at her hands and admired her wedding ring, a thick gold band without jeweled adornment. "Seth bought me this ring when we married, when we needed 'diamond money' for other things. I loved it because it was simple and real and solid gold. Like my Seth." She looked at Thea with tears in her eyes. "I never wanted any other ring. Or any other man."

Thea's eyes filled, too, and she thought of her own diamond engagement ring hidden in the jewelry box at home. A promise never kept. She knew her experience didn't compare, but it had given her a glimpse into the Mary-Alice kind of love.

"The diamond brooch is just a thing. But I'd like to have it back because Seth gave it to me on a special anniversary."

Mary-Alice dabbed at her tears with the edge of her sheet. Thea yanked a few tissues from the box, kept one, and handed the others to her friend, who blew her nose.

"Thank you, my dear." Mary-Alice wiped her wrinkled cheeks with a clean tissue. "Did you happen to see the television coverage of the speeches before the unveiling?"

"I was actually there, dear one." Thea patted the moisture around her eyes, hoping she'd still have mascara left after her blubbering. She appreciated the change of subject, though this train of talk was also sensitive. "But no, I didn't see any coverage. Was it well done?"

Looking proud, Mary-Alice said, "Kenneth was a star, wasn't he? I mean, Nick was perfect and the mayor was perfect. But my Kenneth stole the show!"

Thea agreed he had done a superb job. While the conversation was so upbeat, she took the liberty to mention Cottle's failure to appear.

"So I heard," Mary-Alice said. "I just don't understand it. He'll be here for the judging, you say?" Her lips drew into a thin line and she wore a look that said he'd better be there on Saturday. Or else.

Though one could only imagine what an "or else" moment from Mary-Alice might look like. Tea with no scones? Cream, but no sugar? Maybe a little private prayer-slap?

"By then, I intend to be in fine shape to judge right alongside Dr. Cottle. It will be interesting to hear what he has to say for himself! His behavior has been less than professional." Mary-Alice tensed, working the edge of the blanket with nervous hands.

Since tomorrow was her target release day, Thea didn't want her overly excited. She turned the topic back to the elder's happy place.

"Boy, Kenneth sure did impress me. He seemed so anxious, but then pulled himself together when it was camera time," Thea said. "He should do more of it. Maybe become a newscaster or something."

The comments changed Mary-Alice's countenance into one of joy. "Good idea. I told you he had done Little Theatre in his community, didn't I, my dear? He's talented and photogenic, too."

"I'll have to catch him on TV, then," Thea said, though it was hard to imagine the sweaty, toothy mess of a man coming off well on the tube.

"I worry about him, sometimes." Mary-Alice's blissful look changed to one of reflection. "He is looking for an identity through his acting. Perhaps it is because he's adopted."

"When he finds the right lady and gets married, he'll see himself as a man of worth to someone else. Should help, right?" Dr. Thea, on the job.

"Oh, yes. But what if it doesn't happen? If only he could see himself as God sees him, he would quit looking for significance in acting. Or others." Mary-Alice's words were heartfelt and tender. "I pray for him all the time. And for my daughter, Louisa. I wish you could have known her before the divorce."

"She's divorced?" Thea asked. Though she could see why.

"It's the old story. Her husband of thirty-one years had an affair with his secretary," Mary-Alice said. "At first, Louisa thought they might work it out. She was crazy about him. But he had been carrying on for twelve years and a child was involved." She made a little forlorn sound of sympathy. "You see, Louisa couldn't have children."

No wonder Louisa was such a grouch. She had plenty to be angry about.

"So, my happy, charity-loving daughter has turned into a man-hater. It's the saddest thing. Still, with God comes great healing. If she would put her trust in Him, all would be well." Mary-Alice twisted her wedding ring thoughtfully.

With this new knowledge, Thea was not about to turn down her friend's request.

"I'll do it. I'll be your private PI and you don't have to pay me, either," Thea grinned, taking Mary-Alice's hand again. "You've already . . . what do they say? Paid it forward. In friendship, in kindness, in prayer."

The old woman glowed. "Oh, thank you!"

Then Thea remembered her earlier question. "Remember I asked if anyone in your family could be involved in the thefts or your assault. Is it possible?"

"No. But it wouldn't matter to me if they were," Mary-Alice said.

"Why not?" Thea asked.

"Because, I forgive my own."

21

Thea drove beneath the new quilt show banner attached below the arched "Welcome to Old Town Larkindale" sign. The banner moved gently with the air current in all its red-lettered glory. Semicircles cut into the white background fluttered back and forth, giving Thea the impression of a flamenco dancer's dress.

"Good job, Heather Ann!" Thea called out the window in case her Signs & Banners Chair was within hearing distance. At last, things were trending in the right direction.

She arrived at the Antique Emporium the same time as Lyndi. Thea hesitated, key pointed into lock, until she gave her employee the once over. Today, the purple-haired one radiated sixties splendor with her hair caught in a ponytail to one side. Bands of stark white fabric separated her mod mini-dress into pink and orange symmetric squares. White patent leather Mary Jane's gave her a little-girl look.

"I know, right? The Mary Jane look is wrong. I need go-go boots. But I only found one boot. Weird." Lyndi rotated a bare leg around. "Can you see where I missed a whole strip shaving my legs this morning? It looks like a Mohawk."

Laughing, Thea unlocked and opened the door. "You are nuts. Get in here."

"Did you see it?" Lyndi asked, once inside. When Thea shook her head, still grinning, Lyndi said, "If I'd have worn boots, I wouldn't have seen it either. At least it's dark in here. Maybe no one else will notice."

They did their opening preparations, making coffee, getting the cash box, fussing over the booths, until all was ready. Thea flipped over the sign to Welcome and unlocked the door. To no one. Where was everybody?

"By the way, I have some good news," Lyndi said, leaning against the front counter, twisting her finger around a side pony strand.

After all the bad news on the radio, Thea could use some good news. "What?"

"I got a call, and the barriers are on their way!" Lyndi did a little sixties Mashed Potato dance on the Emporium's plank floor. "Do you remember this?"

"I wasn't born yet. And neither were you," Thea said. "How *could* we remember?" But she did a few Mashed Potato steps to show team spirit.

And to celebrate the coming of the barriers. The more she thought about those, she realized popping over to the museum to set them up would give her an excuse to question the curator, Ned Hilderbrand. Thea had some opinions on the apparent lack of security yesterday. She probably should keep those to herself. But who knew what she might learn since she was now on the case for Mary-Alice?

After Emby opened the Espresso Café, Thea followed the cinnamon bun aroma to the soda fountain. A few customers clustered near, purchasing sweets from a tray labeled, "Day Old, Still Delicious: Two Bits." She watched them lay quarters on the counter, choosing last night's chocolate chip cookies or tuxedoed cake pops.

"Lemon bars?" Thea asked. In her world, a lemon bar had fruit. Almost a healthy late morning snack.

"Gone," Emby said. "To my pad." She grinned. "I left the patchwork-decorated cookies at the museum. For the guild members who will be helping all week."

"Good idea," Thea said. "Sure appreciated your wonderful spread last night, Emby. It put everyone in a good mood." Thea had thanked her at the end of the night, but what with the publicity banner up and the barriers on the way, her thankfulness spilled over onto Emby again.

Thea took a chocolate chip cookie, mouthed "I owe you two bits" to Emby and turned to go back, colliding with Lyndi instead. They parted, laughing and apologizing.

Emby jingled over to them, the bells on her anklet merry. "Hang loose, chickies." She surveyed Lyndi's mod look. "Groovy."

"Oh, yeah. I'm groovin' for sure. Totally," Lyndi said, reveling in the attention. She started to do the Mashed Potato again, but then stopped, apparently remembering her imperfectly shaved leg. She placed it behind the good one. The result was picture-perfect ingénue.

Making her way between mostly empty espresso tables, Thea aimed for the "free coffee" table she always set up and poured herself a cup of Apricot Crème. She added creamer and sugar, then spun smack into Lyndi again. The coffee spilled onto Thea's new blueberry-colored T-shirt.

"Oh, wow," Lyndi said, looking horrified. "I hope it doesn't stain."

"Why are you shadowing me?" Thea asked, taking several napkins and blotting the wet spots. Now her hands were sticky, too. "Do you want something?"

"Actually, boss-lady, I do," Lyndi said. "I wanted to go put up those barriers at the museum. I feel guilty they weren't in place yesterday. And, you know I love the museum." She picked up a napkin and pressed against the coffee marks on Thea's top.

"I've got it!" Thea brushed her hand away, annoyed. Both with Lyndi's stalking and her attempt to spoil Thea's museum plans. "I mean, thanks. I can take care of it."

Adjusting her attitude, Thea said, "Lyndi, I was hoping to go over to Hastings McLeod myself and oversee the barrier setup." She knew this was tricky territory.

Lyndi nurtured a dream to work with antiques full-time. Not in a small-town store, but a big-city museum. Her anthropology classes at the local community college were the basis of her promising career. And Thea knew her employee's resumé would benefit from any museum time.

"You don't think I can do it?" Lyndi looked wounded.

"You do everything well. I want to talk to Mr. Hilderbrand, the curator. I need to get some information for Mary-Alice." Thea added the last part because she knew it would be persuasive. Luckily, it was also true.

"Oh, well . . ." Lyndi still didn't look convinced.

"Besides," Thea pulled out her secret weapon, "you don't want to go out where anyone else can see the Mohawk leg, do you?"

Lyndi gasped. "Whoa, Nellie. No way, José," she said, hiding her leg again. "Why it would be . . . nefandous,"

"Unspeakable?"

"Totally."

To Thea's astonishment, the museum had more than a few cars in the parking lot. Once inside, she saw a number of people nosing around. A security guard stood at the entry and an older woman docent welcomed Thea, asking her to sign a guest book.

After doing so, she inquired about the curator and was told he was mingling among the unexpected crowd.

"Isn't it wonderful? I've never seen it so busy on a Tuesday," the docent said. "Of course, we are normally open Wednesday through Saturday. So I guess it's why I haven't." She smiled as if she was the cleverest docent working any museum.

Thea followed the docent's directions and came upon the eternally red-faced Ned Hilderbrand, chatting with a family in one of the quilt rows. She noticed the barriers were already in place and positioned well. The only thing missing was a white glove lady.

Hilderbrand finished with the group and they walked on, admiring the antiques and quilts. He extended his hand toward Thea. "Ah, Ms. James. Nice to see you again."

"If you have a few minutes, could I talk to you?" Thea explained she wanted to ask him a few questions. And because they were of a sensitive nature, referring to the quilt theft, could they speak privately?

"Of course. Follow me." After Hilderbrand had led the way into his comfortable office and offered her a chair, he took up residence behind a massive desk crafted from a swirling-patterned wood. He ran his hand across the black inset covering the desktop. "She's my prized possession. Straight out of Old Larkindale National Bank. Circa 1908. Isn't she a beauty?"

"Gorgeous. What'll you take for her?" Thea asked, admiring the dark red-brown finish buffed to a high gloss. She wasn't serious, of course. But could think of several buyers who might be interested. Looking up at Ned, she said, "Looks like a Chippendale piece. Mahogany?"

"African mahogany," he said, stiffening. "And I wouldn't sell this desk for any amount of money."

Whoops. "Forgive me, Mr. Hilderbrand. The antique dealer in me escaped her cage for a minute. If I had such a treasure, I wouldn't sell it either."

He gave a well-I-never sniff and straightened his laptop with manicured fingers.

"What did you want to see me about?" Ned Hilderbrand rocked back in his leather chair, peering over half-glasses, in command. "As I said, I can give you a few minutes."

"I do have some questions," Thea said, pulling her Thea-do-list from her bag where she had jotted down a few points. After Mary-Alice's earlier request to find out what happened, Thea felt empowered. Commissioned to duty.

She leaned forward and, with a boldness she actually did feel, said, "With such a valuable item as 'Larkin's Treasure' on display, I expected to see extra security."

Okay, technically, it wasn't a question.

Hilderbrand sat forward, too. "Ms. James, did you know it takes only fifty-eight seconds to steal a priceless painting right off a wall? In the presence of visitors?" He took off the half-glasses and placed them on the desk before he continued.

"I assure you we are serious about protecting our artifacts from theft. In fact, we have been raising funds for a new security system to better guard all our *objets d'art*. Not just one quilt. On loan." He leaned back, clasped his hands, and placed them in his lap, as if he just issued a final decree.

"Are you saying your security system is . . . inadequate?" Like a total failure?

"Not at all. But it's a bit of an antiquity and needs to be upgraded," he said. "We are considering a new system to detect intruders when they approach the building. Closed-circuit cameras with motion or infrared detection. Our current system is outdated."

"What about security guards?" Thea asked. Apparently, anyone could just walk in and help himself to a cool one-of-a-kind item. Though there were sure a lot of rusty gold pans on display. Those should be outside in a box, labeled "Free to a good home." Like puppies or kittens in a box outside of the supermarket.

"Security guards?" Hilderbrand inhaled and gazed heavenward, as if looking for help. "We do have an excellent security guard. He comes on duty when the museum opens. He was here last night at 7:00 P.M. When we formally opened the doors."

"But, Mr. Hilderbrand. People were in and out all afternoon, setting up for the unveiling." Frustrated, Thea wondered if she was missing something here. "I didn't see a guard anywhere!" Well . . . not until after 7 P.M.

"Correct. As I just said, the guard works only when we are open to the public. But I was here and everything appeared to be in good order."

"If having a valuable quilt stolen right out of the display case is good order. . . ."

"Ms. James, there is no need to be rude. Obviously, I am appalled at the turn of events." Hilderbrand spoke matter-of-factly, studying his slender fingers. He checked his watch. "It just emphasizes our need for a new security system."

"But . . . but. . . ." Thea felt like she had drifted onto the funny farm.

She shifted herself into grovel-ready mode. "I don't mean to be rude. But how this theft will impact the Blocks on the Walk Quilt Show on Saturday concerns me. We had hoped for big crowds. Oodles of visitors to Old Town. A renewal for Larkindale."

"If this morning is any indication, you will have your oodles." When he said the word *oodles*, Hilderbrand made quotation marks in the air with his fingers, showing a brief facial movement, promising the start of a smile. But not delivering.

"What do you mean?" Not as though she expected him to make sense. But hope sprang eternal and so on. Thea scooted to the edge of her chair.

"The crime scene investigators were here rather late. I thought I'd just clean up the glass and display area this morning. But those barriers of yours were waiting when I got here and so, with a little help from the company guys, we put them out."

"Yes, thanks. I fully expected to spend the afternoon setting it all up."

"We weren't even quite finished when my docents knocked on the door, ready to work. I thought of having one of them clean up the display area mess, but I didn't want her cutting herself on the shattered glass." His hands waved about like graceful birds as he explained where all the players stood on the museum stage.

"I decided to open the museum and just do the cleanup while it was quiet. The docents could help with the barriers. Only," he said, "several people came inside at once. Past the security guard, mind you." He arched one brow, as if to signal his cynicism at her prior complaint. "Then more came in. And more. They've been streaming in all morning."

"How nice. But what does it have to do with Saturday's show?" Thea asked.

"The traffic we are experiencing is a result of the negative publicity from last night. They came to see the empty case. The broken glass. The scene of the great quilt heist."

"How crazy!" Thea couldn't believe the fiasco had turned positive. Maybe plenty of people would stop by for the show, after all. Rather like slowing down for a car wreck. The horror factor mixed with a natural curiosity held people's gaze.

Whatever the magnet, Thea had new hope the masses would swarm into Old Town like bees to a honeycomb. She gave herself a mental high-five.

"Before I go, I have one more question for you." A question she had meant to ask Mary-Alice but didn't. Since it was a little awkward.

"One more." He brought his laptop into a work position. Thea's time was at an end.

"Did you actually see the quilt in the case?" she asked. "I mean, are you positive it arrived here from the State Quilt & Textile Museum? And can you verify that?"

"You asked three questions." Ned Hilderbrand flipped open the laptop lid. His ruddy complexion flamed. "Don't be ridiculous. You insult me, Ms. James. I have gone over all this with Detective Brewster."

He glanced up, a dismissal in his eyes. "If you have any further questions, I suggest you speak to him."

22

Driving back to the Emporium, Thea wondered if she and PI work had a future. The chat with Ned Hilderbrand had been rough. And her attempt to relieve Odette of information the other night was nothing to boast about either. Where were those wonderful diplomatic skills Mary-Alice had mentioned? Did they go home early? To dawdle over at the Durtles?

Thea noted the time on her wristwatch. Close to 3:00 P.M. Her tummy rumbled, reminding her lunch had been a no-show. A condition almost epidemic these days. Dr. Cottle, Prudy, lunch. . . .

She turned the Wrangler into the Gas-n-Go parking lot. A fill-up could wait a few days, but food could not. What about her mobile cupboard? Maybe the perfect morsel lay forgotten in there. Jumping out of the Jeep, Thea circled around and opened the back, leaning in. She sorted through the sacks and the occasional box full of groceries.

Rats. All canned food or dry goods. She picked up a bag of Veggie Thins, then a cereal box labeled, Co-Co-Nutios. She discarded both, fancying something marshmallowy. Or crunchy. Or even the least bit gaggable.

Were there any other snacks hidden in the Jeep? Thea checked the back seat. Rats, no munchies. Her gaze fell to the pink sewing basket on the floor. Uh-oh. She'd forgotten about it. And about all the donated merchandise inside for the Members Boutique. They needed to be dropped off at Nellie McGraw's, so she could price the items and add them to the merchandise already collected. Thea set the basket on the front passenger seat. Then, with a click on her key fob, locked the rig and proceeded inside the Gas-n-Go Mini-Mart.

The business, a glass and cinderblock wonder, had been built only last year. Thea considered it the repository for all her favorite candy bars. But today, her tastes ran to the more elevated culinary options housed in the hot case. With a pair of stainless tongs, she chose a crispy chicken taquito and placed it in a white, wax bag. It looked lonely. So she added a beef taquito to the bag and folded over the top. Maybe it wasn't farm-to-table dining, but at least she wouldn't be picking squashed Co-Co-Nutios from the floor mats.

The kid at the counter rang her up between rescuing his thick glasses from the end of his nose and giving them frequent shoves back to the bridge. In spite of the glasses and a spotty complexion, his blue eyes were large and fringed. His nametag read "Delbert."

"Hey, Delbert. You make these taquitos yourself?" Thea tossed him a little female attention. "I bet you're a good cook. They're almost gone." It oughta make his day.

"Yes, ma'am. I do make them. I apologize if there aren't enough left for you." Delbert peered into the hot case where a few of the deep-fried tortilla rolls lay in wait. "Do you want me to bag up the rest of these?"

Did he just call her ma'am? Great. Plus, he thought she wanted to eat them all.

"Oh, no! I couldn't stuff them down, thanks. I have two here already." Obviously, he didn't realize she ate like a baby bird. Except for pancakes. Tempted to buy a candy bar, Thea decided to wait and come back when there was a different clerk on duty. And reminded her sweet tooth of the emergency bar stored in the Jeep's glove compartment.

"You women sure love your taquitos. I sold a bunch of them to some twin ladies a little while ago. They were going on a picnic to Little Larkin Falls." Delbert stuffed some napkins into a plastic bag, along with her taquitos, and handed it to Thea with a receipt.

Could it have been Prudy? Off co-picnicking? When Thea needed her as quilt show co-chair?

"How interesting," Thea said. "Twins. Do you remember what they looked like?"

"They looked like each other, ma'am. They were sisters, too."

"Amazing. Did you happen to get their names?"

"Hmm." Delbert stroked the patchy stubble on his chin. "Rowdy and Dowdy? Toobie and Doobie? Hard to say. . . ."

"Prudy and Trudy?" Thea asked.

"Yes!" Delbert seemed proud he'd remembered their names. "Bought taquitos with salsa and sodas. I bet they're having a blast. Anything else for you?"

Thea grumbled a negative reply and returned to her rig. She sat without turning on the engine, considering this new wrinkle in her quilt show plans. Time to change her attitude. To worry any more about whether Prudy would do her part only wasted Thea's time and energy. And made her hungry. She opened the bag and bit off the end of a taquito. Not bad for gas station gourmet. Thea downed half of it before she started the Jeep and drove back to the Emporium, chewing all the way.

Once back in the store, Thea made a cup of tea and tucked herself away in her office. She wanted to call the guild members who were helping with the show and make sure they had enough support.

As she unfolded her to-do list, she thought again about her little investigation on behalf of Mary-Alice. Thea hadn't learned much yet. Or had she? If only she possessed a partner-in-crime as they say. Someone with whom she could talk over the case. A Dr. Watson to her half-baked Holmes. A Tommy to her Tuppance. Or George to her Nancy Drew. If her sister, Rosie, hadn't been away on her honeymoon, what a great side-kick she'd make to Thea's sleuthing self. The thought sent a wistful smile to her lips.

She could talk to Betty, but the feline's communication skills needed work. The logical choice should have been Renée. To Thea, the disintegration of their friendship birthed yet another mystery. A whodunit she couldn't untangle. Reconciled to be spying solo, Thea put aside those concerns for now.

After making calls to a few guild members, things appeared to be on track. But of course, only Thea knew that. It had been a while since they had all met together as a group and given committee reports. Perhaps she could arrange another opportunity for the ladies to share information. A Midweek Info-Meet. Then everyone would have a complete picture of the progress. It might be easier to find gaps in coverage or notice other problems.

The Emporium could work, using Emby's Espresso Café. But would it give them enough room? Probably a bit crowded. Thea knew she'd be on duty, babysitting the Emporium door, letting each person in upon arrival. Unless she left the door unlocked. But then passersby would see folks talking inside and try the door. And walk right in.

Thea didn't relish kicking people out of the store. Where else might they meet? She wanted a setting to pamper the quilters. Luxury for her hard-working team.

Wait. How about a meeting at the Lake House? Her mother's Jane Austen–themed garden parties always made news. Or at least gave the guests something to talk about, even brag about, to their friends. This wouldn't be an Austen event, but Mum's roses were magnificent this time of year, preening their faces in the sun, begging to be seen.

She punched in the number.

"Of course, I'll host the quilt guild ladies, luv." Mum sounded like she had been wishing someone would ask. "We need a bit of a distraction, don't we? And, my darling, there's a new goldfish in Lake Nora waiting to meet you."

Christened Lake Nora by Thea's father, the small pond sported a feeder stream covered by a tiny footbridge. Set among pink and yellow rose bushes, it held an enchantment for Thea, even in her youth. She and Renée had often played the afternoons away, alternately chasing butterflies, splashing through the creek with bare feet, or having a tea party on the patio, wearing full dress-up regalia.

Rather like the little girls in Thea's antique picture. But they were in time-out.

"Your grandmother will probably stalk all the quilters. She misses it, now the arthritis has advanced. But she has her line dancing classes to keep her busy." Mum's disapproval singed the phone connection. Normally, the two women were always in agreement and lived together in harmony. But Gram's foray into line dancing didn't jell with her daughter-in-law's proper sentiments. It strayed too far from Nora's idea of a British grandmother's personae.

"Wonderful, thanks," Thea said, snubbing the censure. "I'm thinking about 4:00 P.M. tomorrow afternoon. It's before dinner, so maybe serve a snack to tide them over? I'll tap Emby for some goodies."

"Nonsense, luv. You leave it to me. It will be easy for our Harriet to whip up some small sandwiches with tea."

Easy for you, Mum! Not for Harriet. Thea laughed to herself. Still, she knew it would give little pause to the housekeeper who worshiped her mother. Harriet considered it a calling to "see to" her beloved employer. And everyone Nora loved.

"Sounds perfect, Mum." Thea rang off and looked at her list of quilters to call. It included some she had spoken to earlier. What a lot of work and chatter ahead. She wasn't in the mood. If only the quilters had something set up like Mum's prayer chain. One person called the next on the list, and that one contacted the subsequent name. Maybe Thea would suggest the idea to the members at Mum's tomorrow.

Since no option was yet in place and she couldn't slough it off to the picnicking Prudy, Thea called the members, one by one, inviting each to her Midweek Info-Meet, disguised as Afternoon Tea. Even Prudy.

Lyndi had just turned the Welcome sign to Closed when Thea finished. Glad she had no quilt event scheduled for this evening, she said good-bye to her employees, locked up the Emporium, and headed for home. She needed a night off.

And as Mum implied, after the last two disasters, time for a distraction of her own. Thea's goal for the evening was tea and stitchery time with her quilt.

And sweet, dreamless slumber.

23

Okay, girls. Time-out's over. You can come back and hang with us," Thea said to the children in the antique print the next morning. Of course, she meant herself and Betty when she said "us." Best company in the house. Maybe on the block.

She carried the picture from the porch into the living room and hung it above the television. "I hope you are ready to behave." She wagged a severe finger at both, but more pointedly at the Renée image. Swirly glass and a lovely frame wouldn't be enough to save them from the antique shop's sale aisle if they couldn't get along this time.

Humming the chorus to "Clementine"—the melody easy to remember because it was the same as that of the verse—Thea picked up Betty's water and food dishes—vintage Bauer bowls in the ringware pattern—and ferried them to the kitchen sink. The cat preferred a fresh bowl with her fresh water, so Thea dug in a lower cabinet and pulled out two more, one green and one yellow, to satisfy the fussy feline. She ran water into the green. Careful not to spill any liquid, Thea carried both bowls out to the porch and placed them on Betty's plastic cat mat.

When she had filled the yellow bowl with food, she shook the Kitty-Yum-Yum's box like a maraca, their prearranged signal for fresh food. But Betty did not appear. Thea had seen the calico this morning in the bedroom, grooming with gusto. In sync with her mistress's morning ablutions, actually. Where had she gone? She had to be in the house.

Whenever Thea left for work, she preferred the cat cozy in her back-porch domain. Everything needed had been provided there: a soft kitty-bed high on a table, from which she could enjoy an outside view through a large window, her drinking and dining bowls, a cat tower for frisky moments, and of course, her private, covered ladies' room.

Shaking the box all the way around the living room, Thea did a little cha-cha. An earlier call to the hospital had revealed the good news Mary-Alice would be released today. Later, Thea planned to visit the Wentworth Mansion and judge her friend's condition for herself.

Opening the front door, she shook the box, just to check. Betty could not exit the house, Thea had made sure. But still . . . what if? She hoped no Durtle cats would hear the delicious kitty crunchies in the box and come running over for an extra breakfast.

No cats came.

Just as Thea started to shut the door, an orange, black, and white streak whizzed over her foot and out front at cheetah-speed. Betty dashed over the driveway, across the lawn, and cleared the Durtles' fence as if she was a cat-thlete in competition. Thea thought she heard a crowd chant the letters, "C.A.T.! C.A.T.!" Instead of "U.S.A.! U.S.A.!" But it must have been her imagination. There was no one in sight.

Why was her cat so drawn to those hooligans next door?

"Not funny, Betty," Thea said, stepping out onto the green-planked porch, closing the door behind her. At least she wore crisp white tennies today instead of her clogs. She'd reasoned out if she hoped to be a good gumshoe, she might need a good running shoe. Now Thea loped across the lawn, stopping at the Durtles' fence. Behind her, she heard her phone ring. *Rats.*

"Mornin', young lady," Mr. Durtle rose, slow and unhurried, from a tangled flowerbed. "Lose your cat again?"

Thea's phone continued its insistent ring. She looked back at the house. Should she grab the call? No . . . better take care of Betty first. "Sorry. My sneaky kitty slipped outside and jumped your fence. Again." Thea felt an unseen presence and glanced up. High atop the porch roof, a couple cats lay, watching the interaction, tails twitching.

Mr. Durtle dragged himself toward her, staggering like a movie monster, wincing at every step. Thea automatically leaned into the fence as if to keep him from falling.

"Do you need some help?" Thea asked, looking toward the gate, hoping he didn't.

The old man's form appeared as gnarled as the tree roots that threatened to trip him.

"No, thank you. Takes a minute to get goin' when I been crouched down putterin' in the weeds for so long." Durtle wore a surprisingly clean long-sleeved denim shirt. The knees on his jeans were dark with the stain of moist soil, his hands encased in heavy-duty work gloves. Perfect if he had committed a crime and Thea had interrupted him burying a body. Where was Mrs. Durtle?

The woman in question sat at the usual window, now open. Her silver hair in flyaway mode, gathered up on one side into a clip-on flower of bright blue. She looked like a little girl ready for a party. Thea's heart stuttered as she was reminded even Mrs. Durtle once was young. Once had dreams and fell in love with her best beau. Perhaps she danced in the moonlight, swirling and laughing. Never knowing she would live out her last days petting cats through the window.

A bony hand reached out to the ledge below, where Mrs. Durtle's long, cadaverous fingers stroked Betty's colorful coat. The cat seemed in feline heaven, her eyes squeezed closed as she leaned into her pet massage. What a little two-timer. And when had this relationship started?

Arriving at the fence, Mr. Durtle straightened up some. He might have been close to six feet tall if he'd been completely unbent. Up close, his watery gray eyes blended into an overall grayness of complexion. Thick white hair combed straight back in a 1940s style gave an impression of vibrancy, in direct contrast to an otherwise frail appearance.

Thea looked from him to his wife framed in the window, then back. "I see your wife has a new admirer. Betty might not want to come home after all the pampering." She smiled at him and he returned it, showing a nice set of pearly dentures.

"Viv is loved by all cats," he said. "And she loves them back. Always taking in strays." He waved toward the roof's cat population and the front porch, where an orange tabby stretched beneath the sun's rays, savoring the only sunny patch.

"Viv," Thea said aloud, liking the sound. She hadn't known the Durtles' first names.

"Vivianna, actually," Mr. Durtle said, his voice warming. "We met at a USO dance when I was serving in World War II. I never saw a more beautiful sight than my Viv, smiling at this homesick soldier. With a flower in her hair."

Thea felt herself transported to another time. "Have you ever thought of writing your experience down? I bet a lot of people would be interested in your story, Mr. Durtle," Thea said. Sometimes she forgot that everybody *had* a story. She jotted a mental note to mention Durtle and the Mrs. to Cole. Might make a great profile piece.

"I'm Martin . . . Marty," he said. "After all, we're neighbors."

"Okay, Marty." Thea stuck her hand over the fence for a shake. "Thea."

"Yep, I know that," Marty said, returning the handshake, then gesturing toward Viv with his chin. "She keeps me informed. Got a smartie-phone and stays on top of all kinds of things. Been reading about the quilt show mess you've had."

"Right," Thea said. Wasn't all of Larkindale informed by now? But she found it interesting Mrs. Durtle was a techno-nerd. A book and its cover and all that. One couldn't tell at first look.

The phone began to ring again and Thea tensed, glancing back at the house.

"Let me get your cat for you, Thea." Marty took off toward the wife-in-window, slow as ketchup poured from a new bottle.

Hurry! Maybe she should give him a few taps on the . . . no, no. Delete the idea.

While she waited, Thea did a few nervous taps of tennies against grass. The effect was unsatisfactory. In a short time, Durtle returned and lifted Betty over the fence into Thea's receptive arms. The cat settled in as if nothing unusual had ever taken place.

Thea thanked Marty and turned to go home. Then she stopped, stirred by an inner nudge. Obviously, the Durtles needed support. What kind of neighbor ignored these creepy but kindly folks? Thea didn't want to hear the answer. Besides, didn't someone say there were things better left unsaid? Silence is golden? High-five to them. But taking heed of the nudge, she faced him once more.

"Mr. Durtle . . . er . . . Marty? If you or your wife should ever need help, please call me. A ride to the store or the doctor? Maybe I could bring something home for you? Name it. I'm right next door." She rattled off her phone number, sincere in her desire to be a better friend. Or a friend at all.

"Say, now." Marty's face animated and became all crinkles and ear-to-ear affability. "It's mighty nice of you. Could you give me the number again, slowly? I'll write it down for the Mrs." He pulled a ballpoint pen from behind his shirt's pocket protector. Taking off his glove, he began to write on his hand, asking her to repeat a number or two.

"Got it," Marty said, giving her a two-finger salute, rather like an old Cub Scout. "And you do the same. When you need something, you call us. We're always here."

No kidding. Thea thanked him again, waved to Mrs. Durtle who merrily waved back, and walked toward the cottage. Betty lay draped over Thea's arm, limbs lax, as if in a cat-atonic state. Thea wondered if the cat-loving Viv had supernatural skills in those bony hands. With all the recent stress, a magic massage might be just the thing.

Maybe Thea would make the first call between neighbors for help.

Back in the house, she arranged the sleeping Betty in her comfy cat bed and closed the door between the back porch and the kitchen. Thea stepped into the living room, past her undisturbed quilting bag. Last night, she hadn't had the chance to pull her Tail in the Rail quilt out before she fell asleep on the sofa. Betty's habit of snuggling a bit too close, like around Thea's neck, had woken her enough to detach from the cat and go to bed.

On the side table, the answering machine flashed like the pulse on a heart monitor.

What now? Thea hit the play button.

"This is Dr. Cottle's secretary again, speaking on his behalf. Unfortunately, he has a conflict in his schedule this weekend and will not be able to participate as a judge in your quilt show. We wish you much success with your event."

Thea hit pause. Great. Now she had no head judge. No big name to lend authority to the entire endeavor. Mary-Alice was going to be so mad she could spit. Though Thea couldn't imagine the gentle elder ever doing such a thing.

Thea wasn't sure, but it sounded as if the secretary read from a script. Could be all her customer service training. And had the call come at this hour on purpose? When most people would be at work? Thea generally left the house earlier than today. Did the secretary know her schedule?

With a kind of dread, Thea played the second message. It was from Prudy, thanking her for the invitation to her aptly named Midweek Info-Meet. "I'll be there if I can, but I'm not feeling well. And Trudy has something else to do, so she can't make it."

Fine, since Thea didn't remember requesting Trudy's presence. Though the woman did have quilt show judging experience. Maybe . . . ? No. She'd already admitted her twin wanted her to influence the judging so Prudy might win Best of Show.

When would this week end?

24

These negative notions knocked about in her brain as Thea drove to the Emporium. Turning into Old Town, she barely noticed the quilt show publicity banner attached to the archway. She parked and hiked along the cement walkway, picking up her pace to open the Emporium on time.

Lyndi stood at the entrance, waiting. A few customers lingered nearby, perking up when Thea stuck the key in the lock. They looked so eager to shop, she couldn't deny them entry and swung the door wide.

"Step right in, folks," Thea said, extending her hand in a sweeping motion. She scampered in behind them and turned on the lights. Throwing the keys to Lyndi, Thea said, "Can you do the honors, please? I'll get the coffee going."

"You got it, boss-lady." Lyndi unlocked Thea's office and disappeared inside with both their purses and the combination to the safe. Before long she was at the front counter, sorting cash into the till. Separated into the slots by denomination, portrait side up, all facing in the same direction, just the way Thea had shown her.

Soon the store bustled with activity, though most of the people poking about were unknown to Thea. Wednesday had never been a busy shopping day in the antique trade. Not like Saturdays. Had folks already started drifting into Larkindale for the big quilt show? The prospect did a bit to bolster Thea's earlier adverse expectations.

She sold some teacups and saucers to a collector, including a chintz set she'd had her eye on. Someone bought a Vaseline glass dresser tray. Another purchased a set of fireplace bellows, circa 1835, for use at his mountain cabin. With its original red paint and folk-art style, Thea could imagine the item given new life in a new century. A few more interesting antiques were sold by lunchtime. A profitable morning.

Mariana dusted shelves and whatever sat on them. Lyndi browsed through booths, looking for anything to enhance the special exhibit she had been assembling for the museum entry this weekend. Naturally, she expected her community college instructor to check it out and shovel extra credit her way. In big scoops.

A couple more gals would be in soon to fulfill the second part of the business agreement each had signed with Thea—booth rent combined with a certain number of hours worked in the Emporium. These ladies would help Mariana cover until closing, so both Thea and Lyndi could pop out to Mum's for the Midweek Info-Meet.

But first, Thea was itching to visit Mary-Alice at the Wentworth Mansion. While she waited for their clientele to dwindle down, she considered how excited Mary-Alice would be to hear a full report on their case. Or cases.

Finally, Thea found her chance to slip away between customers. "See you later at Mum's," she said to Lyndi. And was gone.

Facing the grand door at Wentworth Mansion, Thea expected the housekeeper, Birdie-with-the-shifty-eyes, to answer the door-bell. But when she pushed the button and the Westminster Chimes rang out, Kenneth let her in instead. Disappointing, because Thea had a couple questions to fly by Birdie.

"Welcome," Kenneth said, all politeness as he opened the door. "Please come in. Auntie's expecting you."

Thea stepped inside the foyer, overcome with an impression of calm and grace. Unlike the other evening, when Detective Brewster and company had garrisoned here. She eyed the ficus plant from which Thea had rescued Mary-Alice. Or pushed her into the pot, according to Louisa's retelling of the story.

A little quiver of unease passed over Thea and she asked, "Where's Louisa?"

"Napping," Kenneth said.

Good news.

Kenneth led the way to the sitting room and opened the door for Thea, ushering her inside and taking a few steps in himself. Mary-Alice reclined on the chenille chaise, serene under a colorful lap quilt, looking quite like her old self. Moxie lounged in her mistress's lap, round brown eyes following Thea as she entered.

"Oh, my dear. How nice you're here. How about some tea?" Mary-Alice beckoned her to sit in the Queen Anne chair. On the table between them, a blue and white flower-patterned teapot sat on a tray. A matching creamer and sugar were situated to each side of the pot. Mary-Alice's half-full cup was pulled near.

"We need another cup!" Mary-Alice said, looking toward Kenneth. "Could you ask Annette to bring another? If you don't mind. . . ." She smiled fondly at her nephew.

"Don't go to any trouble," Thea said and meant it. She would be attending Afternoon Tea at Mum's before long. But Kenneth slipped out like a shadow, apparently eager to please his great-aunt.

"Now," Mary-Alice said, leaning a little toward Thea, cupping a hand around her mouth in a secretive manner. Though they were the only two in the room. "Tell me what you have discovered so far, Miss Detective." There was a conspiratorial look in her eyes.

Even though Thea knew this question was coming, she hesitated. What had she learned that was of any value to her friend?

"Well . . ." Thea said, "I may have a couple of things." She went on to tell Mary-Alice about her talk with the museum curator, Ned Hilderbrand. Leaving out their combative comments, Thea related Hilderbrand's theory that the quilt thief may have found an access point into the museum.

"I think it was during the afternoon setup time. And then he returned, gaining access to the inside through the point he had provided. And somehow, finding himself inside, the thief had stolen 'Larkin's Treasure' between the hanging of the exhibition quilts and the beginning of the formal unveiling event."

"It sounds plausible," Mary-Alice said, staring off while she petted Moxie. "But if it happened that way, how come no one heard the crash of glass?"

"I still need to work it all out," Thea said. "Though people were in and out. And Mr. Hilderbrand says the security system is severely lacking. They are raising funds for a new one."

"I see," Mary-Alice said, drawing her brows together with displeasure. "I wish we'd known beforehand. Perhaps someone could have donated a security system to the museum."

Thea knew Mary-Alice, had she been informed, might well have provided the funds needed. And the family's heritage quilt would still be displayed in the Hastings McLeod Museum. Instead of taken who-knew-where. By some unknown person.

A gentle warning knock on the door and Kenneth came in with a fresh pot of tea and a matching cup and saucer for Thea. She reached out and took the cup and saucer, thanking him, trying not to let her hand shake. Thea didn't think rattling vintage china at teatime was polite. She laid her tea things on the table.

"You sure did a great job introducing the quilt the other night," she said to Kenneth as he rested the replacement pot of tea on the tray and carried the empty one to the bookcase by the door.

"Thanks." He smiled with his sizeable teeth. "It was a great evening. Until . . ." A shadow passed over his face, wiping away the smile, and his lips got stuck on his gums. In his misery, he didn't seem to notice.

"Poor boy," Mary-Alice said. "Don't worry. The old quilt will turn up. I know it."

"Let's hope so," Thea said, pouring some tea and offering to refresh Mary-Alice's cup, but receiving a head shake. "Kenneth, did you happen to see the letter Mary-Alice was looking for the night of the quilt show soirée?"

"Letter?" Kenneth snapped out of his dark place. "What letter?"

"The one from the California State Quilt & Textile Museum," Thea said and plunked a couple cubes of sugar into her cup. The tea splashed over one side, but she was not deterred. Thea added a third cube.

"I saw it over there in the linen press, between some quilts. In fact, I was trying to decide if I should read it when Odette found your aunt on the floor and screamed." Thea sent a look of sympathy to Mary-Alice, then stirred some cream in her tea, noting her tea-making steps were out-of-order. Cream first. "I quite forgot about it afterward."

"In here?" Kenneth had opened the doors to the old cabinet and rifled through the folded quilts stacked inside. "Where?"

Thea turned in her chair and pointed. "It was inside the Log Cabin quilt. The third one down with the stripey blocks. I shoved the envelope back in when I heard the scream, and then ran upstairs to check on Mary-Alice here." Thea gazed fondly at her friend. "Just wondered if you knew what was in the letter?"

"I'd sure like to," Kenneth said, now pulling out quilts and shaking them.

Startled by his reaction, Thea wondered if his eyes were doing the mood-swing-change-color thing again, like at the museum. But he was looking away, focused on finding the letter among the vintage coverings.

As her nephew trashed her quilt collection, Mary-Alice put a hand to her mouth, eyes wide with a what-in-heaven's-name look. Moxie's head popped up and she barked at the commotion.

"Kenneth!" Mary-Alice said while trying to soothe her canine companion with gentle strokes. "What are you doing? Can't you see you are upsetting Moxie?"

He pulled out an exquisite sampler quilt in Granny Smith green and white, shook it, then flung it on top of the rest. "How are we ever going to find out the secret to great riches with 'Larkin's Treasure' gone unless someone tells us? Maybe there was something in the letter. You could help me hunt." Kenneth kicked the quilts to the side, while his aunt looked on, horrified.

"Whoa. Sorry I brought it up." Thea wasn't sure what to do, here in Mary-Alice's domain, with her own nephew going wild. He sure was a multifaceted fellow.

Amid the quilt-tossing and Moxie barking, Thea placed her teacup on the table and rose, ambling over to Kenneth's side as if for no reason. She didn't want to upset him more. But by now, the cupboard was literally bare. He stared into the emptiness and then felt around inside, in case he'd missed the envelope.

"Let me help you put these away. I know just how Mary-Alice folds them. And I *should* know after coveting them so often," Thea said, scolding her greedy self.

She put her hand on Kenneth's shoulder in a good-buddy gesture. Instantly, he relaxed, as if coming out of an obsessive trance. Turning to his aunt, and apologetic now, he said, "I guess I got carried away, Auntie. You know I love the old quilt and all the family history, even though it's not my history." Kenneth cast his eyes down. "What with it coming to Larkindale for a week, I expected to be able to examine it and maybe solve the mystery of the riches. But now . . ." his voice trailed off.

Head bowed, hangdog expression, and shoulders drooped, Kenneth appeared the personification of deep dejection. Moxie made an empathetic whimper.

Mary-Alice put the pup on the floor and outstretched both arms to her grand-nephew. He nearly ran to her and leaned in for a hug, his aunt enveloping him, patting his back.

"There, there, Kenny. You're my own nephew. The quilt is your history, too."

Kenneth stayed in her arms for a while, then drew back and sat on the edge of her chaise. He took both her hands in his and beheld his beloved great-aunt.

"I forget sometimes."

Thea could see his eyes were blue. The storm had passed. She picked up a quilt and folded it carefully, then another, while watching them interact. What kind of love was this? A great love for the unlovely, she guessed. One she needed to nourish.

She thought of the Durtles, whom she had ignored and judged wrongly for so long. Yet, conversing this morning with Mr. Durtle ... Marty ... had shown her his kind side.

Maybe Thea was too interested in beautiful dark curly hair and dimples.

"I know you don't always feel a part of the family because you are adopted, Kenneth. Perhaps others make you feel that way," Mary-Alice said. "But I assure you, when my darling niece brought you home as an infant, after longing for a child all those years, you couldn't have been loved more."

Mary-Alice's face had an angelic aspect, and she smiled at him with so much tenderness Thea felt her eyes moisten. She concentrated on properly folding the quilt in hand, listening.

"I don't know," he said, as if doubtful of his connection to the Wentworths.

"God Himself created adoption. I wonder, dear boy, if you are saying I didn't become a part of God's family when I was adopted as a daughter through Christ? Because I cannot agree with you there," Mary-Alice said.

"No, I'm not saying that, Auntie. But it can be hard to grasp," Kenneth said, "when your only experience is being adopted by humans."

"Yet in a way you are the more fortunate of the two of us. You have been chosen and adopted by your parents. And you can be chosen and adopted by God Himself. You will understand better than most how precious it is. . . ."

How tender Mary-Alice's attentions were to her great-nephew. Thea wondered how many times Kenneth's aunt had encouraged him like this. Or opened her Bible and read him truth, hoping it would pierce his heart and bury itself deep within.

Such patience. Such love.

When had Thea last cracked open her Bible? She was ashamed she couldn't name the day. It was too long ago. The remembrance of the ancient words settled about her like a cozy quilt.

Thea felt like an intruder and wondered how she might leave the room without giving offense. She noticed Moxie facing the door, looking first at Mary-Alice and then back to the door. The dog needed to go out. Perfect.

"I'm just going to take Moxie outside," Thea said in a whispery voice, trying not to interrupt. She placed the last quilt inside the linen press. "You finish your chat, kids."

"Oh, thank you, my dear," Mary-Alice said, still holding Kenneth's hands in hers. "I'm afraid I've been ignoring her." Then turning protective, she reminded Thea the dog must be leashed because of her small size. After all, birds of prey cruised the foot-hills, searching for small, unattended animals to whisk away for dinner.

"I know right where the leash is," Thea said, picking up Moxie, hoping the dog wouldn't be vexed by the "Eau de Betty Parfum" clinging to Thea's clothes. She eased the door closed behind her and tiptoed down the hall, carrying the white fluff ball under her arm.

Thea passed through the kitchen where Annette, the cook, washed vegetables in the sink, using a handy pull-out faucet. It might be nice to have a cook like Annette to broaden Thea's culinary world of peanut butter and sweet pickle sandwiches. Dressed in a real apron with ruffle trim and big pockets, Annette's brown hair was caught up in a simple ponytail. She had the built-in benefit of smooth, olive skin and big hazel eyes. No makeup needed.

Annette turned off the water and said, "I can take her out for you, Miss. Just let me dry my hands first." She reached for a towel.

"It's okay. I'm happy to do it," Thea said, hoping nothing messy would ensue.

She lifted the leash from a hook on one side of a cabinet and clipped it to Moxie's collar. Thea leaned down to gently lower the dog to the floor. But Moxie jumped from her arms in one majestic leap. Nails tapping double-time against the hardwood, she strained in place against the leash, targeting the great room's French doors.

Since Moxie wasn't anything like a bull mastiff, Thea was able to stay upright. Still, she stumbled after the dog, rushing to open a door before Moxie threw herself against the glass. They spilled outside. Behind her, Thea thought she heard Annette's laughter.

Moxie dragged Thea past the patio to the soft grassy area and stopped. Thea looked away, giving the dog some privacy, watching the serene lady statue pour water from her urn. The afternoon sun reflected like diamonds in the pool below.

Gone were the bistro tables and chairs, hanging quilts, and dessert buffet of Sunday evening's soirée. There were no violins playing Mozart. Only the sounds of water falling. No police hulking about. No canine officer guarding the gate. All was calm and bright.

Thea let Moxie wander for a while, giving the pup some sunshine, grabbing some vitamin D for herself. She followed the lax leash wherever the dog led. They ambled around to the side of the house; Thea stepped on large natural stone pavers set in pea-gravel. Along the fence, a variety of bushes grew high, with low-growing plants adding spots of color here and there.

The dog sniffed about some, before finding an enticing shrub, then stopped. She pulled on her lead, lowering herself belly to the ground, and attempted to army-crawl beneath the bush. A few dead leaves got stuck in her white coat.

"No, Moxie!" Thea jerked back sharply a couple times. "You'll get all dirty."

But Moxie strained harder and made excited you-gotta-see-this noises, digging.

"Oh, all right." Thea knelt down to see what Moxie wanted to show her. Lifting a limb around the bottom of the bush, she brushed away some leafy debris. "This better not be a dead rat, girlie."

Wagging her tail, Moxie barked at the object, which seemed to shine. What was it? An old piece of glass? Last year's Christmas tinsel? Maybe it was The Lone Ranger's silver bullet. Thea chuckled. Always cracking herself up.

The branches were so heavily foliaged it was hard to identify what was partially buried there, even if she squinted. Thea began to sweep away more leaves, excited, as if someone had lit Fourth of July sparklers in her stomach. She reached in and took hold of a round metal shape. It came away from the dirt as if it weighed nothing at all. Thea blew on it and gasped.

Moxie had found Mary-Alice's antique brooch.

25

Thea rubbed away the mud and tiny roots attached to the brooch, careful not to stick herself with the pin hanging crookedly off the clasp. She fastened it for safety. Wishing for something to clean it off with, Thea surveyed her surroundings. Some stiff dead leaves served to knock away more dirt stuck along the diamond-laced edges. The pink center stone glittered in celebration.

Even filthy, the brooch was beautiful.

Wouldn't Mary-Alice be pleased? Thea stood, unable to stop a big grin. "Come, Moxie. Let's go see your mistress. You can give her your Christmas gift early." She leaned down and ruffled the dog's fur, brushing away a few unwanted outdoor accessories. Untangling the leash, she let Moxie sniff a bit more, though whatever she found next couldn't top the brooch.

Questions began spinning around in Thea's head. Had Mary-Alice accidentally dropped the brooch out the window? Or had someone else done the honors? And why? It was so valuable, wouldn't one just pocket the thing?

Or it could have been pocketed and buried later.

Perhaps it had been disposed of to lead the police to the wrong conclusion while he or she whacked a sweet old lady. What was it called? A red herring. Thea had read about such clues planted in mystery stories to throw the reader off the trail. Maybe it would work in real life. Like in Mary-Alice's case.

If someone tossed the brooch outside, how had it ended up under the bush? It could have fallen through the branches, but then it shouldn't end up buried, right? Or the brooch-chucker could have dropped it in plain sight from the window, marked it with his or her eye, then buried it during the party. Would anyone have noticed? Thea thought not.

She looked at Moxie, wagging her tail, panting a little.

"Did you find it somewhere, Moxie? And bury it for safekeeping? Are you showing it to me now so I can give it to Mary-Alice?" Perhaps Moxie was a part of the mystery. Or she had created the mystery. But how could Thea confirm it?

"You are as good a communicator as my Betty."

Thea walked across the lawn and onto the patio. Moxie trotted along, tail flagging, as if she had completed her assignment and now anticipated a reward. Like lap-time. Opening a French door, Thea entered and released the dog from the leash. But Moxie stayed in the room, not scurrying down the hall toward Mary-Alice like Thea expected.

Did she want to be sure she got credit for the amazing find?

Annette had finished showering her veggies and now busied herself trimming fat from several steaks. She looked up, appearing pleased. "Special dinner tonight because Mrs. Wentworth is home. A marinade bath for the steaks and Mr. Kenneth will barbeque."

"Yum. Do you mind if I use your sink over there with the fashion faucet?"

When Annette gave her the go-for-it, Thea put the plug in the sink. God forbid she should lose the brooch down the drain. Her heart staggered a couple beats at the idea. She grabbed the discarded vegetable brush and poured a stream of Bubbly-Wubbly Dish Detergent on it. And set to giving the brooch a gentle scrub.

By the time Thea finished, Annette was at her shoulder, doing a quick intake of breath. "Mrs. Wentworth's lost brooch?"

"Yep. Moxie here dug it up along the side of the house. Isn't she something?" Thea said, holding up the piece, watching it twinkle.

"I'm sure it should go to a jewelry store for a proper cleaning and to have the stones checked, but I didn't want to give it to Mary-Alice all muddy."

"No, of course not," Annette said. Then she kneeled down and rubbed a blissful Moxie behind her ears. "You are such a good girl!"

Thea dried off the brooch and wrapped it in a floral paper napkin, like a gift. She cut her eyes to Annette, still giving Moxie special attention. With a little baby talk thrown in.

"Such a good wittle puppy. Yes, you are. Yes, you are!" The dog's tail wagged back and forth like a metronome set at presto.

"Pardon me, Annette," Thea said, sorry to interrupt the canine compliments. "Could I ask you a question? You might not know, but . . ."

"Sure," Annette said, giving the dog one last "you smart puppy-wuppy" before she rose. "How can I help?"

Thea explained about the official envelope from Dr. Cottle she had found during the soirée. And how she had stuffed it back between the quilts when she heard the scream.

"I wasn't thinking about anything but Mary-Alice then," she said, giving an inner shudder. Not wanting to reveal Kenneth's aggressive search through the linen press, Thea asked Annette her question. "Did you happen to see the letter anywhere? It seems to be missing from among the quilts."

"You should ask Birdie," Annette said. "She might have seen it."

"Is she around?"

"Afternoon off." Annette gave a can't-help-you shrug. "Sorry."

"It's okay." Thea felt only a little deflated and brightened quickly when she thought about the brooch. She held the napkin bundle up to Annette. "Hey. You want to come watch Mary-Alice open this napkin?"

Annette grinned and nodded, her ponytail bouncing. "May I?"

Gesturing toward the sitting room, Thea turned and walked down the hallway. Annette and Moxie followed. A soft knock on the door and they entered, finding Mary-Alice chatting with Kenneth. The aura had changed between aunt and nephew since Thea left, and she sensed they were at peace. Moxie, shaking with excitement, vaulted onto her mistress's lap without even a pretense of politeness.

"Did you have a nice outing?" Mary-Alice asked, teasing the pup's white fur with her fingers, pulling out a burr Thea hadn't noticed. "What have you been up to, little girl?"

"Funny you should ask," Thea said, handing over the fancy napkin gift. "Moxie dug a little something up for you in the bushes."

"Digging again?" Mary-Alice made little tsk-tsk sounds and gave an indulgent laugh. She unwrapped the crude package, layer by layer, until the brooch winked at her from the paper. Staring in disbelief, she caught her breath. "My Moxie dug this up?" She raised tear-filled eyes to Thea's and then back to the jewel. "I can't believe it."

Near the door, Annette was making tiny little claps of celebration.

Seated in a chair opposite his great-aunt, Kenneth slapped both hands on his thighs. "The mystery is solved!"

"Partially solved. We don't know how it got there, of course." Thea said. "I mean, *you* didn't bury it, did you, Mary-Alice?"

"No, I didn't bury it! What a thought." Mary-Alice burst into laughter. Soon she wiped away tears, probably as much from relief as from joy.

"Are you pleased?" Thea asked, milking the situation a bit.

Recovering, Mary-Alice said, "I am pleased, my dear. Just amazed Moxie found my treasured brooch." She hugged it to herself, her smile so wide it would have made the Cheshire cat look disgruntled. "What a wonderful day!"

Annette opened the door to excuse herself, but Mary-Alice raised her hand, motioning for the cook to remain. "Annette, I know Louisa will be so happy to hear about this. She's resting right now. But would you mind knocking on her door? And if she's awake, please go ahead and tell her."

"Me? Oh, yes!" Annette scurried away to carry the good news upstairs.

Then Mary-Alice wanted all the details of Moxie's treasure hunt, so Thea nestled into the lady's chair to give her friend a summary. Kenneth leaned forward and inclined his head. Moxie slept on Mary-Alice's lap.

As Thea took them through the little doggie drama, she also tossed out a couple of questions roiling around her internal agitation cycle. Had the brooch fallen hard and dug itself deep into the dirt? Or had someone given the gem a purposeful burial?

"We'll have to leave it up to Detective Brewster, won't we?" Mary-Alice said. "I must call him. He'll be happy the brooch is back."

It hadn't crossed her mind Brewster might be involved again. Maybe she should not have dug up the piece. Had she tampered with evidence? Would Thea be in the doghouse? On her way to the big house?

Rats. She'd only wanted to see if it might be a silver bullet, shining in the sun.

Plus, Thea had cleaned the brooch with Bubbly-Wubbly Dish Soap. Another no-no. Especially if there were fingerprints to identify the thief. Her buoyant spirit of moments ago fell like a bouquet of burst balloons.

Thea longed to leave. She checked her watch. Before long, she should get out to the Lake House for the quilter's meeting she'd arranged. She didn't want another encounter with Detective Brewster. And she wasn't keen on watching Louisa fawn over the antique brooch. What if she concluded Thea had stolen and buried it herself?

Her thoughts were interrupted by the Westminster Chimes, signaling a visitor. Oh, no. Did Brewster have the gift of prophecy? How could he be here so soon?

Impossible. Mary-Alice still held her cell phone in her hand.

"I'll get it," Thea said, resigned. "I need to go, anyway. Quilt meeting at 3:00 P.M."

She exaggerated, but only by an hour. She stood and kissed Mary-Alice's cheek.

"Thank you for everything, my dear," the elder said. "Kenneth will walk you out, won't you?" The brooch was now fastened to her blouse. She touched it and smiled.

"Of course." Her great-nephew rose, and together they walked into the foyer as another round of chimes rang. "Coming, coming," Kenneth said and opened the door.

Odette Milsap stood on the step, coy in a vintage fedora, pink blouse, and pencil skirt of scarlet. She held a bunch of daisies tied with a yellow ribbon. Nice touch.

"Hi. I came to visit Mary-Alice. Is it okay?"

Kenneth licked his lips, accidentally clear-coating his mega-teeth, a slack expression on his face. Then he glanced at Thea, his eyes spiraling with what-do-I-do-now radar.

"Uh . . . would you like to join us a while longer, Thea?" he asked.

"Sorry, but I have a quilt meeting to attend," Thea said, sweet as shoofly pie.

Translation: *I'd rather chew on tinfoil.*

Watching Kenneth, Odette flipped her short hair with pink-tipped fingers. "You were good on the TV news the other night."

"You think so?" Kenneth asked, not quite charming, but not totally off-putting either.

Once Louisa and Brewster were added to the mix, Thea expected the conversation to liven up considerably. But she didn't have to be there to imagine the scene.

Suppressing a smile, she moved through the doorway, stepping outside.

Odette Milsap stepped in.

26

Thea congratulated herself on an exit well played as she drove through Larkindale and took the scenic route toward the Lake House. Music low on the radio, she rolled down the window, enjoying the fresh air, which had turned brisk. Since she had extra time—an hour to be precise—she turned the Jeep off onto a gravel side road, nobly named Lake Vista Way, and progressed toward a public picnic area situated along Larkin Lake.

Driving through a narrow, forested tunnel, Thea let the scene's shadowed serenity wash over her like a relaxing day at the spa. The canopy overhead blocked the sun, and she flipped on her bright lights. The road wound around gentle curves, then dropped suddenly like a roller-coaster ride. She slowed her vehicle at the bottom, shifted gears, and then powered up and over a hill, out into an open area.

The Jeep rolled to a stop against a log parking bumper. Thea peered through her windshield, but saw no straggling picnickers or figures fishing along the shore. She opened her door and slid out, landing on both feet. A walk down the incline toward lapping water took only moments. There she found her favorite spot to rest and reflect.

Brushing off some pine needles and unidentifiable rubble, she sat on the wide, squat stump, facing Larkin Lake. A soft breeze ruffled the water, stirring the glassy stillness, suggesting turmoil beneath the surface.

She wondered what was happening at Mary-Alice's house. How was Kenneth coping with Ms. Milsap's unexpected attentions? Had Detective Brewster shown up? If so, had it sent Odette into a panic? Obviously, something must have happened in her past to fan such fear of the police in the woman. But what? Another mystery.

Thea pulled off her tennis shoes and socks, digging her toes into the cool sand, then making miniature angels with her feet. So peaceful. Her mind sorted memories like fingers flipping through a file. How many times had she and her little sister, Rosie, played here at the lake's edge? Canoed with Dad and Gramps? Caught minnows in the clear water around the pilings?

Across the lake, Thea could see the Lake House where she had spent her childhood and teen years. There was a certain majesty about the abode. Not like Wentworth Mansion, of course. Not the same sort of grandeur. But the house rose high above the water, set amid tall trees, like the bow of a great ship, inviting one aboard. Only in this case, guests boarded its wraparound deck to enjoy a cup of tea with good company. And a magnificent view of Larkin Lake.

Overcast skies seemed to promise rain. But this afternoon, she hoped those gray clouds wouldn't bother to keep their word. Though the garden might appreciate some heaven-sent refreshment, even a slight sprinkle could douse the spirit of her impromptu quilters' meeting at Mum's, disguised as Afternoon Tea. And send the ladies in search of shelter inside the house.

If only the good weather held. The outdoor quilt show was— Thea did a quick countdown—only three days away. She gave a worried groan.

A rustling behind her caused Thea to jump up from her wooden perch. What was it? She scanned the parking lot and woods beyond, heart knocking around her chest. But she saw no one.

Still, Thea felt a presence. Was someone watching?

She tried to reason with herself . . . probably just a momma deer feeding or a buck rubbing his horns against a tree. Or not. She had no idea about such things. And Uncle Nick was not available to ask.

A bear?

Oh, gosh. Look at the time. Thea picked up her shoes and socks and sprinted to the Wrangler, hopping in, closing and locking the door. Driving back along the forested road, she imagined a howl, then a few more. Wolves?

Too many imaginings were not good. Maybe Thea needed a vacation.

Then she heard words, sentences, low and distinct. Didn't talking animals live in the woods? Like in Narnia? Though talking animals living out of the woods could be a positive. Betty could answer when she was called. And a chatty Moxie might have informed Thea how Mary-Alice's brooch had come to be buried in the bushes.

She drove faster and her damp, sandy foot slipped off the gas pedal several times. The rig lurched and bucked all the way to the main road, until Thea drove a hundred yards or so and pulled into a little rest area overlooking the lake. Next to an open van, a mom unpacked sandwiches from a cooler. A dad and three children appeared to be skipping rocks across the water. What could be safer than children and sandwiches?

Thea sprang out of the Jeep, shoes and socks in hand, her undressed feet striking the sharp gravel, the pain radiating up her legs. "Ow-ow-ow!"

The woman looked over at Thea, leaning against her rig, rubbing a foot against her pant leg to lessen the torture to her tender tootsie.

"Are you okay?" the woman asked, stopping her sandwich selection.

Blinking back tears, Thea said, "Fine, thanks. Just thin-skinned soles." Faking a brave laugh, she wiped the sand off one foot and pulled on a sock, then the shoe. Much better. She repeated the process on the other foot.

"Sure you don't want a sandwich or anything?" the woman held up a baggy stuffed with crushed wheat slices and whatever was squashed between them.

The offering didn't tempt Thea's taste buds. Though she did wonder if any peanut butter and pickle-flavored goodies hid in the cooler. Unmashed. Still, she was headed out to Mum's for a magical menu of scones and wee sandwiches and who knew what else? So Thea smiled at the stranger and called out her thanks, musing at the neighborliness of the act. Kindness was everywhere.

She felt quite the loony lady, imagining those foresty threats in the presence of such normalcy. How ridiculous. The noises had spooked her active imagination until it shifted into overdrive.

She gave herself a mental hand slap. *Snap out of it, Thea.* If she planned to be frightened, there might be a real reason beyond her crazy conjurings.

What had Uncle Nick said? Be extra careful until they knew what had happened to Mary-Alice. And until the perp, if there *was* a perp, had been officially stopped. Otherwise, she might find herself in a dangerous place.

Not much chance considering the state of her sleuthing skills. Which seemed less than limited. She was all questions and no answers. What was Mary-Alice thinking to invite Thea to break open the case of the missing quilt?

Though to be sure, she *had* solved the brooch brainteaser. Pat-pat-pat on the back. All she'd needed was a little Moxie to figure it out.

Thea clambered back into the Jeep, fastened her seatbelt, and reached to turn on the radio. But it was already on a low volume. Another point on her PI scorecard. Thea had just solved the mystery of the voices in the woods.

Move over, Nancy Drew.

Smiling to herself, Thea maneuvered the rig around until it jutted to the road's edge. She waited for the traffic to lighten a bit more. Squinting both ways, she pulled out in the direction of the Lake House. Glancing up at the rearview mirror, something held her gaze even as it grew smaller and smaller. She stared, startled.

The reflection of a vehicle crept out of the forested, gravel road where Thea had just been. It turned onto the highway, then sped away.

Back toward Larkindale.

27

When she arrived at the Lake House, Thea didn't go inside but followed the porch around to the back, taking the steps down to the gracious patio area bordered by Lake Nora and the little stream. Mum fussed over the arrangement of green deck chairs in groups of two or three with wicker accent tables between. A buffet, also of wicker, sat off to one side, supporting a samovar on top, filled with tea. Glasses, napkins, and small plates encircled a vase of fresh-cut pink and yellow roses.

"Will this work for the meeting, luv? I should have liked to import some tea tables from somewhere, but my wicker chairs are dashed few in number. Banished the old chums to the garage. So, I'm trying to improvise with these canvas ones. Looks a bit dodgy though. . . ." Mum stood back, finger on her chin, brooding over the setup. "Not Jane Austen, is it?"

Thea laughed. "What are you talking about? By the time they leave here, every quilter will want a set of the same chairs. The ladies will have room and be comfortable. They can all hear one another. And those side tables will work wonderfully for their teacups."

"No teacups. Change of plan," Mum said. "I thought iced tea would be fun for a summer afternoon. Hence, the samovar on the buffet. I'll add ice at the last minute."

"Even better," Thea said. "Though it is getting mighty cloudy." She looked heavenward, where the cumulus clouds like giant bags of cotton balls did their best to hide the sun. Not entirely successful as stray beams escaped through random gaps in the puffiness. "Where's Gram?"

"Choosing a hat for this indecisive weather. Will the sun shine and unduly freckle? Or does one need a wide brim in case of rain?" Mum smiled, shaking her head fondly. "Either way, Gram needs a hat for every occasion, even a change in the weather."

Thea took her mother's hand and pulled her over to one of the small seating areas. "Mum, since we are alone, I wanted to tell you something, just between us." It wouldn't matter if she told her mother, right? Mum could be Thea's Dr. Watson.

She explained how Mary-Alice had asked her to make a few inquiries about the brooch and the stolen quilt. "And just today," Thea said, her voice edged with excitement, "There's been a break in the case—"

"What break in what case?" Gram asked, balancing a three-tiered tray of desserts in one hand as she descended the stairs. Her floppy hat somewhat crooked, Gram's sturdy form seemed off center, too. To her granddaughter's gratitude, she reached the last step without incident and placed the tray on the buffet. Joining them, she scooched her ample backside into the third chair. "Who's got a case?"

"I . . . I . . ." Thea hesitated. Gram was not so discreet as Mum. Still, this was her grandmother. Better she know the truth of the matter since she had overheard.

"Well, I guess it would be me."

"Indeed? You're a detective now? Like on *Robbery, She Wrote*?" Gram clapped her hands together, quite pleased with the idea. Her periwinkle eyes, which she had bequeathed to Thea, grew big and round with an oh-my-goodness expression.

Trying not to be too specific, Thea repeated what she had told Mum. "Since it's a police matter, we need to be tactful in our discussion, if you know what I mean." She stopped. Maybe the last sentence was much too tactful for Gram to understand.

"You can depend on me," Gram said. "I'm jolly good at keeping secrets. I was just telling your mother the other day a secret about. . . . What was the secret, Nora? And who was it about?"

Mum, put out her hands, palms up, blocking her entry into the conversation.

Gram wore a faraway look as she peered deep into shallow Lake Nora, searching for the elusive secret. The wide brim of her hat threw a shadow over her eyes, turning them pensive.

Finally, she shrugged at Thea. "By Jove, I kept the secret so long, I forgot it completely! Mustn't worry, child. Do continue."

As Thea related the antique brooch's discovery, she couldn't help but enjoy their positive reaction to the news. The perfect antidote to any future verbal floggings from Louisa. Or Renée. Or Detective Brewster.

"You're smashing, luv! Mary-Alice certainly chose the perfect Miss Marple," Mum said, glowing with a bit of pride herself. "Such a talented one, you are."

"After a start like this, I expect the bobbies will query you on all their cases. Put your name on a jingle, eh?" Gram said with enthusiasm. "Capital."

What? Did she mean someone should write a jingle about Thea's detecting skills? Moxie should be included in the tune since she actually found the brooch. Wouldn't it be tricky? The names Thea and Moxie didn't rhyme at all.

"She's saying you'll have to put out your shingle. Like a private investigation firm or a law office, luv." Mum had an advanced degree in Gram Speak.

"Exactly so!" Gram leaned forward, hands twitching. "Have you found any new evidence in the case of the missing crazy quilt, child?"

"Ah . . . do I hear our guests arriving?" Thea asked, standing, motioning Mum to do the same. "Yes, I think so. . . ."

Gram rose and straightened her hat. She bent toward Thea and in a most secretive voice said, "You can rely on me, child. We'll do this together. Or should I say, rather, I'm in?" She hugged Thea with great enthusiasm and kissed her cheek.

Stunned, Thea wondered what just happened. "No, Gram, you don't have to—"

Now Gram put her hands up, blocking Thea's protest. "No, no. You don't have to thank me. It's what I do. I learned it all from TV. Besides, wait until you see what I bought. Spot on for this purpose."

She put her finger to her lips. "Shh . . . Mum's the word." Then, realizing what she had said, Gram began to giggle as she trotted off to welcome the quilters. "Mum's the word . . . mum's the word." Laughter. "Now, doesn't that take the biscuit!"

The ladies trailed in on time, exclaiming their approval of the view, the grounds, the garden, and Lake Nora. Most wore nice dresses for the occasion of tea at Mum's. One woman also wore a hat, and Gram linked arms with her. They clattered down the steps like college girls, hitting hats each time they tried to talk, then breaking into hysterics.

Soon everyone found a seat. Harriet Bixby, Mum's housekeeper, carried in the rest of the tea things and passed out plates. Thea and Mum offered glasses of iced tea to each, followed by Harriet who stopped at intervals, serving the mini-sandwiches.

Prudy, slumped over in her chair, reached for a sandwich and feebly laid it on her plate, as she could do no more. Her arm fell into her lap, and she said nothing.

Thea remembered Prudy had left a message about feeling ill. Maybe she shouldn't have come if she was too weak to eat a miniscule cucumber and cream cheese tea sandwich. Still, recalling Mary-Alice's example of loving the unlovely, Thea sidled over to Prudy and whipped up a little empathy. After all, showing up sick to take her place as quilt show co-chair could mean Prudy's sterling character traits, hidden up to now, had come to the surface. Thea pasted a smile on her face.

"Prudy, you don't look like you feel well. Can I get you anything?" she said.

"Ugh . . . sick," Prudy said, turning her head and waving off Thea's request. Her dark hair, worn loose today, fell over her face, and she wrapped her arms around her chest in a self-hug.

"Well, you let me know if you need something. Food or a lap-quilt? It's a little chilly out here, right?" Thea decided to quit laying love on the woman. There was no response, anyway. Perhaps Thea needed some practice. She'd have to shadow Mary-Alice until she had the knack.

Mum flitted between her guests like a butterfly to verbena, pausing to speak to one lady, patting the hand of another, and filling iced tea glasses. Aunt Elena pitched in to help, and soon, all the quilters chewed and chatted amicably.

Sissy Sloane sat next to Janny Price, who was seldom seen in society. The big-hearted redhead, devoted to her ailing mother, cared for her at home. Sissy must have hired someone to work The Quintessential Quilter in order to be here. Thea knew it wasn't Odette, so she went over to express appreciation for Sissy's appearance at the tea.

"I closed her down," Sissy said. "Wanted to be here and so I just shut my doors."

Astounded, Thea asked, "Right in the middle of the quilt show week?"

"*Because* of the quilt show. It's why I'm here. Besides, I stuck a notice on the door as soon as I got your call yesterday. It isn't like I didn't let them know." Sissy took a sip of iced tea. "Tasty."

Janny nodded in agreement, putting her glass on the table. "By the way," she said, "I heard Mary-Alice was coming home today. It's great news. Have you talked to her?"

"Just came from Wentworth Mansion. She is looking well. Happy to be home."

Lyndi walked over to their group, a vision in a filmy floral dress. "Did I hear you say Mary-Alice sprung her hospital shackles?"

"Yes and looking pretty normal," Thea said with a grin. "In fact, I think she'll be able to judge the quilt entries on Saturday."

All the ladies within hearing expressed their relief at the news. Lyndi pulled a deck chair away from another group and sat in Thea's circle.

"Do you think they'll find out who whacked Mary-Alice? Why would anyone do such a thing? Total creep!" Lyndi said, giving a thumbs-down for emphasis.

"And he stole her antique brooch, too," Nellie McGraw said before she stuffed a mini-sandwich into her mouth, whole. She added something more, but no one could understand.

"I think it was the senile Dr. Wellman. Everybody knows he's had gambling problems all his life. And he was alone with her for a time," Wanda said. "Maybe he didn't whack her, but I'll bet the brooch is already converted to cash to pay off his gambling debts!"

"Whoa. What's this town coming to? I want to move," Lyndi said.

Heather Ann Brewster told everyone to calm down. "My husband, Detective Brewster, will figure this out. Don't you ladies worry. Larkindale is safe and sound."

She grabbed a dessert tray and offered around Harriet's cranberry scones, lemon Earl Grey Tea squares, and mango-rosette-tarlets, maybe to shut them up. Just the aroma of so much gastronomic goodness served to distract the ladies from the fear of Larkindale's demise. Soon the taste had placated every anxious opinion.

"Ladies! Attention!" Gram said, interrupting their free flow of devouring fancy food. "I have an announcement to jolly well interest you all."

Thea stopped to listen, along with everyone else in the garden. A silence fell, with only the sound of ice clinking in glasses. And then that ceased as Gram cleared her throat. Thea smiled fondly. What could her dear, bumbling grandma have to say?

"The case of the missing brooch has been solved. And it wasn't Dr. Wellman what stole it. No, indeed. 'Twas my own granddaughter, our Thea James!"

Oh, no. Thea slid down in her chair. Prudy sat up with new interest.

The ladies gasped as one, with random outcries, "What?" "Why would Thea steal the brooch?" "Did she whack Mary-Alice, too?"

Thea, her face burning, rose slowly from her chair.

"I've got this, child." Gram motioned to her granddaughter, indicating she should sit back down. Then Gram stepped toward the buffet, grabbed a napkin, and dabbed at her forehead.

"Dear, dear. I put it badly. Getting a bit cheeky in my old age, what? I didn't mean to say Thea stole the brooch. Oh, bless me, no!" Gram patted her heart as if she might have an attack soon. "I meant to say Thea, here, solved the case!"

A lot of "oohs" and "aahs" from the members. And a "High-five, Thea!"

Thea stood, momentarily stunned. So much for keeping secrets.

"Actually, I didn't find it by myself," Thea said. "Today when I visited Mary-Alice, I took her little dog out for a walk in the yard. And Moxie found it, buried alongside the house. I just dug it up."

"And Mary-Alice was so gobsmacked, she hired Thea to do detecting for her. And find the thief what stole 'Larkin's Treasure!'" Gram said, every word a gloat for her granddaughter.

"A real detective in our midst!" Nellie said, clasping her hands together.

"Righto, Nellie. And, there's more . . ." Gram said, dragging out the word to hook her audience. "I am to assist Thea in her investigations. Be her partner. Rather a Dr. Watson type." She preened a little for the crowd. "I shall need a new hat, of course. One I can hide a weapon in—"

"Gram!" Thea said. This was beyond control. Did her little line-dancing grandma seriously think she needed to carry a weapon? Thea looked over at Mum, whose face was lined with deep disapproval. Uh-oh.

"Is this true, Thea?" Heather Ann asked. "Are you investigating for Mary-Alice?"

28

Thea didn't want to discuss her private detecting plans. Especially not with Heather Ann. How many minutes until it got back to Brewster and Thea was called into his office for an interrogation? Or worse?

Thea let out her breath in a despondent sigh, waiting on her diplomacy skills. But they were a no-show.

"Are you?" Heather Ann asked again. "Mary-Alice's personal PI?"

"She's not paying me," Thea said. "And, of course, I'm not a PI, as you all know. I'm an antique dealer, a businesswoman."

Even Thea knew her argument was uninspired. Did she have another angle?

"And a new quilter. I'm your caring quilt show co-chair who arranged to have 'Larkin's Treasure' on display for the whole week, leading up to the show. It was stolen on my watch, so I feel responsible." *Yeah, this sounds good.* "Naturally, I want to get it back for us. And for Mary-Alice!"

Mild clapping within the crowd.

"So, if I can inquire a little here or there and help get the quilt back into the museum where it belongs, I'll do it." She put her arm around Gram. "In truth, I can use all the Dr. Watsons I can get! Quilters, are you with me?"

Applause broke out with shouts of "We're with you, Thea." "Good for you!"

Thea gave her grandmother a cheek peck and turned to address the ladies.

"What do you say we dispense with the drama . . ." Thea looked at Heather Ann, ". . . and have our meeting? We have a show to put on in three days!"

Hoping Heather Ann would back off, Thea watched her reaction. The quilter was a bit hard to read, her countenance confused, but she didn't whip out a cell phone and call her husband.

While Harriet, Mum, and Aunt Elena distributed more goodies to the ladies, Thea grabbed her clipboard and began the meeting. "First of all, did everyone see the beautiful quilt show banner hanging under the archway to Old Town?" Thea gestured toward Heather Ann. "Great job! Thanks so much."

The ladies clapped their support for a job well done. Thea clapped loudest.

Then Thea highlighted the accomplishments of the ladies so far: another hat tip to Heather Ann for creating those pristine signs and programs and for Lyndi and Sissy's setup of the quilts at the museum. She mentioned Elena's white glove duties and the use of theme props collected by Wanda and arranged by Aunt Elena with a little help from Uncle Nick. She also noted Emby's refreshment table, receiving happy applause. These women liked their cookies and cake, by golly.

Next, Thea asked for reports from the committee chairs with regard to Saturday's show. "First, let's hear from Janny Price. Award ribbons?"

Janny jumped up, pulling away a strand of red hair from her face. "Ready!"

She sat back down and a rumble of laughter went through the crowd.

"Perfect. Now . . . um . . . how about the Demonstration Chair? Aunt Elena?"

Elena Marinello, already standing by the buffet table, said, "Thanks to all of you, I have plenty of precut paper and fabric pieces for my English Paper Piecing demo outside of the Hastings McLeod Museum on Saturday." She described where her table would be located in Pioneer Park. "Spread the word. Hope we get lots of students!"

"I'll be there, Aunt Elena. Sounds fun," Thea said. "Special Exhibit Chair?"

Lyndi danced her way up to Thea, holding a yellow rose. "It's going to be so cool! Thanks to all who made those mini-quilts of the buildings in Old Town. Our panorama quilt. Didn't it look great in the museum foyer the other night? But there's more. After the show, it goes on permanent display at the Larkindale Courthouse!" Lyndi grinned and handed the rose to Thea. "This is for you, boss-lady. For rockin' our quilt show."

Everyone applauded again for Thea. Except Prudy. Which apparently was noticed by Wanda, who said, "So. Prudy. Our *other* co-chair. You're quiet today. What have you done for the quilt show?"

Harsh. And hadn't Wanda just said snarky things about the old doctor? Her husband probably needed his garage as an anti-Wanda bomb shelter.

Thea wondered how to answer. Or might Prudy answer for herself?

"Ugh . . . sick," Prudy said, writhing in the chair.

After a pause, Thea said, "Prudy's work has been behind the scenes. Trying to contact our quilt expert, Dr. Cottle, and other things."

"Hmph," Wanda said. "I'll bet."

"Has anyone heard from Dr. Cottle?" Nellie asked. Then added, "Unreliable."

Before Thea could reply, a cell phone rang out.

Sissy pulled it from her pocket and checked the screen. "My aunt. Go on without me." She drifted over to the little bridge across the feeder stream to Lake Nora and spoke into the microphone, her voice scarcely audible. "Yeah?"

"We are still negotiating his appearance on Saturday," Thea said, answering Nellie. "I think he'll be here."

Why on planet earth was she assuring these ladies Cottle would come? What if he didn't? What person with similar credentials could step in at the last minute?

Nellie McGraw gave her report. "I could use a few more things for the Members Boutique. You might even put extra fat quarters in a bag. We can sell them, and you can clean out your stash."

It was a good suggestion because fat quarters were popular with any quilter. The pre-cut fabric pieces were purchased separately or tied in a bundle by color or theme. Several quilters agreed to pull together fabric bundles tied with satin ribbon for Nellie.

"I have some stuff in the Jeep for you," Thea said. "Be sure and take it, okay? Also does anybody need more tickets for the friendship quilt raffle?"

Looking at her clipboard, Thea saw a note she wanted to highlight. "Everyone, remember you are invited out to my friend Renée's Heritage House Inn on Friday night."

Even as she said the words, *my friend*, Thea wondered if they would ever be friends again. A sense of loss lay on her heart as heavy as a tombstone, and she swallowed hard before she continued.

"I know some of you will be labeling last-minute quilt entries, getting them ready to hang early Saturday morning. But if you can come, we'll be having a reception for Dr. Cottle from 6:00 to 7:30 P.M.

"Oh. And remember to encourage those who enter a quilt to pick it up immediately after the show. I might have to take home the stragglers. Believe me, I don't have any room in my car to transport them."

Those aware of the Jeep's mobile cupboard gave a hearty laugh at Thea's expense. But she didn't mind, snickering along with them.

Sissy returned, looking pale. "My aunt is at Mary-Alice's. Overheard Brewster taking a call about a break-in. My store, The Quintessential Quilter. Robbed."

The quilters crowded around Sissy, expressing their sympathies.

All except for Prudy, who shifted in her chair and made moaning noises.

And Heather Ann Brewster, who pulled out her cell phone to make a call.

29

With a cup of steaming English Afternoon tea on the table beside her, Thea unfolded her Tail in the Rail quilt. Betty rested on the next sofa cushion over, her furry tummy rising and falling as she slept.

Thea sipped the tea, then worked her needle through all the quilt layers before pushing it back up with her thimble. The repetitive rocking stitch relaxed her after a demanding day. Maybe she could finish quilting a few blocks tonight. If she didn't fall asleep on the sofa.

Her thoughts drifted to Sissy Sloane and the upsetting break-in at her store this afternoon. She hoped Sissy sensed some peace when Mum asked them all to clasp hands and pray. Too bad Thea hadn't thought of it first.

How had Sissy fared with her police encounter? Thea wondered if it was too late to phone. The clock said 8:30 p.m., which made her consider calling. But the police were probably still at the store. Perhaps the place was trashed and Sissy had no time to talk to well-wishers. Still, shouldn't Thea be the first to call and offer to assist? As a fellow Old Town businesswoman?

Three loud knocks on the door made her startle, and she stabbed her finger with the needle. *Ouch!* Thea put her finger in her mouth to stop the blood flow and checked the quilt backing with her other hand. *Rats*. Blood there, too.

Knock-knock-knock!

"I'm coming, just a sec." For pity's sake. Who would be calling at this hour? Someone rude, was who. "Almost there," she said, laying aside her quilt.

Careful not to wake Betty, Thea stuffed her feet into her Winnie-the-Pooh slippers and padded over to the door. She peeked behind the door's window shade into the dim light of the front porch. Detective Brewster did an in-your-face presentation of his badge, holding it right up to the glass.

She sighed, unlocking the door. "Hello, Detective. I expected to hear from you tomorrow. Isn't it a bit late?" She poked her head out of the doorway to see if Officer Threet or his canine partner were about. Justice might be a majestic example of hero-on-four-legs, but he also might scare Betty.

Brewster nodded toward the black and white. "In there. Do we need them?"

Horrified, heart racing, Thea said, "No! I mean . . . no, thanks." She strained to see inside the vehicle but couldn't decipher any human or canine forms.

"Kidding!" Brewster said and grinned.

"Oh." Her heartbeat returned to its normal blip.

"Can we talk on the porch?" He indicated the two padded chairs sitting in front of the window. "This won't take long."

Thea didn't like the sound of it. Only a few questions and we'll drag you off to jail? And, by the way, you get to ride with Justice. Swell. She stepped outside and sat.

"Nice work today, finding the brooch," he said, sitting in the other chair and instantly locking his steely stare with Thea's.

"I thought you were going to tell me I'd contaminated the crime scene."

"Just about to get to it," the detective said. "You did. Except we don't know for sure a crime was committed or if the brooch was stolen."

She smiled. "I was just about to say Mary-Alice could have dropped it herself. Out the window or when she was walking along the house. Or," Thea said, "the dog could have found it on the floor and buried it for later."

Brewster broke the eye-to-eye connection himself and grinned. "Now there's one I hadn't thought of yet. Pretty good at this, aren't you?"

"Aw, shucks. Thanks." Thea felt curiously at ease with the detective tonight. Maybe it was because he didn't seem to be accusing her of anything. Or she hadn't just done something awful like snitching on Odette. Though she hadn't mentioned Moxie. Would he throw it up to her next and indict her for lying?

"You know Mary-Alice's dog found the diamonds, right?"

"I know. In fact, I know Mrs. Wentworth has asked you to make inquiries into the theft of her family quilt. I know you have been poking around in police business," Brewster said, serious again. "I know you are putting yourself in danger."

She didn't have to wonder how he knew. Heather Ann Brewster was how. And if it hadn't been Heather Ann, he would still know. In Thea's world, Detective Brewster always knew.

"So you're not mad about me handling the brooch? Honestly, Detective, I never thought about it until Mary-Alice said she wanted to call you. And how happy you would be that her favorite heirloom was found." Thea looked up to see if he was happy and got caught in the Brewster stare again. *Rats.*

He looked away, almost sad. "I will be happy if you stay out of it," he said. "The brooch business? Mrs. Wentworth cannot say for sure a crime was ever committed. And neither can the police. The details cannot be verified. She has the brooch back. So the investigation is closed."

"What a relief," she said and exhaled. At least she didn't have to worry about . . . what did Gram call it? Damnation of the crime scene? Thea gave a light laugh.

"It's no laughing matter, Ms. James. We still have an active investigation into the possible assault of Mrs. Wentworth. And of course, into the theft of 'Larkin's Treasure.'" Brewster turned to face Thea. "These are both violent situations. Granted, one is still an assertion. But if it is true, then there is someone who might not appreciate your interference. Who might try to stop your meddling."

Interference and meddling? Thea winced at the words as if they were whip lashes. Surely, making a few inquiries for her dear friend was not meddling. And after what she'd said to the quilters today at Mum's? About doing all she could to bring the crazy quilt back to the museum? To her astonishment, when she'd pled her case to the quilters, she had also swayed herself.

Thea was on board whether Brewster sank her ship or not.

"I warned you on Sunday. And have come to warn you again, Ms. James," the detective said. "Please. Leave it to the police."

"Got it," Thea said. She wasn't exactly agreeing, right?

But, just in case, she crossed her fingers.

30

At the Emporium the next day, Thea grabbed some telephone time and called The Quintessential Quilter. No answer. Only a recorded message giving store hours.

Strange.

She trotted outside into the sunshine and ogled the distance from her store to Sissy's. Since the quilt shop stood next door to Thea's antique store, it wasn't a far squint. Thea walked a few extra steps toward Sissy's entrance, peering through windows like a stalker.

Inside, several bodies darted about, shelving big bolts of fabric like library books in the oversize section. The handwritten sign on the door declared the place "Closed Until Further Notice."

A sad pronouncement on the state of affairs in Larkindale.

Did they need her help? Thea knocked lightly on the door. Either no one heard or everyone ignored her. She rapped harder and massaged her knuckles. Nothing.

Thea shrugged. Maybe Sissy would put a "Help Wanted" sign on the door when she wanted some help. Creeping along the storefront, Thea strained to see inside. Was Odette replacing spools of thread into the display?

Inside the Emporium again, Thea made herself a cup of tea. The almond toffee coffee brewed earlier smelled like dessert. When mixed with the sweet, spicy fragrance of Emby's fresh cinnamon buns, Thea's knees gave way, turning her legs Gumby-like. She needed normal legs today, so she passed on the goodies. Choosing a strong, sturdy Earl Grey, instead.

Lyndi tapped on Thea's office door and stuck in her purpled head. Braids today.

"Hey, boss-lady. This came by courier a minute ago. While you were out for a walk." She handed over a manila envelope. "Hope it's something nice. Like jewelry from your beau?"

"Unlikely," Thea said, not sure Cole considered himself a beau. Turning over the envelope, she felt inside. Not jewelry.

"Can I watch?" Lyndi asked, coming near.

"Absolutely," Thea said, pulling at the glued-down flap. It wouldn't give. She pulled harder and put a power-lifting noise into it. Still stuck. Then she tried to rip open the other end. No dice. Revealing what was inside the package seemed a Herculean task. She worked the flap end again.

"Here. Let me." Lyndi reached across Thea's desk and pulled a pair of scissors out of an oversized mug filled with pens and pencils. Grabbing the offending envelope, she cut open one end and returned it to Thea. "Try now."

Thea looked up. "I could have done *that*."

"Sure you could have. But did you?" Lyndi tapped the side of her head. "Choices. It all comes down to making good choices." She leaned back, waiting.

"Thanks," Thea said with the least amount of sincerity she could muster.

Opening the cut end, she poured out the contents and, gasping, jumped up.

"I gotta go!"

Pushing the Jeep over the speed limit, Thea's breath became ragged. Her pulse beat in her ears. Had something bad happened to Betty? How else could someone have gotten the collar off her cat and cut it into little black bits? Even the heart-shaped "Pretty Kitty" charm had been badly bent.

Along with scraps of Betty's collar had been a note: block letters on black construction paper, written in crayon, the first letter black, next letter orange, then white, black, then orange again. Like Halloween. Or like a calico cat.

MIND YOUR OWN BUSINESS OR
NEXT TIME IT WON'T BE THE COLLAR

Thea turned the steering wheel sharp to the left, aiming for her gravel driveway, almost making it. Correcting, she skidded to a stop in front of the carport, sending up billows of dust. The Jeep rocked in place. Not caring a whit what the Durtles must think, Thea rushed across the lawn, up two steps and onto the porch, shoving her key into the lock.

"Betty! Where are you?" Frantic to find the feline, she ran through the living room and reached for the back porch doorknob. She turned it and threw the door open. The wood banged against the water heater situated behind.

The calico woke at the sound and raised her head from the cozy bed atop the table. "Meow?" She stretched and began to groom a front paw.

"Oh, Betty!" Thea fell on the cat, giving her hugs and kissing her head. Picking her up, Thea carried her into the living room, kicking closed the front door. "You're okay! I was so worried." She snuggled with her pet some more.

Wait. What about the collar and charm? She felt beneath the fur and found them still around Betty's neck. Both seemed in fine condition. At least no one had mishandled her sweet girl.

Instead, someone had bought an exact duplicate of her cat's collar. The charm, as well. Who would know about them? Anyone who ever visited her house. Or heard her rattling on about finding a charm at Pet Pawfect with the exact name she called Betty, "Pretty Kitty."

Thea had no idea who might have sent her the package. And no time to find out.

Now she knew Betty was safe, Thea needed to go back to work. But she didn't want to leave Betty alone in the house until the identity of the menace was known. Mulling it over, Thea considered the Emporium. The cat could hang out there, but the front door was usually propped open in good weather like today.

Betty had an open door policy. AKA if open, escape out.

Where else would Betty be safe? Picking up her cell, Thea dialed the Durtles.

⋘⋙

She arrived at the Emporium, breathless and grateful. Her kitty was having a social outing at the Durtles, with eleven other mongrels. Betty's DNA disclosed not even a hint of mongrel in her tiniest toenail. She had Mayflower-proud lineage. Or Thea was pretty sure she did. One could tell by the crooked whisker.

"Is your cat okay?" Lyndi met her at the door, worried. "Cause if anything bad happened to her, it would be . . . well, you know."

"Nefandous?" Thea was shocked she remembered the word.

"You got it, boss-lady."

Thea assured her employee Betty was fine. "Did you happen to see which courier brought the manila envelope?"

"Nope. Mariana handed it to me."

"Where's Mariana then?"

"Gone home," Lyndi said.

"Never mind. I have work to do for the quilt show. You okay out here?"

"Fine as frog hair. But first, I do have something to tell you." Lyndi grimaced, like it was painful to bring up. "About your Gram."

31

Oh, no. What now? Resigned, Thea did a little bring-it-on sign with her hands.

Lyndi flipped the purple braids behind her shoulders, but they were too short and fell forward again. She took a deep breath and then spoke fast, like the announcers reading the small print at the end of a commercial.

"While you were gone, your mother dropped off your grandmother at the store. Your mum waited, then left her, thinking you'd be right back, though I don't know why. Then your grandmother got tired of waiting for you to be her Sherlock and went off detecting on her own. And she never came back. Honest, your mum is the most beautiful lady. Her skin! And your grandmother, what a cutie-patooty."

Lyndi appeared to present her bad news with a frame of flattery.

"Oh, my goodness! Why didn't you tell me? What direction did she go? What was Gram wearing?" Thea looked this way and that, wondering what to do first. She'd never lost a grandmother before.

"Wait! Let me make a sandwich to take with you." Lyndi took on Thea's frantic persona. "What if your grandmother lost her way and is sitting on a rock in the middle of Fool's Gold Creek? She'll need sustenance."

Good thinking. Then realizing they were both overreacting, Thea said, "Okay, let's take it easy. Breathe . . . focus . . . pant." Or was that childbirth? "I'll walk the business loop and ask around. We'll find her. Everybody knows Gram. She can't have gone far, even in sensible shoes."

"Totally," Lyndi said. "I'll stay here and phone you if she comes back."

"Thanks," Thea said. "She's probably sitting somewhere, having tea."

"Should I call your mum?"

"No! Ah . . . not yet," Thea said. "Let's try and find her ourselves." She dug through her purse and pulled out her cell, pocketing it. Then handed her bag to Lyndi. "Would you mind shoving it in the safe? I'll get going."

Lyndi stuck the purse under her arm, then put her hands together, indicating she'd be praying.

"Thanks," Thea said, meaning it.

⁂

Trying to locate Gram without sending out an alarm challenged Thea's diplomatic skills in a new way. She backtracked to the Babbling Book, hoping her grandmother might be listening to a book on CD until Thea came. She thrust herself a half-body-length into the store.

"Hi, kids. Anybody seen my gram? I think I mislaid her." She gave a general description: floral dress, big hat, gray curls, British accent. It always fit, no matter the day or occasion.

The gal behind the counter had seen her earlier. "Spunky old gal. Came by for a few minutes looking for an Agatha Christie book on tape. We're kind of weeding out tapes now, so. . . ." She shrugged. "Your grandma was carrying a case with her. Looked heavy. She laid it down and almost forgot it."

Thea thanked her and went on to Adeline's Apothecary & Post Office Annex. A tarnished brass bell attached to the door jangled when she entered. Adeline came out of the little Post Office nook to see who'd come in.

"Oh, it's you. Thought it was your grandmother. What a character! Wanted to show me her spy kit. But I just didn't have the time to look at every item," Adeline said, walking up to Thea with a heavy step. "Good to see you, girl."

The postmistress gave Thea a back slap almost knocking her into Tuesday. All woman. And then some.

Trying to catch her breath and speaking with a raspy voice, Thea said, "Did you see which way she went?"

"You got a cold?" Adeline examined Thea's face like a nurse practitioner and put a hand to her forehead. "Hmm. Not feverish," she said. "Your gram went thataway." Adeline pointed over to the town square. "I hope she took a load off. Seemed kind of wobbly. Don't want to see the sweet old dame have a premature heart attack."

Heart attack? Thea didn't like the sound of that. Maybe dehydration was the reason for the wobble. Or it could be her normal wobble. Waving to Adeline, Thea hurried to the little park around the flagpole. No Gram.

She went on to Curly's Miner Diner. But no one had seen the missing senior. Thea wasn't sure where to look next. Those were the usual haunts. If she didn't find her grandmother soon, Mum would need to be informed.

The cell phone rang and Thea looked at the display and answered. "Lyndi. Is Gram at the Emporium? Please say yes."

"No," Lyndi said. "But I got a call from the library. A bunch of quilts were delivered there today to hang up for Saturday."

"Okay," Thea said, sitting down on a bench outside of Curly's. "What does it have to do with Gram?"

"Your grandmother is asleep under a quilt in one of the community meeting rooms. The Gold Rush Room," Lyndi said. "They'd like you to come wake her and take her home." She started to snicker.

Soon Lyndi laughed so hard, she snorted into the phone. Thea joined in the mirth, giggling, gleeful and relieved at the same time. A little good-bye chatter and they ended the call. Thea sat on the bench a minute more, sending up a prayer of thanks, before hiking to her Jeep for the short drive.

By the time she arrived at the Larkindale Public Library, Gram was awake and unable to contain her excitement. She pulled Thea into the Gold Rush Room where several Friends of the Library ladies helped sort through the quilts.

"Wait until you see this, child. I've quite cracked our case!"

"Why did you wander off?" Thea said. "I was so worried—"

"Shh!" Gram put a finger over her lips to shush Thea, who glanced toward the Library Friends, embarrassed. And quiet.

Gram pushed past the ladies to a short stack of quilts, dragging Thea along.

"And what have we here?" Separating several quilts from the others, Gram lifted out a disheveled pile of fabric and spread it out over one end of a conference table. "'Tis our nicked quilt now, isn't it? 'Larkin's Treasure.'"

Thea stared at the ragged crazy quilt, the lovely silk embroidery slashed between pieced edges, patches hanging every which way, all the jeweled memorabilia removed without any respect to its historicity. She saw similarities between the undamaged parts and quilt photographs at Mary-Alice's.

"By Jove, I think you *have* cracked the case, Gram. How did you ever find it?"

"Just some offhand detecting. Instead of waiting for you, I thought I'd take a stab at it with my new spy kit. Quite the thing. You must see this."

Gram set her bag on the table and unzipped it, drawing out assorted tools. She highlighted each: a motion alarm to protect documents from thieves, her bionic ears which could hear a whisper three-hundred feet away, a spy scope, and rearview sunglasses. Had Thea ever seen a secret identity voice changer in six modes? Wouldn't it come in handy? In her wisdom, Gram had added a bag of candy for quick energy and a bottle of water. Plus a grappling hook.

Thea thought the grappling hook a bit over the top. Even for Gram.

"Please, Gram. Just tell me how you came to find the quilt. Here, at the library."

"But I have more smashing stuff to show you."

Thea started putting the spy gear back in the bag. "Later, okay? I'm dying to know how you discovered 'Larkin's Treasure' when no one else could."

"Oh, indeed. Quite-quite." Gram zipped the bag closed and sat in a chair. "Fancy a lesson from your Dr. Watson, do you?" She chuckled. "Once I got to the library, found I was right knackered, I was. Saw quilts in this room and thought I'd have me a look." She blushed and giggled like a young girl. "Had me a nap instead."

"Then, these ladies who've befriended the library got to doing the quilts, ever so nicely. But I say, a loud lot, they were. And I wasn't even wearing my bionic ears!"

A couple of ladies turned to glare.

"Okay, you took a nap," Thea said, mentally tapping her nails. "Then what happened?"

"I noticed them's what did the quilts, made a bodge-job of the folding. Mates of the library don't always know much about quilting. So, I had to refold every quilt. And what do you think I found?"

"'Larkin's Treasure?'"

"Crikey, indeed I did now, didn't I?" Gram wore a wide grin. "I hardly believe it m'self. Do you think I'll get a portrait in the paper?"

"I bet you will. But Gram, how did you recognize the quilt? It looks like it's been practically shredded to pieces," Thea said, a sense of mourning surrounding her over the quilt's senseless destruction. "I don't think I would have recognized it."

"'Twas all tickety-boo, wasn't it?" Gram leaned toward the quilt and flipped it over. "I just read the label, child."

Thea chuckled at the ease of her grandmother's solution. Would she have thought of it? Perhaps. But this was Gram's triumph, and she must be awarded her stars. Just like any good Watson.

Thea pulled out her cell phone. Even though the quilt was in no condition to be shown at the museum, she called Mary-Alice, knowing the former owner would be thankful to hear the news.

Then, because she didn't want another personal visit from the police, Thea called Detective Brewster. She and the quilt would stay put, and Gram could show him her spy kit, which had no bearing on the case, of course. Thea had already decided not to tell him about the threat to Betty. Why give the man an "I told you so" opening? He could keep busy identifying the "Larkin's Treasure" thief.

Last, Thea called Cole and arranged for a lovely portrait of Gram on the *Larkindale Lamplight's* front page. Story on page two.

32

"Goodness, Betty. It's Friday. Quilt Show day minus one." Thea cuddled the cat an extra long time, then gave her free reign of the sofa.

"Do you think I'll win a ribbon on my Kitty in the Cabin quilt?" Betty stretched a response.

Thea started the quilt as a lay-about mat for Betty. But after hours of piecing and stitching, she changed her mind. No way was the little furry seam-ripper getting her claws on Thea's possible prize-winning masterpiece. Now deemed a wall hanging, thank you.

As she dressed for the day in a purple quilt-show-logo shirt, she remembered how thrilled Mary-Alice had been with last night's call about the discovery of "Larkin's Treasure." Thea loved giving her the news. And though the quilt did not look its best, her friend assured her Dr. Cottle's associates at the California State & Textile Museum could repair it good as new.

Of course, the wonderful family trinkets, jewels, and mementoes sewn into the design were lost to her and to history. But most of it would look eye-catching as ever, once the restorers worked their magic.

Mary-Alice had urged Thea to call Dr. Cottle's office and ensure he was coming to fulfill his judge duties. And she would do so, right after she called Prudy. Between Mary-Alice and Thea, they had hatched a little private-Prudy-plan.

"Almost showtime, baby. Aren't you excited?" Prudy asked. "I know I am!"

"Absolutely," Thea said. "You sound like you got over your illness fast."

"Oh, right. I was sick at the tea," Prudy said, her excitement dropped to simmer. "All better now. I mean, haven't you ever noticed how when you feel terrible and get well, you feel better than ever before?"

"Kinda," Thea said, not completely convinced. But perhaps Prudy had a point.

Or . . . maybe Prudy faked her illness at Mum's so she didn't have to participate in the discussion and reveal her lazy behavior.

"Just wondering if you talked to Dr. Cottle yesterday," Thea said, moseying into the kitchen, looking for a breakfast food group item. Muffins? Ice Cream? If she ate it in the morning, wouldn't it fit into the classification?

"Now why would I? Remember, I was sick. Didn't call anyone."

"We are going to need someone to be the Best of Show judge tomorrow. Don't you think it's getting a bit late, Miss Co-Chair?"

"Hey. I already suggested my sister. She'll do it in a pinch," Prudy said, sounding like she was ready to pinch her sister.

"Let me work on it. I'll let you know if we need Trudy to pinch-hit." Smirking at her own pun, Thea rang off and called Cottle's office, getting hold of his administrative assistant, Ralph Galliano.

"I'm a bit surprised to hear your voice at all, Miss James," Galliano said. "Especially today, at the last minute."

Thea put the ice cream carton back in the freezer and sat at her dining table, hungry and perplexed. "Why?"

"Because you've left messages all week: Dr. Cottle isn't needed at this event or any other, when he has already scheduled out the time," the assistant said. "In truth, he's somewhat miffed with you. And with his old friend, Mrs. Wentworth."

"But Dr. Cottle's secretary left messages for me, canceling his appearances."

"Not possible. There is no such person. Someone has been playing a trick on you. I handle all of his scheduling," he said. "In addition, is it true 'Larkin's Treasure'—the historic quilt on loan to you—has been stolen?"

Galliano said nothing more. The symbolic ball was in Thea's court. A lob-zilla.

Taking a deep breath and blowing it out, hoping she hadn't blown into his ear and further offended, Thea told him of the week's occurrences from her perspective. Galliano took it like a sport, saying they had a real mystery at hand. He was gratified to hear the Wentworth quilt had been uncovered and would convey the news to Dr. Cottle immediately.

By the end of their conversation, it was agreed that Dr. Cottle would attend the reception in his honor this evening and judge the show with Mary-Alice tomorrow.

And they agreed to keep that information quiet for now.

Thea dressed up a bit for the reception at Renée's, slipping on a silky pink tank top, jeans, a black velvet jacket, and little heels. She thought she looked snazzy, as Uncle Nick would say. Too bad she had to snazz over there all by herself, but Betty was a dull date.

When she arrived at Heritage House, Thea pulled the Jeep in close to the highway. She didn't want to get hedged in should Renée act especially evil tonight.

As she crunched her heels in the red gravel parking lot, Cole came from the other side and they met in the middle. Thea decided the evening had promise.

"May I?" Cole extended his elbow, his eyes admiring, dimples disarming. Dressed in business casual, with black slacks and gray shirt, the sleeves rolled to three-quarter length, Cole wore his clothes as if tailored just for him.

"Of course!" Thea smiled up at him and took the proffered arm.

They headed up a curved stone path to the house, set back among the pines. Heritage House seemed immense, with its lodge-like exterior. It rose two-and-a-half stories high, with a green-gabled roof and custom lava rock part way up the wood siding. The entry door boasted lava-rock molding, making a majestic welcome to visitors. Thea walked inside.

Dr. Cottle, of round spectacle fame, conversed with the twins in front of the floor-to-ceiling fireplace. Typical. Prudy didn't dig any worms but caught the biggest fish. She smiled and flipped her long locks, brushed to a crazed shine.

Thea glanced up at Cole, his "wowza" expression sparking her confidence. Hey, maybe *she* had caught the biggest fish. Maybe he's partial to blondes. Thea gave her head a victorious toss, but her moussed mane didn't move.

She was enjoying her daydream when Suzanne Stiles entered and broke apart Thea's secure little fantasy. She'd forgotten Suzanne was a blonde, as well. Flamboyantly so. The mayor tapped Cole on the shoulder to get his attention.

"May I speak to you in private, please?" Mayor Stiles asked Cole.

"Ah. . . ." He hesitated, looking to Thea. "Do you mind?"

"No . . . go! Go!" Thea said. It wasn't as if they were on a date.

"I'll give him back in just a few minutes," the mayor said, now taking Cole's arm and leaning against him as they walked away.

"Been outclassed again?" Renée's sarcasm stabbed at Thea, and she whirled around to face her so-called friend.

"What is your problem?" Thea asked, stepping over a self-imposed line friends never cross. Maybe she had finally accepted Renée was not her friend.

Renée seemed surprised. "My problem? Looks like you're the one with problems to me. Man problems."

Thea trembled with anger, clenching her hands. She wanted to do something. To Renée. But she stood there, incensed and mute. All those years of traveling through life together? Being best friends? What had happened to the two of them?

She turned and strode toward the fireplace, where Dr. Cottle chatted with Sissy and Aunt Elena, the latter only partway attending the quilt expert's remarks. Her gaze was fixed on Thea. Excusing herself, she approached her niece, enveloping her in a comforting hug.

"I saw you two talking," Elena said. "Didn't hear the words . . . don't have to know." She patted Thea's back as if she were her own baby girl. "Something has happened to Renée. Everyone can see it. I'm going to pray for reconciliation between you."

Did she even want her aunt to pray? Thea didn't know.

Aunt Elena kindly moved them away from such a painful subject. Instead, they chitchatted about the guild for a time.

When Thea's anger had dissipated, she searched out Cottle again. Sissy had moved off and in her place was Kenneth, who represented Mary-Alice for the evening. They all agreed she should rest at home tonight in order to be ready to judge tomorrow. And Kenneth had brought a date. Who could it be?

Thea leaned in for a better look.

Odette Milsap!

33

Thea couldn't believe it. Kenneth and Odette. He must have won her over with his TV performance. Maybe he was incredibly photogenic. She must remember to watch the footage for herself.

Could Kenneth be a maiden-magnet disguised as an unattractive actor?

The possibility stopped Thea from languishing any longer in self-absorption. Her mood brightened. Next to her, Aunt Elena did an eyebrow lift, showing her mutual amazement. They both smiled at the scene.

Sissy stood off to the side and Thea joined her, asking, "How goes everything in the store?"

"It's cool, thanks. Not much of a break-in. Stuff knocked over," she said. Sissy's high hairstyle, backcombed without pity to enhance her height, was adorned at intervals with sparkly hairpins, bringing a Christmas tree to mind.

"Anything stolen?" Thea asked.

"New books. Worked out though. Inventoried the stock," Sissy said.

Thea wasn't sure what to say and nodded. To her right, she saw the mayor returning with Cole. They made a cute couple.

Mayor Stiles winked at Thea and said, "See? I said I'd bring him back."

Cole didn't stay with either of them, but moved around the room, snapping still shots with his camera. The mayor watched Thea, then leaned near.

"You know," she said, "the man is smitten with you."

"Pardon?" Thea said. "What did you say?"

"Cole is polite to me. And I am more than polite to him because he is the press and I have a career to build," the mayor said. "But he is taken with you, my dear. Don't waste it. He's a keeper."

"I . . . I won't," Thea said. She'd been right. This night definitely had promise.

Mayor Stiles walked away, gracefully, to continue building her career.

Near the fireplace, Kenneth's voice rose. "What are you saying? There is no secret to riches in 'Larkin's Treasure'? And I've been lied to all my life?"

"No, no. Of course not," Dr. Cottle said in a soothing voice. "You know how legends get blown out of proportion over time. The myth of the quilt has become overblown with the telling. The great value is in its historicity."

More people drew closer to hear. Kenneth dabbed at his forehead with a napkin.

"What about all the jewels and period pieces sewn into the quilt?" he asked, his voice rising. "Aren't they worth something? A small fortune at least?"

Dr. Cottle replied with a gather-'round-little-children expression on his face. "The creator of the quilt knew, after the great hardships of those pioneer days, fortunes could be made and lost in a short time. According to an old diary, Hastings McLeod's descendant understood this truth: after faith, family is the most valuable of all riches.

"So she stitched little mementos into the quilt in the period style: a gold cross, a pendant filled with a baby's hair, the chain from her grandfather's pocket watch, a wedding band, a button from a best suit, lace from a wedding dress, and other representations of her family's lives lived across time. To her, these represented great riches, greater than all the gold mines in California."

The small crowd seemed enthralled.

Everyone except for Kenneth, who stormed off, leaving Odette behind. He mumbled his way across the room, pushing people aside, and rushed out the door.

Amid the shocked responses, Thea ran after Kenneth, wanting to reason with him for Mary-Alice's sake. She followed him down the stone path, more slowly as her heels got stuck between rocks and she had to take care. When her feet found the gravel, Kenneth was already tearing out of the parking lot.

Without his headlights on.

Thea managed to climb into her Jeep while he was still in sight and sped after him along Larkin Lake Drive. She flashed her brights on and off, hoping to get his attention. But he drove on, apparently not noticing or caring he was driving in the dark.

Pulling the Wrangler close behind Kenneth's vehicle, Thea flashed her high beams without ceasing. She sensed rather than heard him shouting into the wind and throwing things out of the car. Some of them struck Thea's windshield, scaring her into sudden swerves.

She fought to keep her rig on the road, her eyes on the drama ahead. Kenneth approached a corner, driving too fast, and clipped a row of mailboxes, knocking some over. His vehicle went out of control, spinning, until it came to a stop in front of Thea's horrified eyes.

Pulling over and running to his aid, Thea could tell Kenneth was hurt. Badly. She cradled his head as he slumped forward against the steering wheel, and repeated over and over, "You'll be okay, Kenneth, you'll be okay." She hoped it was true.

He muttered something, and Thea leaned close. "What?"

"All a big waste of time . . . all my trouble . . . for nothing," he said, his voice no more than a whisper.

What did he mean? Then Thea saw him grasping something in his hand. The ancient gold pendant containing the baby's hair. And then, she knew.

It had been Kenneth who stole "Larkin's Treasure" and cut off all the mementos thinking they must be extremely valuable or might lead him to the mother lode.

Was he the culprit who clobbered Mary-Alice as well? If so, how sad she would be to learn the truth. All of it.

As Thea pulled out her phone and called 911, she pleaded with God for the life of Mary-Alice Wentworth's beloved great-nephew.

34

When Thea arrived downtown at 8:00 A.M. to check the quilts hung all along Main Street, she could not quit thinking about Mary-Alice. By now, she must know Kenneth had stolen the family heirloom quilt. And might be her attacker. How must she feel?

The Quilt-Without-Guilt Guild member-machine chugged along without a hiccup. Already, visitors lined the streets. Curly's Miner Diner was something of a gold mine itself today as people went in and out of the doors like ants on an anthill.

Thea decided to check on the progress at the Hastings McLeod Museum and found Mary-Alice already there. Impressive, considering she'd just been released from the hospital a few days before.

"My friend! I'm so sorry about Kenneth. His accident and . . . well. . . ." Thea didn't know how to finish. She'd almost come to like the man.

"I know, my dear. Me, too. The doctors say he only has a concussion," she said brightly. "He'll be out of the hospital soon."

"Are you angry?" Thea asked.

"More disappointed than angry. I understand why he stole the quilt, and it saddens me he felt insignificant enough to take such an action," Mary-Alice said. "I'm not sure if the state will let him off scot-free, but of course, I forgive him."

"You do?" It hadn't even been twenty-four hours since Mary-Alice had learned of his deception.

"It's so easy to recall offenses against us and forget the blessings, isn't it?" Mary-Alice said. "Kenneth has blessed my life immeasurably. Should I hold this one offense against him? Shouldn't I forgive?"

"But it's more than one offense. What about conking you on the head? Do you forgive him for that?"

"Isn't this exquisite?" Mary-Alice gazed at a lovely quilt in a Rose of Sharon pattern. "Did you know Jesus is referred to as the Rose of Sharon?"

"No . . . how lovely," Thea said. "But can you forgive him for attacking you?"

"Oh, he wouldn't hurt me, my dear. I'm his second mother. It was someone else."

Someone else? If so, then Mary-Alice's attacker was still at large.

Dr. Cottle had not yet arrived to join Mary-Alice for the judging. Since the quilt entries were hung both in Old Town and in Pioneer Park, Thea worried the ribbons wouldn't be attached to the quilts in time for folks to show off their awards to the attendees. What kind of victory was it to be proclaimed the winner after everyone had gone home?

Where was Prudy? After all her fawning over Cottle at the reception, she had grabbed the responsibility of making sure he appeared by 10:00 A.M. and the judging would begin. Already past 9:00 A.M. History told Thea to release her inner worrywart.

She wandered past the folks enjoying the local heritage quilt display, saddened "Larkin's Treasure" wasn't the star of the show. Aunt Elena did her white glove lady thing again, charming everyone. Nellie busied herself arranging merchandise in the Members Boutique, the center of quilting commerce. Outside, Pioneer Park made a meadowy setting, with lines of quilts swaying in the soft breeze. Thea thought it reminiscent of long clotheslines, hung with sheets or blankets.

"Howdy, Thea!" Renée's husband, Howie, gave a cheery wave from the raffle table. Then handed over some bills toward a chance or twenty at winning the friendship quilt.

"Renée loves this quilt. I'm trying to increase her luck."

What a nice guy. Beside him, his wife glanced up at Thea, then looked away.

"Howie, have you seen Dr. Cottle today?" Thea asked. "Prudy was supposed to bring him out for the judging by 10:00 A.M."

"Let me ask Renée," Howie said, turning to her, then back. "She says Prudy came to the house early, checked the doctor's room, and found it empty. Thought he might have taken a cab. I didn't notice one. Maybe he caught a ride?"

A death-like dread gripped Thea and she excused herself, rushing to the parking lot, firing up the Jeep. She covered the miles to Heritage House like it was located down the street, parking again on the red gravel. Spotting a server, she asked for Dr. Cottle's room.

"He has the cabin by the pool. Over there." The woman pointed to a rustic building on the edge of a great lawn. Behind it, tall trees loomed.

Thanking her, Thea charged across and knocked on the door. "Dr. Cottle?"

No answer. A low moan. Thea jiggled the knob, and the door gave. She repeated his name and got a groaning response. "In here."

She found him sitting on the side of his bed, nursing a head bump. "Dr. Cottle! I'm so sorry. Do you want me to call an ambulance?"

"No, I'll be okay. Though I never saw it coming," he said. "Can't say I think much of Larkindale hospitality."

"Neither can I," Thea said. "When you didn't turn up on time, I asked around. The rumor is you caught a cab. . . ."

"Obviously, still a rumor." Cottle stood, steadying himself. "May I ride in to the show with you?"

"Are you serious?" Stunned, Thea could see the little man had gumption.

"Very. I didn't come all this way to whimper in my room and not do my job. I promised Mary-Alice. With what happened last night, I must help her have a successful show today." Cottle brushed his thinning hair and straightened his bow tie. "How do I look?"

By noon, the judging had been accomplished and ribbons attached to the winning quilts both in Old Town and Pioneer Park. Dr. Cottle had arranged an impromptu ceremony for the Best of Show award to take place before the media. All were gathered at the museum for presentations and pictures, including Uncle Nick, there at Thea's request. Curator Hilderbrand and the security guard stood nearby.

Thea had to pronounce Prudy's watercolor quilt extraordinary. Prudy had said it was her best work with a twist. Upon viewing it, Thea saw not only precise points and perfect hand quilting, but also exquisite detail in the appliquéd border. The twist.

In Thea's mind, the skill shown in Prudy's quilt had earned its blue ribbon and the right to be chosen Best of Show. Though it pained her the littlest bit to say so.

"Congratulations. Your quilt is lovely, Prudy."

"It is, isn't it?" Prudy said, beaming. "And congrats on your honorable mention for your little wall-hanging." She sounded almost sincere.

"Thanks!" Thea said, appreciating the sentiment. Maybe she had misjudged Prudy.

"By the way, I'm surprised Cottle made it to the judging," Prudy said, leaning toward Thea with a conspiratorial tone. "How many events did he already miss this week?"

Straightening, Prudy took herself and her snide remarks over for a snark-session with Trudy, leaving Thea overjoyed at the loss of her company. And wondering if she, like the little girls in the antique picture, needed a time-out.

All the blue ribbon quilts had been transported over to the museum from Old Town and hung beside the Pioneer Park frontrunners in a kind of winner's semicircle. Pictures were snapped and admirers drew close. Dr. Cottle and Mary-Alice walked alongside the quilts, stopping often to confer, pointing out a flaw or highlighting a marvel of workmanship. Finally, they seemed to agree and Dr. Cottle positioned himself behind the podium brought from inside the museum. He tapped the microphone to make sure it was live, glanced around as if to be sure all the important parties were present, and began to speak.

"Ladies and gentlemen. I'm pleased to award the Best of Show ribbon to. . . ." He walked over to Prudy's quilt and tapped it, giving a few claps with raised hands to start the applause. The quilters gave a standing ovation for Prudy's stunning quilt.

Easy to do, since they were already standing.

Prudy clapped for herself, jumping up and down in place. Trudy offered a thumbs-up. All around her, Thea saw the enthusiasm from the other quilters for the fine work. Gram, Mum, Aunt Elena, Lyndi, all applauded.

Thea joined in.

"I'd like the quilter who made this fine quilt to come up front and let me congratulate her," Dr. Cottle said and Prudy rushed to the podium. "I'd like to, but can't. Because this quilt was not made by anyone present today."

Thea's mouth dropped open, and the crowd stilled their celebration.

"What do you mean?" Prudy said. "I'm right here!"

Cottle turned to her. "Indeed you are. But you did not make this quilt."

"Well, I never!" Prudy said.

"Right. You never made it." Cottle turned back to the audience. "This wonderful watercolor quilt was made by famed quilter and author, Natalie Twinkle. It is pictured in her latest book, *Quilting with the Twinkle Touch*. It is, in fact, one of three quilts she sold. I've seen it before."

A communal gasp sounded.

Undeterred, Prudy said, "I have the book. I used the same pattern."

"You have the book because you stole it from my store!" Sissy said. "Thief!"

"What do you have to say now?" Cottle asked.

"My label's on the back!" Prudy said, her gaze darting around.

"Easily done. You can sew a label on any quilt and call it yours," Cottle said. "That doesn't mean it is."

Prudy edged away, and the quilters crowded in. She grabbed a quilt dowel from a bin full and held it up like a weapon, grabbed Gram and, knocking off her favorite hat, slipped the rod across her neck. "Back off!"

For a moment, it seemed as if all sound was suspended. Silence, only interrupted by Trudy's horrified gasp.

Then Thea rushed Prudy, pulling her co-chair away from her flummoxed grandmother, who began to look for her hat. The security guard, aided by Cole and Uncle Nick, dragged off a screaming Prudy.

"My sister, Trudy! She did it!"

35

In the evening, a few family and friends met at Heritage House for pie and coffee. Or maybe *not* friends exactly, because Renée was there. The talk turned to the mysterious week now behind them. Thea, Uncle Nick, Aunt Elena, and Cole sat at a giant farm table with their hosts, Howie and Renée. With cutlery clinking against the plates, they turned to Uncle Nick for his insider police information.

"Why did Prudy ever go on her head-bonking binge?" Thea asked.

"Simple," Uncle Nick said. "She wanted to win Best of Show with a quilt she hadn't made. Mary-Alice was too good of a judge. So was Cottle. They both needed to be removed, at least temporarily. And I understand Prudy suggested her sister as a replacement judge?"

Thea nodded. "Her sister refused. But if there had been no one else . . . ?"

"Prudy's plan was shrewd. She pretended to be Dr. Cottle's secretary and left messages for you, Thea, canceling his visits. Then left messages for him, impersonating you. It might have worked if you had given up. You didn't, even when she sent you a shredded cat collar as a warning."

"Awful." Thea shuddered. "But why did she fake the flu at Mum's tea?"

"It was Trudy," Nick said. "She pretended to be the sick sister while Prudy made a visit to The Quintessential Quilter. To get a certain book."

Thea had thought something was off about the twin. She didn't guess what.

"Who stole the brooch?" Elena asked.

"Prudy again. She tossed it out the window, making it seem Mary-Alice was robbed. Giving a false reason for the assault." Uncle Nick speared a piece of peach pie. "She threw out the cell phone, too. So no one could call while she sneaked back down the old servant's stairs." Nick further revealed Prudy had pocketed the letter Thea found, later tossing it as a thing of no value.

Maybe a copy could be retrieved from Cottle since it was an official document from the State & Textile Museum. But, good heavens. Who would have expected Prudy to be so tricky?

"What a shock for her twin. Did she leave town? Isn't she some kind of accessory to the burglary at Sissy's quilt shop?" Thea asked, trying to use police lingo. Since she was a PI and all.

"Reliable scuttlebutt says Trudy isn't considered an accomplice because she had no idea of Prudy's plans, though she agreed to fake her sister's presence at the Lake House meeting," Nick said. "No law against it as far as I know."

He added another syrupy peach to his uneaten pie bite, looking at it with longing before returning his attention to Thea. He explained Trudy would be standing by her sister while incarcerated. "Once it's all behind them, I think they both plan to go back east."

"What about Kenneth stealing 'Larkin's Treasure'?" Renée asked, directing yet another question to Nick.

"Kenneth had copied the key to the display case, using the one on the chain Mary-Alice had been wearing that night. It was in her valuables, bagged and given to him at the hospital. He rode with her, remember? But during the setup for the unveiling, he found a moment alone in the museum. He crashed the display case glass to make it look random. Then he couldn't be linked to the quilt by the key."

Nick then informed them of Kenneth's impromptu morph into crime. "Until he saw the key among her personal belongings, he had no intention of stealing the quilt."

Uncle Nick sampled the pie and between bites moaned his compliments to the chef.

"Kenneth's a good actor," Elena said, ignoring Nick's not-so-elegant pastry praise. "I never suspected him."

If the surprised looks around the table were any indication, no one else had either.

"I heard he may have to go to trial for stealing the quilt," Howie said, giving input for the first time. "Looks like Mary-Alice's forgiveness won't get him off this time."

"Technically, the quilt belongs to the State Textile & Quilt Museum, so it's way beyond family business now." Nick went on to say that Odette Milsap had declared she'd wait for Ransome "till he gets out of the pokey." An unexpected happy ending.

Uncle Nick patted his stomach and smiled at Renée. "Great pie."

Thea gave a covert glance across the table at Renée's reaction to the compliment. Would she be smug? Faux humble? It seemed she was neither. Instead, she watched Thea, something unreadable in her gaze. Something familiar. Acceptance?

No. Couldn't be. Thea shook it off.

"Okay, this has been bothering me all along," Thea said, pushing her half-eaten pie to the side, not wanting to give Renée the satisfaction of eating it all. "Do we know why Odette was so frightened to talk to the police? It was upsetting."

Thea didn't mention her own role upsetting Odette's interview with Detective Brewster. No need to murk up the waters, right?

"I know the reason," Uncle Nick said. "And it was a good one, at least in her own mind. A sensitive family matter. Odette will reveal it when she's ready. But, in spite of her fear of talking to the police, she has never broken the law."

"So, what *has* she done?" Renée asked, but Nick said nothing more.

"Nick, don't tease!" Elena tilted her head in an appealing way and placed a hand on his arm. "Tell us what you can, for heaven's sake!"

"Yes!" "Please tell us. . . ." "We'll keep it quiet," from around the table.

He gave in. "All I can say is she has a family secret kept over many years. Sissy was never told," Nick said. "For Odette, a police interview could lead to a background check, and she feared the ugly truth would be revealed. She worried it might change everything for Sissy and her standing in the community."

"Well, who doesn't have a family secret?" Elena threw up her hands, incensed. "Poor Odette. She's going to get an ulcer, worrying so much." There was a sympathetic murmur of agreement from the guests.

"Just one more question," Thea said. "Does anyone know who followed me to the lake the other day? I know I was being watched."

"It was me," Cole said, his grin an apology. "Your uncle's suggestion."

Thea rolled her eyes. "I'm not a baby!"

"But you're my princess," Uncle Nick said and winked.

⁂

When the pie and chatting was done, Renée leaned across the table and whispered to Thea, "Would you mind coming outside a minute?" Her countenance held none of its former malice.

Still, history taught Thea another verbal whacking could be waiting beyond the door.

With reluctance, she trailed Renée to the lovely pavilion where weddings were often scheduled. Thea's hands felt Kenneth-clammy as she sat on the bench, facing her friend.

Or rather, ex-friend.

"I'm so sorry!" Renée said, with an unexpected burst of humanity. "I've been the worst friend. I felt so unhappy and blamed you."

Had Thea heard right? "I don't understand," she said. "What did I do?"

"Something I didn't expect." Renée paused and studied her wedding ring, as if to organize her thoughts. "You became popular and poised while I was away. Before I went to Europe, I was the woman of the day. The bride, fussed over.

"But when I returned, here you were, heading up an important cultural event with a drop-your-daisies handsome boyfriend. All eyes were on you. I'd been displaced. I didn't like playing second violin when I'd always been concertmistress.

"My behavior was inexcusable, of course, but I'm asking you to do just that. Excuse it. Besides . . . I hate the distance it's created between us. I miss you." Renée touched Thea's arm. "Can you ever forgive me?"

Thea stared, shocked at the declaration. At least now she understood why Renée had been so antagonistic. Simple jealousy.

She thought of Mary-Alice and how easily she forgave one who hurt her. Could Thea let go of past offenses and forgive? Or trust Renée to be a blessing again? Thea was no Mary-Alice.

One thing she knew, Thea did not admire the person she had become in the midst of this situation with Renée. Maybe it was time to begin again.

"Okay," Thea said, not at all sure it truly was okay. "I'll try."

"That's all I ask. Thank you!" Renée gave her a joyous hug. "Wait. I'll be right back." She dashed across the lawn into the house and back out with a big package. Which she presented to a still stunned Thea.

Unwrapping it, Thea recognized the colorful quilt inside. "This is yours, Renée. It's—"

"The friendship quilt! From the show."

Thea looked up. "But Howie bought all those tickets so *you* would win."

"And I did win!" Renée said. "But I want to give it to you. An investment in our friendship. Or maybe a dividend, long overdue."

Thea smiled a little, tracing the intricate pattern on the quilt. "It's lovely. Thanks."

The gals sat and chatted for a time, catching up on what had been left unsaid. As they rose to go back to the house, Thea sensed an inner nudge to reach out to Renée. Should she risk it? Nothing ventured and all that? Thea tossed out a casual invitation.

"Ah . . . would you and Howie like to come to dinner tomorrow night? I'm cooking for Cole and the Durtles."

"Are you making your Uncle Nick's famous spaghetti with the secret sauce?" Renée's expression turned optimistic, as if she hoped for a yes.

"No," Thea said. "Remember he won't give me the recipe until I get married?"

For a minute, it looked like Renée might say something sarcastic about Thea's single state. Or her cooking. But Renée's expression gentled into a sweet smile.

"I'll bring humble pie for dessert," she said.

"Just come," Thea said, grinning. "I have a terrific antique print I want to show you. Bought it while you were away, because it reminded me of . . . us."

Renée beamed and Thea had a feeling from now on, those two little girls in the picture would get along just fine.

Group Discussion Guide

1. When reading *A Stitch in Crime*, what elements engaged you immediately? What emotions did it stir in you as you read?

2. There are several themes in this book. Did one stand out to you? Why?

3. What scene resonated most with you personally in either a positive or negative way? Why?

4. Have you had an experience similar to one in the book? How did you react to it?

5. Who are the key characters? Did one of them remind you of yourself or of someone you know? How?

6. Do you have a Mary-Alice mentor in your life? If so, how has that affected you?

7. Would you want to meet any of the characters? Did you like them? Hate them?

8. If you could counsel one of the characters, who would it be? What would you say?

9. Was the ending satisfying? If so, why? If not, why not? How might you change it?

10. What do you think will happen to the characters next?

11. Where *could* the story go after *A Stitch in Crime* ends?

12. What would your life be like if you lived in Larkindale? In this story?

Want to learn more about Cathy Elliott
and check out other great fiction from
Abingdon Press?

Check out our website at
www.AbingdonFiction.com
and find out about more Quilts of Love books at
www.quiltsoflovebooks.com

At these sites you can
read interviews with your favorite authors,
find tips for starting a reading group,
and stay posted on what new titles are on the horizon.

Be sure to visit Cathy online!

http://cathyelliottbooks.wordpress.com/

We hope you enjoyed Cathy Elliott's *A Stitch in Crime* from the Quilts of Love series. There are twenty-five books in the Quilts of Love series, and they include cozy mysteries and romantic suspense, historical romance, Amish, women's fiction, and contemporary romance. We hope you'll read and enjoy other books in the series. You can find out more about the books and see quilt patterns from the series at www.quiltsoflovebooks.com.

Here's a sample chapter from Carolyn Zane's *Beyond the Storm*.

1

7:00 a.m.

"Good morning, Rawston, heart of the American Midwest! We've got seven a.m. straight up on your Saturday, May 3rd, and you are listening to Mike and Julie on 101.5 K-RAW. Keep it right here for traffic and weather on the tens as head meteorologist Ron Donovan's got some breaking news about a thunder boomer headed our way, right after this!"

———

The bell over the Doo Drop-In Hair Salon's front door jangled as it opened. "I got wings!" Isuzu Nakamura shouted as she did every morning when she arrived for work. As usual, she gave the door a healthy, window-rattling slam.

"Mmph." Twenty-eight-year-old Abigail Durham, the salon's owner/operator jerked awake and blinked around the break room. Ah, man. She'd been dozing. And the day hadn't even begun. What on earth had possessed her to stay out so late last night? Isuzu's massive purse crashed onto her workstation table and moments later, Abigail could sense her standing at the door, frowning as she sat up and peeled a granola bar wrapper off her cheek.

221

"You look terrible."

Abigail yawned up at Isuzu-fresh-as-a-lotus-flower-Nakamura. She might be tiny in stature, but the dainty Japanese national was as tough as the acrylic she used for her customers' French-tip nails. Isuzu rummaged through the cupboards. "I make more coffee. You stay out too late at Kaylee bachelorette party last night?"

"Golly, mom. Why do you ask?" A person would never guess that Zuzu was three years younger than Abigail, the way she acted like such a granny at only twenty-five.

Isuzu dropped the metal coffeepot into the sink and turned the water on, full blast. "You wear two different shoe."

"Oh?" Abigail frowned at her feet. "Oh. Don't worry. I'm not actually here yet. I just came down to check my appointment calendar. I don't have anyone till 8:30."

The smell of the coffee beans Isuzu had ground began to tease Abigail awake. "So? How was party?"

"Kaylee hated it . . . so, it was fun." Dancing and party shenanigans had never been the virginal bride's bag. Probably would have left before the whole thing started, but Kaylee wasn't one to hurt anybody's feelings. Had Kaylee been an animal, she'd have been a dainty, coal-black poodle, all soft curly hair, soulful brown eyes, and perfect manners.

"Too bad you miss Friday service at church last night. They dedicate big, fat baby to Jesus. Baby cry and smack pastor in nose. Blood everywhere. Very exciting."

"Ah. Yeah. Well. Next time." *As if.* Abigail ducked her head and crossed her eyes. Church on Friday night? Isuzu needed to get a life. Sunday morning was enough for any normal person and even then, only if one couldn't come up with a good excuse for sleeping in.

The door jangled again, and Isuzu glanced up. "I do prom nail for my niece, Brooke, this morning. She invited to prom dance with nice boy tonight. Fresh coffee in two minute, okay?" Isuzu pointed at the hissing machine and then rushed to greet her niece, leaving Abigail to mull over memories of last night while she waited for her java to perk.

Kaylee's bridesmaids had gone all out. A piñata filled with party favors and gifts, line-dancing lessons, and some dude named Bob Ray Lathrop—part-time personal trainer—had dressed as a cop, arrested Kaylee for "breaking hearts everywhere," and then proceeded to do a dance that had everyone howling. They'd all taken a turn on the dance floor with Bob Ray, and he'd passed out business cards and coupons for one free personal training session down at his gym, The Pump.

But, to Abigail's way of thinking, the best part of the night had arrived too late. "*Whoooie!* Get a load of the Marlboro man!" one of Kaylee's bridesmaids had shouted over the blaring country music, just as Abigail staggered off the dance floor and flopped into a chair to rest up. Craning to see, Abigail had snapped to attention. *Oh, my. Yes, indeedy. Cute, cute, cute. Real cute.* He wore his plaid shirt untucked, and his Levi's and cowboy boots gave the impression that he'd just climbed off the rodeo bull. In her professional opinion, he could use a good haircut, but it was hard to tell as he'd covered most of the offense with a backwards ball cap. She ignored the niggling voice of caution that cried, *Anybody that good-looking has to be a womanizing jerk. Don't you have enough scar tissue on your heart from meeting guys like him in places like this?* Feeling rebellious, Abigail had pointed her fingers, like twin revolvers, at cowboy-man and pulled the trigger, then blown at her fingertips.

"Abigail! He saw you!" the bridesmaid had shrieked and ducked her head in a fit of laughter.

"Uh-oh," she'd said and laughed. Right about that time, the bride, killjoy-Kaylee, began making noises about heading home. Seemed the bachelorette had family arriving from

Seattle over the weekend and wanted some beauty rest. Plus, her fiancé had called her twice, which Abigail had razzed her about, teasing that he was probably worried about Kaylee's virtue.

"Marlboro," as the girls had nicknamed the newcomer, stood just inside the door, arms folded—making it obvious he spent time in the gym—and surveyed the joint for a few minutes. Then, much to the bridal party's delight, he strode across the room and asked Abigail to dance. It had been like something out of a movie.

"My hero!" she'd shouted for the benefit of the girls. They'd all catcalled and whistled as she'd skipped out to the dance floor after him. Abigail's hands had felt feminine in his work-roughened ones, but his touch had been gentle and polite and his smile genuine. He was all beautiful teeth and twinkling eyes and five o'clock shadow. He'd taken enough time to slap on a little aftershave that morning. Armani. It wasn't cheap. Abigail knew this because she carried it at the salon. *Mm-mm.* Such deep blue eyes. And eyelashes? Long enough to sweep her off her feet.

As she reminisced, Abigail found a mug and poured herself a cup of coffee.

"Come here often?" he'd asked in a deliciously rich baritone.

She'd leaned back in his arms and grinned at the dopey line. "Nope. You?"

"To be honest, the only reason I'm here now is because I just finished some work I was doing on a charity project and I'm starving. If I come here at all, it's usually with a group of work buddies for burgers and to catch the game scores."

"Sounds fun." *Charity thing. Yeah. Sure. Whatever.* It was true, however, that Low Places offered burgers as big as your head and a trough of fries for a song.

"Your boyfriend mind me asking you to dance?"

She'd laughed. "No boyfriend. No husband." He'd seemed inordinately pleased, which pleased her. Inordinately. "You?" she ventured.

"None of the above." He was probably feeding her a load of baloney, but she was a sucker for a pretty face.

"Ah. What about a girlfriend or wife?"

"Nope. I'm relatively new to the Midwest. Haven't lived here a full year yet."

"Welcome to Rawston," Abigail murmured and smiled into his shirt. *Oh, yes.* He was a great dance partner. Nice and tall, which made her 5' 6" plus heels feel perfect.

Just as things were getting interesting, Kaylee appeared at her shoulder and announced that the clock had struck midnight and she was leaving the ball. And, since Kaylee had driven most of them, it was time to bid Prince Marlboro adieu. Abigail's friends were all laughing as they pulled her off the dance floor.

"Goodbye," Abigail had mouthed and thrust out her lower lip in disappointment.

"Next Friday?" he'd answered, seeming just as disappointed.

What the hey? Maybe this time it would be different. Maybe he was that rare combination of good-looking and unmarried good guy. *Eeh.* Probably not. But she'd nodded anyway, grinned, given him a thumb's up, and that had been that.

Abigail couldn't wait for Friday. She opened the fridge for some creamer and suddenly remembered.

"Oh, no," she muttered and stared at the refrigerator door. "I forgot to ask his name!"

"What?"

"Nothing. Hey, Zuzu? I'm gonna go home and shower." She headed toward Isuzu's nail station. "I'll be back in by 8:15 for my first appointment. Aunt Selma is scheduled for 8:30. Oh, and if she gets here before I do, put her in the chair and give her a magazine."

"Okay. Look at this polish Brooke pick. Nail going to be perfect for tonight." Isuzu held up a bottle of sparkly color and waved it at Abigail.

"Hey, Brookie-cookie. How you gonna dance without any ice under your feet?" The Olympic hopeful and her figure-skating twin brother were the local celebs. "Excited?"

Brooke snorted and laughed. "Uh, yeah? To finally dance with a normal boy, and one who won't be tossing me into the air and then not catching me? Totally."

"What's his name?"

"Nick Gleason." Her face flared crimson, and Abigail had to wonder if there was more to the story than that. "He's my best friend."

"That's cool. Friendship is more important in a relationship than the mushy stuff, trust me." Abigail sighed. "Not that I'd know. I haven't had a date with a friend in . . . ever. But hope springs eternal."

7:10 a.m.

"*It's time for weather on the ten's with head meteorologist, Ron Donovan.*"

"*Thanks, Jack! Right now, we've already got 72 degrees; looks like it's gonna be a sizzler today. There's a cold front moving in from Canada, bringing a strong chance of a thunderstorm arriving by six or seven o'clock tonight. Possibility of some hail and lightning, so park in the garage and keep the kids and pets inside this evening. Stay tuned here for any changes in the storm's severity and direction. Traffic and weather brought to you by Quilty Pleasures Quilt Shop.*"

"Thanks, Ron. Hey folks! If you're looking for some family fun, be sure to head over to the 17th annual Rawston Quilt-o-Rama May 17th and 18th. That's just two weeks away, so be sure to put it on your calendar. My family went to that last year, Julie, and I gotta tell you, the quilts are beautiful, but the food? Oh, man. Good eats down there at the Rawston Taste!"

The thing Justin Girard appreciated about living in a small town like Rawston was the charm, he thought as he snapped off his radio and pulled the keys from his truck's ignition. Partially because the city planners insisted on it and partially because the shopkeepers down here had a ton of civic pride, all the shops in the entire Old Town area were required by city ordinance to have western storefronts and covered wooden sidewalks. Barrels and baskets of flowers were encouraged, as were benches, twinkly lights, and alfresco seating for diners. The stores all had catchy names like Quilty Pleasures, Quick Draw McGraw's Art Supplies, and The Sarsaparilla Soda Fountain. The trees that lined the streets were huge and shady and a hundred and fifty years old if they were a day. The area was so quaint and welcoming that even in times of heavy recession it flourished.

This friendly, slow-lane lifestyle was new to Justin. Last summer, he'd transplanted from the East Coast to escape the rat race and a failed relationship and also because he needed to be closer to his grandparents. They still lived by themselves but were now in their eighties and beginning to have some health problems. Since he was the only one in the family who wasn't saddled with a spouse and kids, Justin had been elected to head out to the Midwest to help them and to keep an eye on things.

For the most part, small-town, middle-American life really agreed with Justin, except that he missed his friends and family. Although he had to admit, venturing out on his own for dinner last night had been a step in the right direction. The place he'd selected? Normally, he avoided the bar-and-grill scene in favor of a drive-thru window. And dancing had certainly been the last thing he'd expected to be doing. But the smell of charbroiled burgers wafting from Low Places had been more than his rumbling gut could ignore as he'd driven home late last night, so he'd given in to his hunger pangs and pulled into the crowded parking lot.

Loud country western music greeted him before he even got out of his rig, and he'd followed the thrumming bass through the front door. When he'd entered the room, a tall, curly-headed blond was jumping to the beat and was obviously the life of a bachelorette party. Even from across the room, he could see she was different. A real spitfire, yes, but there was something else. Something unpretentious and oh-so-joyful. As he'd laughed out loud at her antics, he decided that he had to ask her to dance before the night was over.

Her huge green eyes seemed to miss nothing, and she had a single, deep dimple in one cheek that only appeared when she laughed. Her hair was wonderful—wild, shoulder-length blond stuff done up in a big old mess of curls that was losing its gravitational hold with every jerky dance step. Like a compass needle to due north, her carefree abandon had drawn the attention of every guy in the place. He'd zeroed in on her, a decision that had given him second thoughts in the middle of the night. A pang of guilt had him regretting his promise to meet her next Friday night. Just because he'd lived here for a year and hadn't met some nice girl who shared his beliefs didn't mean he had to start looking in bars.

He shook his head. *Focus on business, Girard.*

The pungent smell of hair chemicals assailed him as he stepped into the upscale hair salon.

"I help you?" A petite Asian lady sat painting the toenails of a kid who he assumed was her daughter. They were both pretty as porcelain dolls.

The nail lady eyed him with suspicion. Must not get a lot of guys in tool belts looking for hairdos and nail jobs. "Uh. Yeah." Justin fumbled in his shirt pocket for her info. "I'm supposed to talk to somebody named . . . uh, Abigail Durham. She around?"

"Abby? No. You just miss her. She go home for little bit. Maybe one hour. I give message for you or you come back later."

Coming back held no appeal. "Yeah. Okay. Tell her Justin Girard stopped by?" He dug around in his shirt pocket some more and produced a business card. "I'm donating the labor for the Quilt Fair food cart? I hear—since Jen Strohacker is having a baby any day now—Ms. Durham is taking over her job for the high school booster club."

"Yeah, yeah. Abby doing that. She used to be Rawston Rah-Rah so she think she qualify for running little restaurant." The nail lady seemed to find that hilarious. "This long message. You want to wait and tell her? Sit there." She waved at a comfortable grouping of chairs in the corner. "Sit, sit, sit! She be here later to work."

"Oh, no. I just wanted to tell her that I ran into a bit of a permit problem, and we need to talk before I put on the awnings. City ordinance won't allow us to build it the way it's designed without more fees. It's going to be expensive, so we need to discuss options. Have her call that number when she gets a chance, okay?"

"It's 8:10 here at K-RAW 101.5 FM. Hey, Julie, don't know about you, but I'm already sweating. Feels like you could just grab the air and wring it out, huh?"

"Yeah, Mike, you know I've been thinking about starting a new fad and making all my clothes out of beach towels. Attractive, yet functional."

"Hey, that'd be cool! Make me something fetching?"

"Aaanyway! We've got a set of concert tickets for the fifth caller in our Name That Hair Band contest sponsored by Doo Drop-In Hair Salon! So let's wake these sleepyheads up with some rock and roll! Who's performing this oldie but goodie?"

A refreshing shower, some fruit, oatmeal, and a huge cup of coffee later, Abigail felt as if she'd rally. She lingered another moment on her back balcony lounge chair, knowing that in a few minutes she'd be inside for the rest of the day. It would be too hot to do otherwise. Feet propped on the deck's railing, she jotted down a quick grocery list as she watched a small cloud, like a puff of meringue, float across the crystal clear sky. Ron Donovan predicted a T-boomer, huh? Wouldn't be his first misdiagnosis. Wouldn't be his last. Seemed like he'd been wrong every day this week. Even so, she added batteries to her list. Her flashlight was dead.

Man. It was gonna be a hot one. Tiny beads of sweat were already collecting on her upper lip. She'd changed out of her sweats and mismatched shoes and into a bright, flowery mini-skirt, a periwinkle blue tank top and flip-flops. Wielding the blow dryer in this heat would no doubt make even this skimpy ensemble too much by midday. A quick glance at her watch told her Aunt Selma was due any minute now. She was notoriously early for everything.

Standing, she stretched and then paused, straining to listen to a low rumble in the distance. *What was that?* Leaning over the railing, she glanced up and down the street, looking for the semi-truck that sounded as if it was rumbling by. But there was none. She eyed the lone cloud with skepticism. Wasn't thunder, that was for sure. Must be traffic from the next street over.

Skipping downstairs to her salon, Abigail headed to her whitewashed, antique lobby desk. A quick scan of the appointment book told her she had five haircuts, a perm, a complex color job, and two prom up-dos. Busy day. She dropped the pencil on her blotter and stepped back to survey the newly decorated room. The cream n' java paint she'd chosen for the lobby walls last month looked perfect. Chic. Especially with the brown and blue curtains she'd made herself. She'd splurged on a fabulous blue vase for the coffee table and kept it filled with fragrant white roses. A special shelf held her *North American Hair Stylist of the Year* award and other trophies, certificates, and honors. Abigail was good at her craft. And people knew it.

It had taken her three years to achieve this magazine-cover perfection for her shop. Three years of garage-saleing and sanding and scraping and painting and arranging everything just so. But it had been worth it. Between her creativity with the shears and the beautiful salon, she was attracting new business in droves. Luckily, she was able to add two part-time stylists and a manicurist last year to deal with the overflow. She was even thinking about renting the spare room to a masseuse.

Then again, though Abigail loved her salon—and Rawston— an offer hovered over her, never far from her thoughts. Abigail had received a call from an exclusive salon in Los Angeles, one that catered to a number of celebrities. The money would be great. And it would be nice to finally bust out of small-town USA with the small-town busybody mindset. But she'd miss her aunt. And her friends. And her clientele. Some more mulling would have to happen before she made a decision that drastic.

Just outside her plate glass window, Selma Louise Tully's 1972 Oldsmobile Cutlass Supreme, driven by Selma herself, jumped the curb for a moment before settling back into the parking spot in front of Abigail's salon. The car was an ungainly machine that seemed to drive Selma, rather than vice versa, and had more than one dent to make that case. Riding so low in her seat that she had to peer through the spokes of the steering wheel, Selma regularly drew goggling stares from folks who thought the car careened down the road without a driver.

Selma was as saucy as a plate of spaghetti and never failed to infect everyone she met with her unbridled enthusiasm for life. Though she was eighty-seven, she was still glass-shard sharp, and her dry sense of humor and boundless energy made her seem decades younger. She'd just renewed her driver's license for another five years and ran the quilt shop two doors down—Quilty Pleasures, one of the most famous quilt shops, among the quilting set at any rate, in America. She wore her white hair in a close-cropped cap, and her clothing was usually gaudy enough to glow in the dark. She claimed it kept folks from stepping on her.

A blast of hot air charged into the room along with Selma. "Hi, honey. I'm early. Came straight here from home. Wanted to give you some extra time to turn me into a bombshell for the Quilt Fair. I have to look good for my adoring fans." She grabbed Abigail into a crushing embrace and standing on tiptoe, noisily kissed her cheek. "Hey, Zuzu," she called and climbed into Abigail's hair chair.

"Hi, Auntie Selma," Isuzu called back as she guided Brooke to the blue light machine to cure her nails. "You getting ready for quilt people to come mob you?"

"You know, I've been doing this thing for years, and I still get butterflies."

"That's because every year fair get bigger."

Isuzu was right. Selma's darling shop was a seriously big deal in Rawston and not simply because of her huge selection of vintage fabrics and notions. Nor was it a destination point because of the treasure trove of beautifully crafted quilts that hung from every wall and the high rough-hewn ceiling rafters. Though those things were true, the real reason for the shop's notoriety was the annual Quilt-o-Rama Selma founded seventeen years ago. What had started as a little quilt show was now an event that literally took over the streets of Rawston as quilters from all over the nation flocked to partake of the festivities. Quilts dangled off railings, gutters, rooftops and any other thing that sat still long enough to act as a display stand. The carnival atmosphere consisted of a nationally renowned quilt contest, sack races, pie-eating contest, Mrs. Grandmother America pageant, quilting bees, and more.

Abigail was rummaging in her closet for a cape for Selma when Isuzu shouted, "Oh, Abby you have message from handsome guy who come in for you."

"Seriously?" For a second Abigail thought it might be the guy from last night, until she remembered they hadn't exchanged names. "What'd he want?"

"He leave his card. Call him. City won't allow you to build booster food cart. You fix. Very expensive problem."

"*What?*" Abigail moved to the door and stared at her, completely flummoxed. "You have got to be kidding me! The Rawston Taste is in two weeks! And we don't have our new *food cart?* For the love of—" Spinning around, she gave Aunt Selma's cape an agitated snap before she fastened it around the old woman's neck. As if she didn't have enough to do already for this Quilt-o-Rama booster club deal. Now she had to fix the food cart?

"Try not to let the stress get to you," Selma clucked sympathetically. "You just do what you can do, and then let the rest go. It seems like every year there's a crisis. Which reminds me, you know each year I host the team speed-quilting contest?"

Zuzu's niece, Brooke, laughed from across the room. "That just sounds hilarious."

"Oh no, missy. This is serious stuff. Even an Olympian such as yourself hasn't *seen* competition until you've witnessed a dozen teams of quilters come in from all over the United States and start quilting Saturday morning and not stop until Sunday night. The prize is six thousand dollars for the charity of your team's choice. The quilts are all auctioned off for that charity, too."

"Whoa." Brooke was impressed.

"Yeah, whoa. Well, anyhow, The Rawston Raw-Edges have not won in six years, and we're tired of eating crow. We've all been trying to come up with a great theme, but so far," Selma stuck out her tongue and blew, "*Ppfft*. Nada. Zippo. Thelma Edwards suggested a garden patch theme with flowers. Mae Dewsbury suggested berries or grapes. I'm thinking those are just . . . oh, what's the word?"

"Mind-numbingly dull?" Abigail yanked her shear drawer open and stared inside. What was she looking for again? *Ooo, this food cart thing honked her off.*

"Okay. I might not put it that way, but sure. Anyway, I don't know what is wrong with me, but this year I just can't seem to think of a winning theme. Nothing seems to . . . to . . . to just *jump out* at me, you know?"

"That's cool." Abigail was only half listening as she was still fuming about the guy who'd just dumped the food cart problem in her lap. Thank heavens Jen Strohacker was coming in at ten. Maybe she could help her untangle some of this mess.

"I know God will eventually show me the perfect idea, because I've been praying over it for some time now," Selma said. "I'm sure that I'll know it when I hear it."

Abigail closed her eyes so Selma wouldn't see her rolling them. *Like anyone—let alone God—cared about cool ideas for quilts.* All her life, Abigail had listened to Selma natter on about the tedious subject of quilting. All those little pieces of material, making all those little designs and filling them with all those little stitches. . . . Just thinking about it had her falling into a coma on her feet. Because, *come on. Who cared?* A quilt was a quilt was a quilt. *Booooring.*

"*Quilting isn't just sticking pieces of material together,*" Selma liked to say, "*it's about putting the pieces together.*" Abigail wanted to ask, "*Putting the pieces together? Sticking the pieces together?* What did that even mean? And why should I care?" But she didn't because she loved her quirky aunt, and so she tried to listen and feign interest.

The bell over the door jangled. Isuzu's sister-in-law was here to pick up Brooke.

"Hey, Mieko." Abigail put on her professional façade of tranquility, though on the inside she still fretted. "You guys have something going on today?"

"I've gotta get the kids up to the Southshire ice rink for a training session with their coach," Mieko said.

"On Saturday?"

"Every day." Mieko sighed. "Monday through Friday the kids practice from three to seven, then we have to drive back in time for school. It's a hassle."

"Wait, you're talking three *a.m.?*"

"Yeah."

"Wow! And you and your husband still have to work all day at the restaurant?" Abigail occasionally ran over to the Sakura Garden for sushi. As far as she knew, aside from Isuzu pulling some evening shifts in the kitchen, Mieko and her husband were the only people who worked there. "When do you guys sleep?"

"Sleep?" Mieko laughed. "What's that? The kids sleep in the car to and from, and I doze while they practice. It all works out. And, in the end, God willing, it will be worth it. Come on, Brooke. Tyler's waiting in the car and he's hungry. Let's go!"

Abigail looked back and forth between mother and daughter. "Are we still on to put your hair up this afternoon for prom?" she asked Brooke.

"Oh, yeah!" Brooke was wriggling like a puppy.

Mieko's smile was exhausted. "Four-thirty. Okay. Zuzu! You coming to help roll sushi tonight?" Isuzu answered in Japanese, but because her head was bobbing, Abigail figured that's where she'd no doubt go after closing.

"And I thought I had a busy schedule," Abigail deadpanned as she began wetting down Selma's still thick, snow-white hair.

Selma tsked. "They are too busy. Everyone is these days. Busy, busy, busy. No time to sit back and enjoy the splendor of God's creation. The devil must get a real charge out of all this stuff we think we need to do."

"You preach, sister!" Isuzu shouted from her station.

"Who needs it? I'm telling you, Zuzu, I miss the good old days. The days where people turned off the boob-tube and went outside and visited with their neighbor—"

Abigail tuned the sermon out. Nobody ever said anything about her having to help build the stupid food cart. That was *his* job. For pity's sake. She was a volunteer. She had already put dozens of hours in on this project, and all she ever got was complaints. Well, this was the last time she was ever gonna step up to the plate. Let some other poor slob take the heat. Just as soon as Selma was out of here, she was going to call this goon and give him a piece of her mind.